"If you will but cooperate, you may find that you enjoy the experience," said the Prince.

Dia's flesh crawled at the thought. "And if I refuse?"

He eyed her up and down with something very like contempt. "It will be no particular trouble for me to take you," he told her. "I'd had some hope that, in this situation, you might bow to the inevitable."

"I had rather by far that you killed me, sir," she said, her voice flat with hostility.

"Ah, no, I cannot." he told her. "There are rules, you know. You may choose to kill yourself once I have done with you," he added indifferently. "Or you may choose to go on living. It really does not matter, my lady. Whatever you choose, the end will be the same and Great Septha will finally regain his place in this world."

As the sense of his words penetrated her shock and anger, she began to see that Maermat had nothing to lose. And now, as she realized that bedding her was not a means to an end, but the end itself, Dia began to be truly afraid ...

The Rise Of The Phoenix

by Dawn Rivers Baker

Brighid's Fire Books
P.O. Box 41
Sidney, New York 13838
(607) 563-7523
www.brighidsfirebooks.com

Brighid's Fire Books is an imprint of Wahmpreneur Books.

Brighid's Fire Books
A division of Wahmpreneur Publishing, Inc.
Post Office Box 41
Sidney, New York 13838
U.S.A.

The Rise of the Phoenix

Copyright © 1999 by Dawn Rivers Baker. All rights reserved. Produced in the United States of America. Except as permitted under the Copyright Act of 1974, no part of this publication may be reproduced or distributed in any form or by any means without written permission of the publisher.

ISBN: 0-9713278-1-5

Cover art ©1999 by Shelly Russell

CHAPTER ONE

Lady Dia of Shae reined in her sweating horse at the top of a long rise, halting her small entourage to allow their mounts a few moments of rest. She looked around with eyes narrowed against the glare of the relentless sun, still only a reddish golden ball low on the eastern horizon. Now that the Great Dark had receded for the year, the world would gradually change from a frigid wasteland to a bright and brutal inferno. Already, the air was very warm and a slightly damp breeze blew steadily out of the north, gently rustling the budding grass under the horses' hooves. HighSun was still some months away, but Dia would be glad to reach her destination and the respite it offered.

The valiant animals that had carried them for mile after weary mile were also beginning to give way to the cumulative stresses of endless heat and light. Dia slapped her stallion's neck affectionately. "You shall have the coolest and most ill-lit stall I can find for you presently, old friend," she murmured to him gently, adding with a smile, "and so shall I."

Dia had graciously declined when her father had suggested to her that she might like to accompany her brother, Daerus, to Ormaerand to make their courtesy to the Emperor. She had said very simply that she did not think life at court would suit her. Since her father was inclined to agree, he had let the matter rest, but they both knew that eventually she would have to take herself off to court, whether she would or no. Dia had a duty to perform as a child of Shae. It had become the custom for the children of the Great Houses to present themselves to His Imperial Majesty upon attaining their maturity. Privately, Lord Loraed had little use for Emperor Kaerkas but it would not do to offend him. The Emperor's likely response to the insult implied by a failure to perform that duty would be both decisive and excessive.

Of course, nothing would have persuaded the Grand Duke and Duchess to part with their only daughter during the Season of the Great Dark, when the world was plunged into half a year of darkness and the snow piled as high as the second floor windows of Shae Manor. But, now that another year had dawned, the snow had melted, the air had warmed, and his Grace had no excuse to offer should the Emperor take it into his head to wonder what had become of Lord Daerus' twin sister.

Lord Loraed had reached the stage of beginning to consider and discard various ultimatums for the most likely means of getting the girl out of the house. Thus it was that, when Dia had entered the dining hall of her ancestral home a fortnight since, and surprised her sire with the news that she intended to join her brother at court at last, his relief was so great that he did not even pause to wonder what had prompted this sudden capitulation. Nor did he waste his time arguing with her about her proposed style of dress. She set off, adorned in light leggings, with a loose-fitting tunic rather than a decent overdress -- and of linen, rather than silk or even satin, Dia's mother had thought despairingly -- such as she often wore about the estate. His grace, in spite of some inevitable misgivings, was too well pleased that he would not be obliged to order her to Ormaerand to balk at piddling things like her wardrobe. So, he had waved his only daughter on her way, charging her with graceful messages of his duty to the Emperor, and her grace the Duchess with loving ones of her pride in the Grand Duke's heir.

"At least she has covered her head," said her Grace, adding with a shake of her head and a regretful sigh, "She looks like the veriest peasant."

"I expect she knows that very well, my dear," was the Duke's gruff reply. "No doubt she finds it amusing."

His grace could not have known, of course, that her brother was responsible for Dia's abrupt decision. She had awakened very suddenly from a sound sleep the day before her departure, with the sense of his familiar presence in her mind. *Awake at last, are you?* Daerus had said to her. *You are still a mighty sound sleeper, my girl. It is to be hoped that you do not snore, as well.*

They had been able to do this for as long as she remembered. Being twins, they had been closer perhaps that most siblings, but their many schemes and bouts of mischief were often aided by the Talent they shared. It had certainly kept them quiescent on many occasions when they might, they felt, have otherwise died of boredom.

When they had been ten years old, Phoebus, the priest of the Phoenix who served her father's estate, had informed their father that these twin children of Shae were possessed of the Talents of the TimeKeepers. Lord Loraed was somewhat alarmed by this revelation, but Phoebus had serenely informed his Grace that there was naught to fear.

"Why?" Lord Loraed had asked suspiciously.

"Because the priesthood of the Phoenix is a passel of withered, pious fools, paying homage to a dead religion," Phoebus had replied with the unearthly calm that was habitual to him. "Is that not the common opinion, your Grace? Of all the Great Houses, only Shae retains its hereditary ties to the TimeKeepers." He had smiled faintly, then. "I do not suggest that either your heir or his sister enter the priesthood, your Grace. That is not needful. Indeed, there have been no new TimeKeepers since the death of the last age, and there will be none for a hundred generations or more, if need be, until once more a Phoenix rises from the ashes of Chaos to guide us to peace and order."

Lord Loraed, who had been bred to regard the TimeKeepers with deep respect but disliked being lectured as much as the next fellow, sighed. "In that case, good Phoebus, one wonders why you bring the matter to my attention?" he ventured.

"It were best, I think, to give them some training, if we are to prevent them from becoming nuisances to themselves, each other and everyone around them," Phoebus had replied with uncharacteristic bluntness.

"They already are," his Grace muttered feelingly.

Phoebus had actually chuckled. In anyone else, Lord Loraed would have called the priest's glance sly. "All the more reason to begin their instruction as early as may be convenient, my lord -- with your permission, of course," was all he said.

Lord Loraed having no further objection to make, Daerus and Dia were taught many of the Secret Ways of the TimeKeepers. They were strictly enjoined to reserve their talents for those circumstances when such abilities were truly needed, lest they rouse the mistrust of their fellows -- a caution that the feisty twins heeded scrupulously, for they knew that the priesthood had fallen into disrepute. That did not, however, keep the them from maintaining their close mental contact, even when Lord Daerus left the Shae estate to attend the Emperor's court.

Well, brother? she had replied.

Never better, sister, he had said.

So. You wake me from a sound sleep simply for the pleasure of my conversation?

And still she is a shrew when she wakes. Really, my dear, you should try to do something about that. Only think of your poor, as-yet-unknown husband ...

Daerus!!

His chuckle echoed in her mind. *Make ready to travel, my dear, he said. You are needed in the palace.*

The matter is urgent?

Why else would I wake you at this hour? he asked, managing to sound injured. Then, laughing again, his presence faded. Trust Daerus to tell her nothing more than that. Still, Dia was not fooled by his lighthearted manner. She knew from that brief contact that something momentous was afoot and she trusted him enough to set forth almost immediately to join him at court.

As tired as she was, it was difficult for Dia to pause even long enough for her noble steed to catch his breath now that the end of her journey was in sight. She was in no particular hurry to attend the Emperor's court but she was eager to get inside the thick palace walls and away from the unremitting sunlight. Wistfully, she recalled the last age, ended these two years, when the world had not stood still, when day had followed night in hours instead of months, and the world had been fair and friendly under the gentle hand of Ageless Phoenix.

That first HighSun had been most difficult, filled with fear and famine and madness. Now, the people seemed to be adjusting and seemed perfectly resigned to blizzards, floods, droughts, scarce food supplies and only about four months of the year when it was neither too hot nor too cold to accomplish anything. There was even a sort of brooding gloom that abode among them, as if the Great Dark continued to stalk the land and its people even after it had receded. She had first noticed it when she had left the Grand Duchy of Shae and began to ride through neighboring Ormaer, and she had wondered if the capital and its denizens trailed those same shadows about like worn cloaks. If there was such a thing as a mood of the land, it seemed as if the mood had become one of dark anticipation; yet, no one else seemed affected, as was Dia, by this sense of some great beast about to pounce.

Shaking off such somber reflections, she nudged her tired horse into a canter, for she had spied a lone horseman emerging from the unguarded gates of the capital. *How kind of you to ride out to meet me, dearest,* she sent the thought with a humorous inflection.

As well for you that I do, he replied, surprising her with his grumbling. *Garbed as you are, you would likely suffer any number of insults from his Imperial Majesty's servants.*

Why, Daerus, one might think you were ashamed of the odd appearance your sister presents, she said in wholly feigned astonishment.

I suppose I should have known better than to imagine that ***you*** *would give the matter a thought,* he replied, sounding so bitter that she thought she must have misunderstood him.

After a moment's pause, she sent him a gently reproachful thought. *I do beg your pardon, dearest, but you* ***would*** *have me join you here.*

There was an even longer pause. Then her brother said, *Indeed, my dear, I do not mean to snap at you so. In truth, I would not have inflicted the Emperor's court upon you at any time were it not for the fact that I am desperate.*

And that puts me in my place, she said, laughter rocking her "voice". *I might have known this was not a mere case of my brother pining for my company.*

Oh, surely, you **must** *have known better than that!* he instantly replied in an attempt at his usual bantering manner.

Dia grinned at him as she crossed the intervening space between them, but she was both baffled and concerned. Her normally lighthearted brother was haggard and there was a haunted look in his eyes that she had never seen before. Even more alarming, their mind-link, which should have grown stronger with physical proximity, had thinned and dimmed as she rode closer to him. She was not completely closed off from him but she was being held at a distance, something Daerus had never done to her before.

"What ails you, Daerus?" she asked as soon as she was within hailing distance. "You look dreadful."

"Too much revelry, no doubt," he tossed off negligently, regarding her intently and searchingly.

"You do not look as if you have been enjoying it, my love," Dia said with a wry half-grin.

As she returned his gaze, she found herself moving rapidly from concern to alarm. There was a darkness about her brother that filled her with foreboding. She had been wondering if the city of Ormaerand bore the same gloom as the countryside, and could not imagine how Daerus could stand being there. Now, it seemed she had her answer. Would she, too, grow dark and tired and empty if she remained in this place for very long? At that moment, it seemed that her brother was almost a stranger.

"Now, for the love of Chaos, Dia, don't nag at me," he snapped irritably.

Dia said nothing. This was not her brother, this peevish, dissipated-looking fellow. Something was very wrong here. "I beg your pardon," she said at last, and a bit stiffly.

He did not seem to notice. "Yes, well, never mind that. I will have to present you to his Imperial Majesty as soon after we arrive as may be and, Dia, as you love me, let me have none of your odd ways. It is of the greatest importance that the Emperor be pleased with you."

She digested that for a moment in silence. "I suppose I should be gratified that my reputation precedes me," she said lightly. When Daerus said nothing, only tossing her a disgusted look, she exclaimed, "Daerus, ***what*** is the matter with you?!"

"Nothing!" he almost shouted at her. "Do as you will! No doubt it matters not at all to you how you may shame the House of Shae. I must have been mad to imagine I could look to you for aid in this pass."

"Mad, indeed, my dear, to imagine you could look to me for aid when you will not even divulge what the problem is," she told him, restored to calm. "Our mother sends you her dearest love, by the bye. I must hope that you will not return to Shae until you have recovered your misplaced manners, for I fear she will be sadly grieved." Daerus did not respond. "Come, twin, surely you did not inveigle me into making this tedious and uncomfortable journey for the sole purpose of picking a fight with me. Fire and ashes, you could have done that from the comfort of your chair and saved me the trip!"

"Indeed, sister, I have no wish to quarrel with you," he muttered, his irritation disappearing in an instant, to be replaced by that vague desperation she had seen before.

Dia sighed, finding it surprisingly difficult to converse with her brother for the first time in her life. Really, she ought to be able to talk to Daerus even if she did not have access to their habitual mind-link. "It is also to be hoped that, when you locate your manners you will also find your sense of humor. No doubt you packed them both away in your trunk, finding that you would need neither while you were at court."

A reluctant chuckle reassured her. Whatever was amiss, Daerus was still Daerus. She supposed some misfortune had befallen just before he'd set out to meet her, for he had certainly seemed his usual happy-go-lucky self when he had called her here. Dia was sure he would tell her all when he had recovered his composure. In the meantime, they had passed through the gates of Ormaerand and Dia looked about her with interest.

The capital city was neither a large city nor an attractive one. She had often thought as she rode north that House Ormaer had some obscure affection for ugliness, but she'd expected better of the Emperor's home. The houses were plain and unadorned, built closely together of a dark grey stone with slate roofs. None of the homes or businesses was very large, for the Great Houses of the empire preferred their own lands to residing in close proximity to court. That was only practical; Dia knew, for example, that it would have been most difficult for Lord Loraed to administer to the needs of Shae from the confines of this city.

Dia could only be thankful for that expediency. She had thought she was used to seeing people trailing the darkness about like a forgotten garment but the aura was much worse in the streets of the capital. Back in the Grand Duchy of Shae, her own people took advantage of this time of relative comfort to conduct business, repair their homes and farms after the ravages of the Great Dark and prepare for the exigencies of HighSun. Here, all was noise and confusion as the townsmen reeled about in what seemed to her to be an endless, desperate gala of gambling, drinking and wenching, with the occasional brawl erupting for a change of pace, and none of it appearing to afford the participants much pleasure. Embarrassed, she averted her eyes from a pair of townsmen enthusiastically coupling before an abandoned tanner's stall. There were even a few bodies sprawled in corners and alleys, grey and stiff in death and contributing a rancid, nauseating stench to the bright darkness.

Perhaps, she thought, *I have been too much shielded from such things.* Curious, she cast a sidelong glance at her brother. The aura did not seem to be affecting him any more than the wild gallivanting of the people, and he rode on oblivious. *Are the denizens of the capital always like this? Is he used to this dreadful darkness or has he even noticed it?* she wondered. It certainly looked ominous but it *felt* much worse.

"I suppose I have grown accustomed to it," Daerus answered her unspoken thought with a shrug. Dia took some comfort in this proof that their mind-link might be seriously weakened but it was still there. "It does not disturb me, in any event."

"I envy you that insensitivity, brother," she told him. "If the honor of Shae were not resting upon my shoulders, I confess, I would turn tail and run from this place as fast as poor Coer could carry me. Tell me, is the palace any better?"

Someone else's eyes glinted at her from her brother's familiar face. "I will leave you to judge that for yourself," he said, pulling his mount to a stop. "We have arrived."

As soon as she looked at the palace, she had her answer. It was much worse. Dia had not even noticed it as they approached, so occupied with her fascinated horror at the chaos in the streets as she had been. Now, she looked upon her Emperor's palace and her sense of foreboding expanded another notch. *Great Phoenix,* she thought, *I cannot even see it!* Indeed, the place appeared to her less as the massively imposing structure that it was than as a gaping, hungry black maw. She felt a profound reluctance to enter the building, for surely such a place would suck her mind and soul out of her body so that it would seem as if she had never been.

Dia had a notion she now knew what ailed Daerus. Convulsively, she shivered.

Really, my dear, such fanciful notions as you have! Daerus said to her mockingly. *When did you become such a romantic? Your reputation will be sadly tarnished if this becomes known at Shae.*

Dia grinned, burying her misgivings deep in her mind. *'Tis a wonder if my brains are not baked out of my skull. No doubt an hour or two in the coolness of the palace will restore me to my perfectly ordinary self,* was her retort.

Pausing only long enough to give her servants instructions on the care and disposition of her horses, Dia joined her brother at the entrance. He was talking to a wizened little man with elaborately coifed curls and an unpleasantly knowing leer. "Really, Lord Daerus, you should know not to bring your whores into the palace by way of the front door!"

Dia stiffened. *I **did** warn you, Dia,* her brother reminded her gently.

Aloud, he remarked, "One wonders how you can have become the Emperor's chamberlain, Oshaed. It cannot have been because of your keen mind or your exquisite manners." He paused, while the little man drew himself up, offended. "This is my sister, my lord fleawit. See to it that she is properly housed and that her quarters are close to mine."

Oshaed's leer became more pronounced as he raked Dia with his glance. "Are you a protective brother, my lord? I would never have thought it. That will certainly present his Imperial Majesty's guests with a bit of a challenge."

Dia, who had had almost as much of this style of conversation as she cared to tolerate, lifted her chin and fixed this offensive lord with the stare she usually reserved for impudent maidservants and overly-familiar guardsmen. How dared this shriveled little creature so address a daughter of Shae! As Oshaed returned her gaze, the impudence slowly drained from his expression, to be replaced with a look of sullen chagrin and a flush.

"Never mind exercising what passes for you wit, sir. Just see to my sister's quarters," Daerus retorted, smiling grimly as he observed that silent exchange. Gesturing, he added, "We will wait in that antechamber."

Feeling as if she had just stepped into a cesspool, Dia allowed her brother to guide her past the chamberlain and his knowing leer. She asked mildly, "Is the Emperor very fond of his chamberlain?"

"Nobody is fond of his chamberlain," Daerus replied shortly.

"Then, you do not think his Imperial Majesty would be terribly upset if my lord was found some morning with his throat slit?"

Daerus smiled faintly. "Very likely not."

Dia nodded with a satisfied smile. "That is good to know," she said as she entered the chamber through the door her brother held open. Once inside, she fixed him with a keen, worried glance and said without preamble, "Very well, Daerus, tell me of this urgent matter that required my instant presence in this elegant brothel."

"Determined to get yourself a lodging in His Majesty's dungeon, my dear?" he ask mildly. "That is hardly a respectful way to refer to the imperial abode."

"Never mind my manners, my dear," she replied sweetly. "You know I have none. What's afoot?"

Daerus took a turn about the room as, to Dia's further dismay, their mental link grew still weaker. The silence between them continued as the young man paced restlessly. Dia waited.

Finally, he said, not looking at her, "Sister, I would be wed."

Involved as she had been in imagining all sorts of potential disasters that might have been about to befall him -- an imminent duel, a lady-in-waiting with child by him, the prospect of imperial displeasure due to some indiscretion -- these tidings made her laugh aloud. "Well, really, Daerus! It is as well that your future bride is not here to listen to your dismal way of bearing such glad news! The prospect of being a husband would appear to afford you little pleasure."

Daerus tried to smile at her teasing but it was a wan effort. "Do I sound so dreary? I must take care!" he replied.

"Why?" she asked, her grin fading. "Is this betrothal not of your seeking?"

"Of course it is! Really, Dia, why must you forever be looking for ogres and curses?"

"Why, indeed? It surely could not be because you summon me to the palace in such a bang and then deliver yourself of this news as if you were announcing that you were bound for the headsman's block!" He did not reply and Dia went on to ask, "Who is she?"

"Princess Kera," he replied shortly.

"The Emperor's daughter? Your aim is high, my love," she said. "Is the lady agreeable?"

"She does not dislike my suit but will heed the decision of the Emperor."

"A dutiful young lady," she remarked and then paused, waiting. When her brother said nothing, she exclaimed, "Fire and ashes, Daerus, but it is difficult to get this tale from you! What has the Emperor to say? Shall I wish you happy?"

"The Emperor would have me present my sister before he makes his decision," Daerus told her, looking at her at last. Again, the thought struck her that it was not Daerus who gazed at her so speculatively, but someone she had never met.

"The Emperor wishes to make my acquaintance? How very odd. I would have thought he would wish to meet Lord Loraed and his lady. What have I to say to this matter?" she asked guilelessly, thinking but not saying that she had likely arrived at the crux of the matter.

"Now, how should I know? Mayhap he has heard tales of Lady Dia of Shae and wishes for an excuse to withhold his permission."

She was silent for a moment, trying mightily to bring herself to believe what he was telling her and failing utterly. "Naturally, you would have no way of learning his motives," she uttered sardonically. "You did not touch his thoughts?"

"Would I so use my emperor?"

"Why not? It would not harm him and your motives are not treasonous. Besides, he would never know a thing about it." He opened his mouth to argue with her but she did not give him the chance. There was more in the wind than Daerus seemed willing to divulge and Dia suspected it involved a favor he was reluctant to ask. "Well, never mind. I expect I will learn for myself whatever the fell tidings may be."

"You are very suspicious, are you not?" he asked her, his voice silky.

"Have I not reason to be suspicious?" Once again, she had that sense that she spoke to someone she did not know. On an impulse, she deliberately sought to strengthen the mental link that had dwindled to a nadir.

He flinched away from her mental touch, saying, "None of that, my dear."

She stared at him, hurt and not bothering to hide it. "You have never objected before."

Daerus returned her glance, clearly hesitating and searching for something to say. He was rescued by the arrival of a liveried servant, who asked my lady to please come with him so that he could show her to her rooms. Indeed, his obvious relief at being spared the need to fabricate some further explanation that would satisfy her was even more hurtful than his rejection of her mind-touch.

So, Dia unhesitatingly allowed the conversation to come to a close, uncomfortable with her brother for the first time in her life. He dutifully accompanied her to her door, saying before he left her, "We dine shortly. My rooms are three doors further down this hall. Join me there when you have rested and changed."

"What? You mean I cannot sit down to endmeal with the Emperor as I am?" she asked in mock astonishment.

"Dia!"

She chuckled and entered her apartment.

CHAPTER TWO

Colonel Lord Caelon Aerandos stalked down the hall of the imperial palace on his way to his mother's apartments. His habit of movement, more crisp and decisive than was the norm among the nobility, had already attracted the fascinated attention of many members of court. They wondered why he squandered such energy doing nothing more urgent than walking, while disdaining those pastimes that they considered much more diverting and thus worth the effort. He seemed quite humorless to them; he barely drank more than a cup of wine with his endmeal; he had not taken a lady to his bed since he had arrived some time ago. Yet, even as they tried to shrug him off as a dull fellow, they secretly drank in his aura of purposefulness as a starving man might wistfully breathe the perfume of a well-cooked meal, seeing in it a devotion to something more sustaining than pleasures of the flesh.

Caelon was well aware of, and grimly amused by, the fascinated horror with which the Emperor's courtiers beheld him. For his part, on a good day, he eyed them with barely veiled contempt. Was this the much-vaunted imperial court, that was said to impart some sort of worldly wisdom upon the scions of noble houses? It seemed to him that they could learn as much in the back alleys of any town large enough to boast a tavern and a brothel. Surely, it was a very wise man who had said that idle hands bred feeble minds.

On a bad day, his lordship was not so generous and today was turning out to be a very bad day. Caelon was no more prudish than the next fellow but he found himself thinking, as he strode down the hallway, that if he had to spend much more time among the drunken sots and unrepentant whores of His Imperial Majesty's court, he was likely to do something desperate. And, to make matters worse, when he wasn't fending off the advances of another energetic gentlewoman or indulging his male peers in wine-scented conversation, he was listening to addle-brained proposals from the madman on the throne.

With a perfunctory knock, Caelon opened the door to his mother's sitting room and entered without ceremony. She looked up from her needlework and smiled at him. "Really, Caelon, whatever is the matter? You are looking quite ferocious. I am sure the entire court must find you terrifying!"

His scowl softened into the quizzical smile that was more habitual to him. "I had rather hoped for that effect, Mama, but alas! it is not so," he told her.

Lady Tamia's eyes returned to her embroidery. "If there is one good thing to be said about a half year of daylight, it is that there is plenty of light in which to set one's stitches," she remarked. "'Tis a good thing your father and I did not bring you here with the notion of providing you with entertainment, my dear. I would have been sadly cast down by your stubborn refusal to enjoy yourself!"

At that, Caelon burst into laughter. "Oh, in that case, I would have made some effort, for if you were to go into a decline over the business, I would never hear the end of it! Come, Mama, admit that if I did find something with which to occupy myself among these wretches, you would be wholly mortified."

"Oh, how can you say so?"

"Easily," he replied instantly, a loving smile on his face that would have astonished much of the court. "So, tell me, which would you prefer? Shall I spend my time with my noble peers, drinking myself into a stupor regularly? Or shall I abide with the ladies instead, to see if my stamina is up to par?" Caelon shook his head, adding as his smile soured, "I had rather seek out the stable hands. At least they spend some of their time usefully."

Her Grace chuckled. "You would not think so to hear what our own Thaerd has to say of them!" she told her son, youthful blue eyes twinkling. "To hear him tell it, the only reason to keep any of them about the place is because His Majesty's guests are so little addicted to *outdoor* exercise that the general ineptness in the stables goes unremarked."

"As if anyone would ride out in this heat! Thaerd is quite absurd, you know."

"No, he just does not approve of *anything* this far south. I am sure, if we asked him, he would say that we would still have a Phoenix if only the Temple of Fires had been built in Aerandos. Besides," Lady Tamia continued as Caelon grinned, "he is a soldier, my dear, and has no taste for the amusements of the imperial guests."

"I, too, am a soldier, ma'am, and Thaerd is a very sensible fellow," Caelon contradicted himself promptly.

"No matter how absurd he might be!" her Grace retorted with a delightful gurgle of laughter. "Now, my dear, what did the Emperor say that has put you in such a temper? I felt quite certain, from his manner since we arrived, that he had some signal honor in mind for House Aerandos."

That question effectively put a period to Caelon's amusement. "Oh, he does indeed," he replied grimly. "He would have my father serving on the General Staff of the Imperial Army here in the capital."

"And what is there in that to put you out, Caelon?" asked her Grace in some surprise.

"Why, nothing, ma'am," Caelon said promptly. "Indeed, the Emperor needs to do *something* about the sorry state of the Imperial Army, if the imperial guard here in the palace is considered the best of them. This latest evidence of His Majesty's military genius is wonderful. He would have us withdraw our own troops from the northern frontier to take up positions closer to the imperial person, and replace them with regiments from his own sorry forces."

Lady Tamia frowned thoughtfully and charmingly. "I would not offend His Majesty for the world, but I do not think his troops would be able to hold the north against the Throk," she said hesitantly.

"They would be about as effective as those kittens you keep about the estate in such abundance," Caelon said in disgust.

"Nonsense, boy," said another voice from the door. "The kittens at least have claws."

Caelon turned quickly as Lord Saeros stepped inside and closed the door behind him. He advanced into the room to greet his lady, placing an affectionate hand on Caelon's shoulder in passing. "Your departure was somewhat precipitous, my boy," he noted to his heir as he bowed over Lady Tamia's hand.

"Why, how is this, sir?" Caelon replied, feigning astonishment. "We had been dismissed. Surely I could not have been mistaken?"

"Did I not bring you here in your capacity as my heir?" Lord Saeros turned now and bent a stern glance upon his son. "Do you imagine that your instruction at the hands of my generals and my stewards is all you will require?"

"Well, if there is more that I will require, I beg you will not ask me to learn it *here,*" Caelon said, making no effort to mask his contempt.

Lord Saeros eyed his son sardonically. "Aye, the baby lord thinks to assume the command of the premier fighting force in the empire without need of learning how best to address imperial machinations! Think you that you can display your contempt for the imperial court so plainly when you stand in my shoes? The Emperor is still my liege, and will be yours; you can no more avoid him than you can avoid my lady's cats."

At that, both Lady Tamia and Caelon laughed. "Now, really," the lady said, "why must the pair of you harp so upon the poor pussies? They do earn their keep, you must confess. Cook tells me there has not been a mouse in the kitchens since I was married!"

"I knew you must have been well dowered, Mama," Caelon said, very much impressed, "but, indeed, I had no notion of the riches you commanded."

Lord Saeros did not smile at this banter between his wife and his heir. "A moment of your attention, Caelon!" he said, throwing back his shoulders and assuming what Caelon undutifully called "commander stance".

And Caelon responded in kind as was expected. He straightened to attention, saying, "Sir?"

"You are to attend me at *all* of my meetings while we are here in the palace. That means informal meetings as well as formal ones. It is for that reason that I brought you here to begin with."

"As you will, sir," Caelon said, bowing. Then, as he moved to the door, he added with a grin, "And I had thought my purpose at court was to acquire the acquaintance and society of my peers. Never was I more disappointed!"

"Off with you, Impudence!" said his father, trying to scowl around the smile that was blossoming on his face.

Caelon quit the room in a much better frame of mind than he had entered it. He strode down the hall, trying to decide which of the numerous saloons and sitting rooms in the palace was most likely to be empty. He did not particularly want to remain closeted in his room, but neither did he want to make himself too accessible to his empty-headed peers by arriving for endmeal any sooner than was absolutely necessary. The closest thing in the palace to an exercise gymnasium was the imperial steam rooms, which Caelon had avoided since he learned, early in his stay, that the courtiers were likely to use the rooms for purposes for which they were not designed. He would have given a great deal for the sort of equestrian exercise arena that Lord Saeros had constructed at Aerandos, to be used for training cavalry units in inclement weather. In truth, Caelon was not used to having a great deal of unoccupied time on his hands; he was restless and felt sure he was growing soft with so much enforced idleness.

He wondered what could have occurred after he had excused himself to his father that had roused that gentleman's ire. Caelon doubted it was simply a matter of wanting him to observe the smooth technique which his Grace used to divert imperial importunities. He'd had plenty of opportunity to observe *that* during that thrice-blighted conference, so he had! A reluctant smile tugged at his lips. Perhaps there was something to be said for acquiring a touch of court polish.

The imperial summons had come to Aerandos at a bad time, for his Grace had been busy about his estate, repairing flood damage and preparing for the long dry spell that had just begun. Still, the Grand Duke of Aerandos knew his duty to the Emperor better than most, occupied as he was with the defense of the empire, so he had placed his well trained steward in charge of the repairs and brought his family south.

But his Imperial Majesty, once the Grand Duke Saeros and his family were ensconced in the palace, seemed in no hurry to get to the matter that had inspired him to summon them. Instead, they had been treated to interminable banquets and insipid soirees, the Emperor apparently determined to demonstrate to House Aerandos the endless congeniality of his court. His parents had been heartily bored by what His Imperial Majesty had referred to as "picking up the neglected threads of their acquaintance", and tactfully refrained from pointing out that none of the minor nobility currently at court were known to them. Caelon had been passed around among the younger visitors to the palace like a platter of savories and soon grew every bit as bored.

So all three of them were pleased when Lord Saeros had been summoned to an imperial audience as they had been finishing a substantial midmeal. Caelon and his father had exchanged a single startled, hopeful glance before attacking the remaining wine in their glasses with what Lady Tamia had laughingly called unseemly haste. Neither of them had spoken of it, but father and son both hoped the summons meant that his Imperial Majesty was finally going to get on with it. Caelon, indulging optimism, thought that perhaps they might be on their way back to Aerandos before endmeal.

Lord Saeros and his heir, therefor, arrived in the conference room and greeted the Emperor with such affability that his Imperial Majesty seemed smugly gratified. Since the cordiality of father and son had nothing to do with their delight in the imperial court, and everything to do with relief at the notion that they might soon be done with it, Caelon reflected that it was as well that the Emperor could not read their thoughts as the TimeKeepers had been said to do. Politely, he bowed to General Kraetus and to the imperial heir, Prince Maermat.

"How may I serve you, my emperor?" Lord Saeros had asked, once the introductions were over and all the men were seated.

"The matter is simple, Saeros," the Emperor said, as if he felt sure his Grace would fall in with his idea without protest. "I find the imperial troops in less than the desired state of combat readiness. You have perhaps noticed the same thing?"

His lingering relief had prompted a mood of hilarity in Caelon and only his father's stern glance had kept him from uttering a crack of laughter at this massive understatement. "Why, yes, your Majesty," Lord Saeros had agreed, "I did make note of a certain ... er ... "

"They're soft and lazy, your Grace," Kraetus had interjected with a grunt. "No need to wrap the thing up in clean linen. I have given the Emperor a thorough briefing on the condition of his army."

"Indeed," Kaerkas the Beast had said, frowning petulantly. "It will not do. Ormaeranda is the greatest empire in the history of the world, but the might of the empire will be judged in the end by the might of the imperial army." He had paused and Caelon felt sure he had caught himself on the brink of unwise speech. "We must improve the men, Saeros, and without delay."

"A wise choice, your Majesty," Lord Saeros had agreed politely.

An awkward pause had followed that courteous remark as everyone had waited for him to continue. Curious, Caelon glanced around the table. General Kraetus was scowling down at the fine grain of the hardwood table under his hands. Prince Maermat wore a faint smile and the imperial visage held nothing but polite interest. Yet, all three men betrayed a taut expectation in the set of their shoulders, in Maermat's narrowed eyes and the Emperor's fingers, which drummed absently and arhythmically on the table.

Now, what's afoot? wondered Caelon. It was quite obvious that his father had been expected to offer to see to the task of sprucing up the imperial army, and it was equally clear to everyone in the room that his Grace had missed his cue. Lord Saeros appeared to be the only one of them who was in command of his face *and* body language; he seemed completely at his ease, his expression politely enquiring. Caelon carefully hid a smile; his Grace certainly knew how to bring conversation to an abrupt halt.

"Hmmph. Yes, well," said the Emperor, with an expression on his face that was very close to a pout. "The thing is that this task will require leadership, Saeros."

"Your Majesty has a very fine General Staff," Lord Saeros pointed out.

"Nonsense!" the Emperor stated. "How fine can they be if they have allowed the army to deteriorate in this fashion?" His Imperial Majesty seemed to have forgotten that a member of the General Staff sat at the table with them. The General's scowl grew blacker.

"The thing is, your Grace, that our generals here in the capital do not have that military tradition so long in their bloodlines as does House Aerandos," Prince Maermat took up the chant, his voice smooth and persuasive. "All the world knows that the soldiers of Aerandos are the finest to be had anywhere."

"Your Highness is very kind." Lord Saeros murmured the formula response, still apparently unwilling to help these three say what they seemed so reluctant to say.

"Kindness has nothing to say to the matter," the Emperor said firmly. Given his reputation, Caelon had no doubts about the sincerity of *that* statement. "Your aid is needed, Saeros. I would appoint you to the General Staff as a special advisor and have you see to retraining the imperial army. Now, what say you?"

"You honor me, your Majesty," Lord Saeros said slowly, his face giving no hint of his opinion of this indication of imperial favor, "but I have duties to my people in the north that must be discharged, and I also must see to my own troops."

"That will be no problem at all," the Emperor said promptly, as if he had anticipated this caveat. "I will send the army to you at Aerandos, and your troops will come here in their stead."

That plan seemed so fraught with disaster, that Caelon remained silent only with the greatest difficulty. Of all the ridiculous notions ... !

"That would not be a very good idea, your Majesty," his father pointed out. "It would be imprudent to withdraw the best troops available from the border of the empire's only hostile neighbor."

"Great fires of Phoenix, Saeros, but you are insulting!" General Kraetus burst out with what, to Caelon, seemed a bizarre reversal of his originally proffered opinion of the imperial troops.

"They may not measure up to the heights of soldierdom that *you* set, but neither will they turn tail and run at the first sign of an engagement! Rest assured, your Grace, our men will fight."

"Of course, they will fight, General," Lord Saeros returned, his voice mild but his eyes glinting. "But will they *win*?"

"A home question," said the Emperor, clearly delighted. Caelon wondered if the man were deliberately needling his general or if he was simply an idiot. Much more of this, and Lord Saeros would need to watch his back most assiduously during the remainder of his stay at the palace.

Lord Saeros sat back, apparently pondering the matters at hand. "I do not think I should care to have the Throk as near neighbors," he remarked absently. "As it is, they are quite close enough." After a pause, during which the company awaited his pleasure, he smiled faintly and spoke again. "Your majesty, you have presented me with a nice dilemma. The easiest solution would be for me to acquire the ability to be in two places at once."

Prince Maermat chuckled, but his glance remained watchful.

"I will consider the matter," his Grace had declared. "There may yet be a way for me to both discharge my responsibilities to my people and serve the empire's needs."

Striding easily down the hall, Caelon considered the matter now. That his father's reaction at being offered a special commission by the Emperor was less than effusive did not seem to disturb a ruler known far and wide for his intolerance to opposition. Caelon found that interesting. He did not think that report had lied or exaggerated; there was that in Kaerkas' eyes that made one hesitate to cross him.

Lord Saeros, Caelon realized, had handled the situation with admirable skill. He had failed to instantly fall in the scheme and volunteered neither action nor information, yet he had managed to avoid placing the Emperor in a position in which an imperial ultimatum would have been justified. They were going to have to volunteer more information before they acquired his Grace's cooperation, much less his army, and that was just as well. The general's hostility was not difficult to fathom but Prince Maermat's calculating gaze suggested that there was more to this very plausible imperial request than met the eye.

All at once, Caelon realized that he was being watched and he cursed his inattention. Automatically, his steps slowed as his eyes darted around, trying to penetrate the shadows. The watcher was unfriendly, instinct told him; the level of malevolence he could feel from that silent observer caused him to wish, not for the first time, that the Emperor would allow his guests to be armed with more serious weapons than their fashionable daggers. This corridor, like the entire palace, was ill-lit and quiet. Waves of coldly brooding menace chilled him, inhuman in their intensity.

Inhuman? Caelon was not a fanciful sort but he had learned not to cast aside those random, instinctive impressions if he would save his own life. Surely, this corridor had not been *this* dark a few moments ago? Those instincts, which had served him so well for so long, could sense that dark menace building, reaching toward a crescendo that could only mean his unseen watcher was working himself up to launch an attack. Caelon's nerves stretched taut as his body automatically prepared for battle, but his mind seethed with helpless frustration. How could he fight what he could not see? What *was* it?

A door latch sounded and Caelon, poised for a fight despite the dimness that seemed to shroud his sight, whirled to his left with his knife in his hand.

"What ails you, my lord?" a sharp, feminine voice asked.

Suddenly, he could see again. Confused and angry, he looked accusingly into the face of a woman he had never seen before. "Perhaps I should ask you the same thing, my lady," he replied sardonically. "I had thought that a female of your obvious breeding would not stoop to spying about the corridors of the palace. Tell me, were you expecting your lover? No doubt it were better to make these little appointments for some time *after* endmeal."

She glanced up at him with eyes the color of a stormy sky. "You are churlish, my lord," she said, her voice flat with hostility and her hands twitching, although she wore no daggers.

He *had* been churlish, he knew. Manners and morals in the palace may be lax, but his hasty words were unforgivable. Still angry, he said, "Forgive me, my lady. I find I do not care to be watched and there is no need for you to trouble yourself with my movements. I have no secrets."

The lady seemed to have mastered her temper and now stared at him sardonically. "On that point, I must beg to differ, sir," she said. "No doubt you have a great many secrets, for I have no notion of what you may be talking about!"

"Do you mean to say that you were not watching as I came up this hall?" he asked her, suspiciously.

Caelon knew, as soon as he had asked her, that she could not have been that silent watcher. That aura of menace had been far too strong for her to successfully hide it now that they were face to face, and her present annoyance was a zephyr compared to the brooding hatred he had sensed. She did not even reply to his distrustful question, merely staring at him with her remarkably fine gray eyes. Those eyes held a peculiar expression, a combination of cynical amusement and the sort of wariness one usually employs when dealing with lunatics.

Aware that he had behaved in such a way as to completely justify her apparent impression that she had encountered a raving maniac, he bowed and suppressed an untimely fit of laughter. "I can see that I was very much mistaken and can only beg your pardon, my lady. You must think I learned my manners in the stables," he told her ruefully.

She fixed him with a stern eye and drew a deep breath. "I expect that any manners you might learn from the stablehands would be a vast improvement, sir," she told him. "Frankly, if the two gentlemen I have encountered since I arrived at the palace are a fair sample of Emperor's court, I had as lief return to my home without further delay."

This time he could not control the crack of laughter her words surprised from him. "How very unhandsome of you!" he said, grinning. "Come, my lady, I have owned my fault and apologized most properly. It is unkind in you to withhold your prompt forgiveness!"

She took another breath and open her mouth to speak, but what reply she might have made him he would never know. Suddenly, as she gazed at him, her eyes widened in astonishment and her irritation seemed to melt away. She seemed amazed by something only she could see and Caelon found himself wondering who she was and why she was looking at him so oddly.

Finally, she seemed to recollect herself, for she released her pent up breath and, in some confusion, dropped a curtsey. "Of course, my lord," was all she said.

"Thank you," and Caelon bowed again, feeling rather irrationally as if he had been robbed of some good sport. "No doubt you will be attending His Imperial Majesty's tedious endmeal, at which I expect we shall be formally presented to each other. There, I shall behave so irreproachably that I daresay you will be astonished and I shall be fully redeemed in your eyes." He reflected, as he made that extravagant promise, that once she had a taste of the rest of the imperial court, she would no doubt think him a model of rectitude.

He turned from her and continued down the hall, entertaining himself with speculations about her likely reaction to that particular treat in store -- or should he rather call it an ordeal? -- his unseen watcher momentarily forgotten.

CHAPTER THREE

Dia watched the gentleman walk away from her down the dim corridor and wondered again who he might be. Everyone she had encountered since she had entered the capital city had been carrying that aura of darkness that chilled her to the marrow of her bones. She had even wondered if fatigue was clouding her sight. It was not until she had been within an inch of giving the impudent fellow a severe scolding that she had realized that he was different. Handsome, certainly, and as arrogant, but to her tired eyes he seemed a blazing beacon of light in an ocean of blackness.

Whatever was the matter with her? She did not for an instant think that she was sickening for anything and she knew that she had always had unusual perceptions and abilities. But nothing like this had ever happened before, where her eyes started playing tricks on her. She turned away from the young man and started toward her brother's rooms, sadly puzzled.

Very likely, none of it meant a thing. Not the peculiar things she was seeing. Not the very odd, bone-deep chill she had felt just before she had opened her chamber door. Not even her brother's bizarre moods and haggard appearance. She would drive herself insane if she spent too much time trying to solve puzzles that did not exist. But, she owned privately, unconvinced by her own arguments, she wished she had Phoebus by her.

Only Daerus knew how much she detested occasions such as the one she would be attending that night. Her mother, thinking to solace her once she no longer had her twin's companionship, and hoping that some local gentleman would catch her eye, had inflicted countless entertainments upon her after her brother had left. Much to her mother's dismay, Dia had gained nothing from these revels except a great deal of practice at hiding her distaste for them. *Poor Mama!* she thought fondly as she paced the silent corridor. *How patiently she bore my ingratitude for her ridiculous scheming! I wonder if she would be pleased to know that those tedious evenings seem likely to do me some good now?*

She could not determine from Daerus' incoherent conversation what would be at risk during this endmeal, but she was determined not to fail him. Bearing in mind his injunctions, she had selected her raiment with some care and entered his room with a flourish. Her flowing gown was of an older design, in linen and crepe of a pale aqua, rather than the silken overdress and close-fitting leggings currently worn by young ladies of fashion. Its cut she thought both demure and becoming; dressed so very modestly, she felt certain to please her suddenly exacting sibling.

Daerus' first words instantly disabused her of that notion. "Great Temple fires, Dia! What do you mean by wearing such a grandmother's gown?" he asked, surveying her in some disgust.

Dia halted abruptly in the act of crossing his room, startled by this unexpected scolding. After staring at him for a moment, she sighed. "I had thought you were worried that I might be taken for a fast sort of female," she said in long-suffering accents. "At least, that is what you were complaining about earlier. No doubt that exquisitely polite Lord Oshaed has already given out his opinion of me. I but thought to counteract the gossip."

"The very thing you, of all people, would be worried about," Daerus told her sarcastically.

"*I* was not worried about it. *You* were. Remember?"

"I know of no reason why you cannot be ladylike and attractive at the same time."

"The man is quite old enough to be my father, Daerus," said Dia wryly. "I am not trying to seduce him, so what matter if my gown is demure?"

"Do not expect me to swallow that tale, sister!" he replied, clearly distracted. "It seems you are determined to ruin all my chances ... "

"Oh, give over, Daerus!" she snapped, completely out of patience with his hysterics. "You are become tiresomely difficult to please all of a sudden! You speak to me in the most general of terms and give me none but the vaguest of directions. If you are not going to give me a round tale, then you must not snarl at me if I stumble, for I am groping in the dark." She paused but he remained silent. Smiling faintly, she added, "You seek the Emperor's approval of me, do you not? And why should he not approve of a retiring girl-child from the country?"

A long pause ensued. The tension in the room slowly dissipated, while a reluctant smile fought for possession of her brother's lips. "A 'retiring girl-child'? Surely, such a role would be much too arduous for you to maintain, my dear," was his overly solicitous inquiry.

Dia grinned. "Brat!"

He grinned back.

"Have we done with brangling? I confess, I am longing for my endmeal," Dia said, taking his arm and hoping that he would not treat her to any more such scenes for awhile.

"I cannot think why you should complain," he replied mildly. "What would you do, if you had no brother to fight with when you are feeling peevish?"

"Do you know, I have no idea," she said, apparently much struck. "I shall have to consider the matter."

"Brat!"

They left the room together, and Dia was a bit easier now that they had revived their normal style of conversation. She had made the painful decision, while she was preparing herself for the evening, to pull herself out of mental contact with her brother completely, until she could discover what had happened to him.

Nothing had ever been so hard for her to willingly do! Her mind seemed echoingly empty; she had never felt so alone in her life. Yet, they chatted easily as they made their way to the throne room, where the Emperor's guests gathered before endmeal, and Dia realized sadly that her brother had not even noticed her withdrawal. She suppressed another sigh.

They came presently to the massive oak doors of Emperor Kaerkas Ormaer's throne room and a pair of uniformed, ceremonial guards sprang to open them. Daerus led her into a vast cavern of a room, filled with little except the reverberation of noisy talk, the glitter of brightly colored clothes and jewels and, overlooking all, the throne. Dia almost reeled backwards at the noise; the gentry in the neighborhood of Shae were much more refined in their social chatter. She had not been expecting such a clamorous babble.

Daerus led her forward and she had not time to distinguish more than an impression of swirling color, restlessness, a liveliness that had a touch of hysteria about it -- and, of course, the ever present darkness. Then she found herself standing before the raised dais on which sat the throne.

She had had no idea of what to expect and she examined the Emperor of the realm with interest. He was a small man, not much taller than herself, and he sat his throne as if it were a tunic that was several times too large to fit comfortably. His figure was compact, if a little pudgy with the approach of middle age, but his face came as something of a shock. It was almost invisible to her, for *his* darkness was so dense that he hardly looked human, and she had to struggle to keep herself from backing away.

"What ails you now, Dia?" Daerus hissed fiercely.

Faintly, she shook her head. If he could not see it, there was no point in mentioning what seemed to her to be growing evidence that she was losing her mind. The chatter of the guests, the swirling colors and, above all, the darkness, seemed to be closing around her. Sternly, she repressed her growing discomfort.

"Your Imperial Majesty," Daerus was saying, "allow me to present my sister, Lady Dia of Shae."

Dia sank into a deep curtsey, as the Emperor replied, "Welcome to court, my lady."

She rose and tried to look into his eyes, but she was blinded by his darkness. "I am honored, Sire," she said.

"A well-spoken child," the Emperor said to Daerus, "and quite the beauty. Why did you never mention how charming your sister is, Lord Daerus? Do you not agree, Maermat?"

It really was unfair of her, but she could not resist. *Did you not tell them how charming I am, twin?* she murmurred into his mind. *But how shocking!*

After a moment's struggle with himself, Daerus replied, "Indeed, Sire, she has improved beyond recognition in the time since I left my home." He bestowed a fatuous smile upon her. "I hardly recognized her."

Score a point for Daerus, she thought, sternly containing her laughter.

Meanwhile, the Emperor had beckoned to a classically beautiful young man with carefully curled black hair, who stood quietly behind his throne. "Allow me to make my son and heir known to you," he said.

Again, she curtsied. "Your Imperial Highness."

"My lady," he replied courteously, bowing over the hand he held and examining her speculatively.

Dia looked into his eyes with a growing sense of confusion. She *knew* she had never met this imperial personage before, yet his glance was startlingly familiar. But even as she tried to remember where she might have seen those eyes or that gaze, a strange kind of lassitude came over her. It seemed that her memories grew far away, as if she had arrived years ago instead of just after midmeal. Oh, merciful Phoenix, what *was* the matter with her?

How long she stood transfixed she could not have said. Again, she experienced that sensation of something trying to enclose her, to swallow her whole. Prince Maermat had not moved, yet he seemed to be a part of her feeling that something was trying to steal into her mind and take her away from herself. Startlement, discomfort and even curiosity slowly faded and a peculiar ringing filled her ears.

She had no idea what the Emperor was saying to her, or what she was replying. No one seemed to notice anything peculiar, so she relaxed and ceased to worry about it. She felt like a puppet; as long as whomever was pulling her strings knew what they were about, and would not land her in a scrape, she was willing to allow them to do with her what they would. It did not matter; nothing mattered.

Meanwhile, it quickly became obvious to everyone present that Shae was currently enjoying imperial favor. Dia and her brother were the object of interested glances and whispered conversation throughout the room. They were even partnered at endmeal by the Prince and Princess, while his Imperial Majesty looked on with smug satisfaction. Dia would have found such scrutiny trying, had she not still been enveloped in that comforting fog. She began to look around with incurious eyes.

Endmeal was a sumptuous affair, with course after succulent course offered at table, and the guests seemed to be drinking a great deal. In fact, the small part of her brain that was not entirely asleep noted, the lords and ladies attending the court were swilling their wine in much the same way as the commoners she had seen when she had entered the city. Fortunately, the guests had lost interest in her, and were busily carrying on countless indiscreet conversations at the top of their lungs. Several improper assignations were made, and any number of vulgar suggestions were shouted across the table amidst bawdy laughter. Dia looked gropingly at her brother but, in truth, she could see very little.

After endmeal, the Emperor and his court returned to the throne room to continue their evening's entertainment. Still sunk in that peculiar detachment, Dia had no desire to participate and retired to an unoccupied corner to watch. Several games of dice flourished and a number of thrashing tapestries suggested that the couples who had retired to hide behind them were enjoying vigorous exercise. Liveried servants were gliding around the room, dispensing wine as the guests drank without pause. A duel erupted from one of the dice games, the combatants snarling at each other as they grappled and the spectators taking bets on the victor. Dia looked about her mindlessly, still undisturbed by the scene. Absently, she wondered where her brother was.

"I had hoped that your brother would stay by you, at least long enough to present me," a vaguely familiar voice seemed to answer her unspoken question with what were, oddly enough, the first words she had heard clearly all evening. "Since I see that he has abandoned you, I shall make bold to introduce myself."

Dia turned and found a gentleman bowing before her, suffused with a strangely compelling brilliance that was almost painful to look upon. She stared at him with dull, apathetic eyes.

Meanwhile, the young man had risen from his florid bow. "I am Caelon of Aerandos," he said.

"Dia of Shae," she murmured, giving him her hand.

CHAPTER FOUR

Dia came to herself with a shock. The lassitude which had overcome her had suddenly evaporated and she was alert once more. It almost seemed that she had been in some sort of trance and, unsure of what she had said in the last hour, and to whom, she looked around her in some alarm. Daerus was nowhere to be seen and, now that she was really seeing the bawdy revelry all around her, she blushed a fiery red in mortification. The thought of what she might have said in her stupor made her feel vulnerable and a little frightened.

Her companion watched her confusion and dismay for a moment and then, in what seemed to her to be the most profoundly understanding tones, said, "Permit me to make my mother known to you."

Dia, trembling, allowed herself to be led along the wall to where a few chairs had been set up for the older ladies. Her heart was racing and she had no desire to be presented to anyone else or, indeed, to do anything but return to her chambers to consider this strange turn of events. Even now, she felt a sort of pressure in her mind, a heavy hand bearing down on everything in and around her. Indeed, it had not been particularly subtle, but it had been terrifyingly irresistible. She could understand how the courtiers around her would have succumbed; that she, trained in the Secrets of the TimeKeepers, and well shielded, could also be helpless against this power left her feeling trapped.

And yet, whatever it was that had taken over her mind had vanished at a touch from this Caelon of Aerandos, who was somehow unscathed by that power, who was a single point of light amidst all this terrible darkness. That apparent immunity bore investigation. She took a deep, steadying breath. "Are you long at court, my lord?" she asked as they walked together down the room.

"Long enough to know that I have no wish to acquire what is politely referred to as 'court polish'," he replied, looking around him with unfeigned contempt. She looked inquiringly and he added, "My father, the Grand Duke Saeros, has business with the Emperor. He required that I and my mother accompany him."

Dia thought there was probably some reason for that and, at that moment, she did not care in the least what that reason could be. She was only glad that his Grace had insisted or Chaos alone knew what would have become of her! "And does he mean to make a long stay?" she asked, wincing at a shrill shriek of laughter.

He hesitated before replying, "To be completely frank, my lady, I hope not." He looked around and added confidentially, "Indeed, I feel as if I had been here for a thousand suns already! But come, here is my esteemed mother, looking to be in need of some unexceptional company."

The lady he was approaching was seated in a velvet cushioned chair, her expression a curious combination of boredom and pained resignation. She cheered visibly when she looked up and saw them approaching. "Caelon," she said gaily, "have you found someone to rescue me? Oh, I do beg your pardon, my dear," she went on to Dia, not waiting for an introduction, "it is very rag-mannered of me, but I can see that you are enjoying this melee as little as I am. Dreadful, is it not? If this affair were not taking place in the imperial palace, one would think this was a company of the lowest street peasants. But I should not be talking to you like this;

one should always preserve at least the *appearance* of respect for the throne -- however little the throne may deserve it! I can see that Caelon's tongue has tied itself in knots, so I shall present myself. I am the Grand Duchess Tamia of Aerandos, my dear ... and I would wager that you must be one of the Shaes. You have a great look of your mother about you, you know."

Dia, feeling the stirring of a sense of humor that had been dormant for most of the evening, glanced at Lord Caelon. He did not look to her at all as if he were having any trouble finding his tongue. His eyes were lit with unholy amusement but he had made no effort to stem the flow. "Lady Dia of Shae, Mama -- if you would but let a fellow put in a word or two."

"How very unhandsome of you!" that lady said with a fond smile for her son. "Now, here is what we shall do," she went on to Dia, lowering her voice, "for I can see that you are feeling quite uncomfortable in the midst of all this. Really, I can't *think* what your brother can be thinking of! But never mind that! I shall be feeling unwell (as we elderly ladies are wont to do) and you shall assist me to my rooms, my dear. It is very plain to me that things will soon get out of hand here, and you are likely to find these affairs quite mortifying, you know."

Dia looked around. Things would *soon* get out of hand? "I beg your Grace's pardon, but it seems to me that things got out of hand quite some time ago," she said ruefully.

"A very proper spirit, my dear," said her Grace approvingly. "Caelon, you shall come with us and if any should try to stop us from leaving ... "

"I shall slice them to ribbons with my dagger," he supplied readily and with the utmost cheer.

"Do hush, you ridiculous boy," said Lady Tamia, choking. "Much as I might enjoy such a scene, I am sure it would create a dreadful scandal." She sighed. "Ever since our Phoenix completed his Time, the whole world seems to have run quite mad."

"Except Aerandos, of course," Lord Caelon said, grinning.

Dia glanced at the Grand Duchess curiously. That was the sort of remark that she and her brother had been taught to keep to themselves. "Do you say that all *this*," and she waved her hand toward the dissipated revelry behind her, "comes about because we have no Phoenix?" She knew her teachings well enough but she was curious to know if Aerandos, too, maintained the ties of the Great Houses with the Temple of Fires.

Lady Tamia smiled at her. "Well, you are certainly better than most. The young people here in the palace seem to know nothing of the Phoenix or his priesthood or even what it all *means*."

"Yes, yes, Mama," Lord Caelon interjected, grinning wickedly, "but I believe the lady did ask a question."

"Yes, I know that, Caelon, and I wish very much that you would stop interrupting me!" Lady Tamia told him severely. "Now where was I?" she went on, ignoring her son's silently shaking shoulders. "Ah, yes. Well, as you know, my dear, we have not had a normal day, with a sunrise and a sunset I mean, since the Phoenix ended his Time. And it *does* seem such a little thing, to be sure, but there is no denying that it is very difficult to organize much of anything when there is no common time for going to sleep or getting out of bed or going out to business or ... oh, all manner of *simple* things! Indeed, Saeros had the worst time imaginable with his men but, you know, you cannot have an army without uniform conduct." She looked around and wrinkled her nose in distaste. "It is really too bad that something similar did not happen here. The Emperor's court seems to have become so dreadfully -- uncivilized. I can only hope that another Time will occur before this poor world falls apart."

"Nonsense!" interjected Lord Caelon. "Only think of how dull the Emperor's parties would be!"

"Oh, do be quiet, Caelon!" said her Grace. "I must look properly vaporish on my way to the doors and it would never do for you to make me laugh just now."

Or me, Dia thought, sternly suppressing her own laughter and assuming a suitably attentive expression. She was more grateful to them than they could know, for their banter had stilled the quivering panic in her belly, further clearing her head. Now, all she needed was enough peace in which to *think*!

"You are retiring, my lady?"

The pressure in her mind increased as Dia turned to face the crown prince. "Lady Tamia is unwell, your Highness. I am escorting her to her chambers," she replied. The Prince took her hand, rather possessively she thought, and bowed to her. Dia felt herself sinking once more.

"Nothing serious, I hope?" he inquired politely, with a bow to her Grace.

"Not at all, Highness" Lord Caelon replied with unabated cheer. "It is merely one of those mysterious female ailments that requires the presence of another female."

Lady Tamia erupted into a terrible fit of coughing.

"In that case," said the Prince, smiling at Lord Caelon in masculine sympathy, "I have nothing more to do than wish the ladies a pleasant rest." He bowed again, adding to Dia, "I shall send a servant to enquire of you, my lady, after firstmeal is served. You have not forgotten, I hope, that you are promised to us then?"

"Of course not, your Highness," Dia said as one in a trance, although she had no idea what they had planned to do together. Gropingly, she extended her hand.

"Excellent," was his reply, giving her no clue.

"Come, my lady," Lord Caelon said, giving the prince an apologetic look and Dia a penetrating one. "I would not press you but if my mother should tumble to the floor in a faint, I fear it would be quite injurious to her dignity." He took the searching hand she had extended, unwittingly clearing Dia's mind once more.

Her Grace mumbled something appropriate and the small party finally got through the doors.

The Duchess enlivened the journey to her rooms with the ingenuous chatter that seemed natural to her. Dia, not required to keep up her end of the conversation since her Grace was in the habit of answering her own questions, gave herself over to some rapid, intense thought. It seemed that she had stumbled upon the answer to what was ailing Daerus and, if she were not very careful, she would fall victim to the same complaint. But what to do? Whoever it was seemed able to cut through the defenses of a well-trained mind as easily as a knife cuts through cheese. How was she to defend herself against such power? Nothing Phoebus had taught them seemed sufficient to deal with this situation.

And who could it be? Her first thought, that it must be Prince Maermat, she rejected. True, that trance-like state seemed to come over her as soon as he touched her hand and his eyes met hers --

the same eyes that seemed to be looking at her from her brother's face, she suddenly realized. Well, then, perhaps our good prince was indeed the culprit. He did not seem to emanate the same sort of Talent that she felt whenever she had been in Phoebus' presence but, then, neither did whatever had come over her feel like any other mind touch she knew.

None of this solved her immediate problem. How was she to spend any time in the presence of the Prince, as it seemed she was pledged to do, and still retain her wits intact? On impulse, Dia inserted a question into one of Lady Tamia's infrequent pauses. "I beg your pardon, your Grace, but are either of you acquainted with my brother?"

"Have you a brother, my dear? Yes, of course you do," her Grace said, still answering her own questions. "Is he also in the palace?"

"Why, yes, ma'am," Dia replied, affecting diffidence. "He has been here for some time and sent home to ask me to join him here."

"I am not certain but what he might have done better than to invite you to such a place as this," Lord Caelon said with surprising austerity. "You will give me leave to inform you that he must be a poor sort of a brother."

"Oh, no, Caelon, how can you say so?" her Grace came to the absent Daerus' rescue. "I expect he thought she might meet some unexceptional gentleman or some such thing."

"*Here*?" he asked, scornfully incredulous.

"Yes, here," her Grace replied firmly. "Indeed, if he is well acquainted among the Emperor's guests, he may very well have someone in mind. And if he is not very good at matchmaking, I am sure that is no fault of his, for he is only a man, you know." She added in an aside to Dia, "Men should *never* attempt to play at making appropriate matches between young persons, for they are perfectly dismal at it, my dear. And yet, one can never seem to persuade them that this is so, for they are always meddling and always making a dreadful mull of it. In any event, I think it speaks greatly to his credit if he has given the matter any thought at all. Is he your elder brother, dear?"

"We are twins, your Grace," she replied, unable to help smiling at the notion of the Daerus she thought she knew bothering his head with her matrimonial prospects.

"Twins? But how intriguing!" Lady Tamia said, looking quite delighted. "This is wonderful, indeed, and how extraordinary that we were just speaking of the next Phoenix! Here we are."

"Your Grace?" Dia asked in some bewilderment. The three of them had come to a halt beside what must be the Ducal chambers.

"Now where was it?" Lady Tamia asked herself, with a charming frown of concentration. Lord Caelon, his lip curling, began to speak but she stopped him with a gesture. "No, no ... don't tell me ... "

"I could not tell you if I wanted to, Mama," he said patiently. "And I do not think Lady Dia can be interested in the ancient sayings of mythical creatures when she is looking so tired."

Dia, who would have very much liked to have heard which of the First Prophesies had caught the Duchess's wandering attention, said with a smile, "It seems you have an unbeliever in your midst, ma'am. How would it be if I came to your sitting room for midmeal? No doubt you will have remembered the passage by that time and if Lord Caelon finds such matters so very tedious, he will be at liberty to amuse himself elsewhere."

Lady Tamia beamed. "The very thing, my dear! I must confess, I will be very glad of your company and should dearly love to present you to my lord. Now, Caelon, do you take the child to her rooms, she looks to be quite out on her feet."

"Yes, Mama," said that dutiful young man in a suspiciously meek tone of voice, as he held the door for his mother. Once he had closed it again, he turned a quizzical glance upon Dia. "You cannot be serious."

"My lord?"

"My lady?" he mocked her. "I fully appreciate your exquisite manners but you will be heartily bored by the time my mother has done reading to you from the sayings of this Phoenix of hers."

"I do not fear it, my lord," she said with calm certainty, adding with a faint smile, "It would be difficult to imagine finding her Grace boring under any circumstances." She turned and slowly made her way back down the hall toward her own rooms. "You do not believe then?" she asked tentatively.

"I cannot bring myself to do so, my lady, despite my beloved Mama's best efforts," he told her.

How very odd, she thought.

"Is it not?" he replied smilingly, causing Dia to suffer another shock. Apparently unaware that she had not spoken aloud, he went on, "Clearly, I am the most undutiful son imaginable."

"Not at all," she said politely. "It is curious, though, that you harbor this disbelief when you have yourself witnessed the end of a Time and need not rely solely upon the teachings of priests. Have you never wondered what had happened?"

"I feel sure there must be some rational explanation that would satisfy a logical man better than the notion that one man died and the world stopped." He added with a shrug, "I have met many men and even seen some die. It is not such a matter for wonder. And, in any event, who has ever even seen this mysterious Phoenix fellow? I do believe that someone must have made him up!"

She nodded without comment, but did not smile at the raillery in his voice. For all he seemed to possess some latent Talent, he did not believe. For some reason, she found that unutterably sad.

"You are troubled, my lady?" he asked into the silence.

"It is of no moment," she replied, feeling subdued and not looking at him.

"Might I be of some assistance?"

"Thank you, my lord, it is very kind in you but it is not needful."

He seemed to accept this rebuff meekly enough, yet, she could sense a certain diffidence about him, as if he were loathe to leave her, that she found oddly comforting. By this time, they had reached her door and he bowed politely. "Then I will bid you a pleasant rest, my lady," he said.

She watched him turn away from her for the second time since she had arrived, only then remembering her dilemma. "Lord Caelon!" she said hurriedly.

He turned back to her readily enough. "Yes, my lady?"

"There *is* one thing that you can do for me," she said, holding out her hand. She spoke tentatively, certain he would think her quite mad but unable to conceive of another remedy to her most pressing problem.

"How can I serve you, Lady Dia?" he asked her kindly.

"You can do this," she said very seriously, indicating the hand he had unconsciously taken with a slight pressure of her fingers. "Any time you see me, anywhere in this palace, come and shake my hand. Indeed, if you can do no more than pause at my door before you retire in the evening, so that I can do *this*, I should be excessively grateful."

During this speech, Dia, widening her considerable sensitivities, felt herself growing, expanding, strengthening somehow, with him and of herself, as their hands held. Indeed, she got the feeling that if only they could stand so for long enough, she could then withstand whatever that mysterious dark enemy threw at her. She held his eyes with her own and saw them assume a guarded, wary expression, although the smile did not leave his face. *You feel this, too, but you do not know what it means,* she said silently, still watching him.

His eyes widened. "My lady?"

"My lord?"

He blinked. "What is all this?" he demanded with a slight, puzzled frown. He looked as if he thought she was playing some trick on him and was fully prepared to give her a severe scold. The notion amused her.

So, she smiled kindly at him. "I doubt I could explain it to your satisfaction, my lord," was all she said.

There was a distinct pause and Lord Caelon's expression turned quizzical again. "Well, and that certainly puts me in my place, and serve me right, heretic that I am." He paused and his voice softened. "Never mind. I think you could explain, if you would, but I will not press you. No doubt you have good reason to keep your own counsel just at this present."

"And, will you ... ?"

"I will most happily perform this small service for you, ma'am," he said, so pompously that she chuckled. "Indeed," he added with rueful candor, "I fancy the difficult part of this duty will be the letting go."

Dia had also noticed an almost embarrassing unwillingness to release his hand, but she did not comment, merely sinking into a thankful curtsey.

Clearly reluctant but without further speech, Lord Caelon released her hand and bowed her into her room.

Dia made her way through the sitting room to the bedchamber, her body weary but her mind running around in the kind of circles that were likely to keep her from sleep until she had contrived some sort of plan of action. *And the first step toward accomplishing that,* she told herself severely, *is to seek some sort of calm.* She donned her nightdress, sat on her bed and closed her eyes.

Phoebus had taught her and Daerus this technique one day when they had asked him how he managed to retain his unruffled demeanor in the face of any manner of confusion swirling about him. Dia sent her mind on an inward journey, sinking deep into herself to find the essential core of her being. It its way, this method of meditation was the mental opposite of the reaching touch with which she and her brother communicated. Rather than expanding, growing outward to touch the mental energies of those around them, one must shrink, drawing inward to focus upon one's central kernel of being. Nothing, Phoebus had told them, no matter how powerful, could touch that essence; as long as they could find it, and take all the time they needed to explore it and to draw as much of it as required to the surface, they could always retain their mental integrity against attack.

Dia had never had occasion to call this facet of her training into practice; living quietly on her father's estate all her life, she had found little that she could not handle without needing to draw upon these deep reserves. Now, sinking further and further into herself, she was astonished at just how profound those reserves were. *How little I have known myself*, she thought in wonder. Breathing slowly and deeply, she could not have said how long she sat so, for she was determined that nothing should hurry her through this first encounter with herself. Really, it was rather too bad she had never done this before; the longer she spent experiencing herself in this new way, the more peaceful, yet joyous, she became. Phoebus had never mentioned this powerful, exalted feeling. Little wonder that the archpriest was always so calm.

Finally, almost reluctantly, Dia opened her eyes and set about considering her situation. She wasted no time wondering whether her brother was under the influence of the same dark fog that overtook her mind during endmeal; that Daerus was in thrall to that mental sludge must be obvious to one who knew him as well as his twin. But, before she could address her brother's mental captivity, she needed to know just what that cloying blackness was and who or what wielded it. Her initial assumption, that someone in the Imperial family was to blame, was based merely on the fact that she had first noticed that darkened aura within the boundaries of Ormaer, and that she herself had succumbed to it as soon as she had come into close contact with Prince Maermat. Yet, for aught she knew, it might as easily be someone else or even some sort of disease of Talent that was spread by proximity or contact.

In spite of her father's consistent accusations of unremitting featherheadedness on the part of his twin children, Dia was not unaware of the political difficulties of the situation. She could not imagine what either the Emperor or his heirs could desire of them that required either subterfuge or mental coercion, for Shae was a loyal and honorable House. Indeed, she realized, his Imperial Majesty had nothing to do but issue an imperial command to acquire whatever object or deed he craved. *Well,* she corrected herself, *almost.* The Great Houses *did* have rights, even in the face of imperial displeasure. If the Emperor, or his heirs, was using some sort of mental power in order to control the children of Shae and, ultimately, the House of Shae, she needed to know the full extent of their plans.

On the other hand, if some outside agency sought control of the Imperial family of Ormaeranda, it could only be for the purpose of some sort of mischief or treason. As distasteful as she had found Kaerkas the Beast -- and she had little difficulty in perceiving why her father had no use for the Emperor and his sycophants -- she had no notion of sitting idly by while someone, powerfully schooled in Secrets of their own, caused their ruler to commit some dreadful blunder or worse.

Yes, she thought, *this matter bears investigation.*

Precisely how she was to initiate such an investigation presented her with another problem. The simplest way of learning more about that dense, dark mental blanket was to allow it to overtake her again. Very likely, there would be no difficulty about that, since she was pledged to the imperial party immediately after firstmeal. Yet, the notion of spending any time with her mind numbed by murky shadows filled her with trepidation. How could she learn anything of the phenomenon if her wits were dulled to all whenever she came into contact with it? And, more importantly to her, how was she to drag herself free of it?

That dilemma, and the solution she had found for it in the person of Lord Caelon, reminded her of the party from Aerandos. Dia wondered why this aura of darkness seemed to have left both Lady Tamia and Lord Caelon unscathed. Could it be simply that they had not been in the palace for long enough to succumb to it? That did not seem likely, for only think of the terrifying swiftness with which she herself, fully shielded, had surrendered to it. Could they be somehow invulnerable to it? She could readily believe it of Caelon of Aerandos, who stalked about the palace blazing light, when a simple clasp of his hand could chase the darkness from her mind. But what of her Grace? And the Grand Duke? Dia saw that she would do well to cultivate their acquaintance.

And what was she to do about Daerus? Was he really as besotted with the Princess Kera as he said, or was that merely another manipulation of the mysterious wielder of darkness? She had only the vaguest recollections of the fair lady with reddish-blonde hair to whom her brother had presented her; try as she might, Dia could recall no distinguishing characteristics of mind or manner that would make the girl stand out in a crowded room. Considering her stupor at endmeal, she could not judge whether or not her brother's tastes truly ran in that direction. She had no difficulty with the notion of Daerus marrying an imperial princess, but she thought it might be a very good thing to get him away from the palace for a time. Long enough, at least, for him to come to himself and learn whether this betrothal was indeed what he wished. She sighed. He would never leave the palace willingly, as matters now stood.

Would it make any difference to her ability to persuade him, she wondered, if she were to attempt to renew their mind-touch? Dia recalled how her twin had flinched away from that touch when she had tried earlier to strengthen it. *Almost,* she mused, *as if he found it painful.* Well, she would postpone such a mind-touch, she decided. Until she better understood what she was up against, it would serve no purpose to inflict herself upon him in such a fashion.

That brought her back to her first decision, to take a better look at the darkness. But how to maintain her own mental integrity? Dia reviewed the experience just passed, the joyous calm of her contact with her inner being, closing her eyes and savoring it once more. Could she carry that untouchable kernel of self with her, holding it in her mental hand and allowing *it* to observed the thing? Perhaps she could retain enough awareness to make her observations in spite of the enveloping, enervating blackness. Likewise, emerging from the fog presented little difficulty if she could keep her wits about her enough to make her way to Lord Caelon's presence once she was quit of the Imperial family.

How fortunate that Grand Duke Saeros had business with the Emperor that had brought him to the palace just at this time! she thought with considerable relief.

Having settled on a course of action, Dia stretched out on the bed. Her last thought before she drifted off to sleep was again of Lord Caelon, and she wondered what he had made of her strange request. Perhaps, she thought drowsily, when they were better acquainted, she would explain the matter to him. Who knows? He might even believe her.

CHAPTER FIVE

Dia knew, before she opened her eyes, that her brother was pounding on the door. She had risen and dressed in some haste, determined to give herself enough time to commune again with that eternal, internal core before she was required to face the dangers of darkness once more. She felt wonderfully refreshed, even more so than when she had awakened from a deep and restful slumber. She took a deep breath, cloaking her skin with a profound calm that she hoped she could carry about with her, and refusing to be hurried.

"Dia!"

She heard several more thumps on the door. Inhaling deeply once more, she went to admit her brother.

Dia wasn't sure what Daerus was expecting, but when she opened her door and he looked upon her, his head reared back slightly and his face reflected amazement and displeasure.

Her brows lifted. "Is something amiss?" she asked him in a tone of polite interest as she ushered him inside.

He stared frowningly at her. "Where did you run away to last night?"

"I did not 'run away' at all, my dear," she placidly replied. "I merely retired some time after endmeal."

"Without bidding our hosts a good rest? I had not thought you were so rag-mannered."

"I supposed I must be just so rag-mannered," she said pensively, "but, as it happens, Prince Maermat met me on my way out and I was able, at least, to take my leave of him." She noticed but did not comment upon the hint of a satisfied smile that greeted this news. "I must say, I am at something of a loss to understand you, twin," she went on. "When last I saw you, before you came to this place, you would have been horrified at the sort of activities that the Emperor's guests seem to enjoy."

"It would do you no harm to learn something of pastimes that are more elegant than hobnobbing with the grooms," he told her severely.

Dia laughed. "More elegant? I am given to understand that dicing, wenching and drinking wine as if it had just been discovered are more elegant than honest work, caring for our beasts of burden?"

"You are beginning to sound like Phoebus, sister," he said with a sneer.

"Thank you," Dia retorted cordially, but she wondered with something like despair if she would ever hear her brother's merry laugh again.

Daerus continued to staring at her disapprovingly. "It is not for you to judge the conduct of your peers," he said.

He is goading me, she thought, her curiosity aroused even as she renewed her mantle of composure. *Interesting.* "So you say," she replied pleasantly. "But, even if I am not to judge them, do not expect me to emulate them, for I had rather throw myself from the topmost tower of this palace." She suddenly grinned as another thought occurred to her. "And, if my father should learn that I had been aping the behavior of my 'peers', as you style them, no doubt he would spare me the trouble and perform the deed himself."

That surprised a laugh from him and hope surged in Dia's heart once more. Perhaps Daerus was not entirely lost to her, if she could still joke him about their beloved, if tiresome, parent. "So, did you merely come here to scold me? Or had you some other errand?" she asked, still smiling.

"His Highness awaits you in the small dining room."

"Ah." She nodded and followed him from the room.

"Why do you not take your meals with the imperial family?" Daerus asked her as they walked down the corridor.

"I have not been invited to take my meals with the imperial family," she replied, "for which I am profoundly thankful."

"Why?"

"Because I have no wish to spend any more time with them than is strictly necessary."

"And why not?"

"I do not suppose you will permit me to say merely that I am not comfortable around them?" she asked, smiling faintly.

"Really, Dia, one would think that you were the veriest country bumpkin!" Daerus expostulated, almost laughing. "There is no need for you to feel intimidated, simply because the Emperor shows you favor."

Dia's backbone automatically stiffened at this insult, drawing her to her full height. "I am not in the least intimidated, and well you should know it," she snapped contemptuously. "I am Shae; I have no thought of being cowed by Ormaer, on the throne or elsewhere!" *He* **is** *goading me, and to some purpose,* she told herself. *Come, Dia girl, pull yourself together.* After a brief pause and a few steadying breaths, she added gently, "I was right, you know. This *is* an elegant brothel, and I give you fair warning, I shall quit the place just as soon as I may."

His eyes went flat with hostility. "Well, here's a high flight. Emperor Kaerkas is a great man; we are fortunate to have him on the throne of Ormaeranda. And, if it is not your place to judge the amusements of your peers, it is even less your place to judge those of your emperor."

"Very likely not. I wish you will tell me why you must needs get angry with me every time I open my lips to speak," she said mildly. "I had thought that my task was to win the Emperor's approval. You never mentioned that I was required to *like* him, as well."

"And how do you imagine that you will win his approval if you avoid him at every turn?" he asked her impatiently.

Dia feigned a melancholy sigh. "Alas, my poor brother is so little acquainted with me that he thinks I cannot be adroit!" She went on confidingly, "That certainly puts me on my mettle! I shall contrive to avoid him at as many turns as I can, and so smoothly that he shall suspect nothing. *And*, I shall expect you to be suitably impressed."

"Oh, stop talking such nonsense!" he said furiously. "And I don't see what you find to laugh about!"

"Very likely not," she said again, still chuckling.

He said nothing for a moment, obviously mastering his irritation. "And what did you think of Prince Maermat?" he asked her with studied calm at last.

She shrugged. "He seemed a pleasant enough young man," she said carelessly. "It is to be hoped that he improves upon acquaintance."

"What is that supposed to mean?"

She looked at him then. "I mean, my beloved brother, that his Imperial Highness is a dead bore."

"And that is your last word?"

"No, how should it be?" she replied in a reasonable tone. "I am barely acquainted with him. I would certainly hope that he can be persuaded to be more amusing than he has been thus far. That awful endmeal last night cannot have shown him to advantage."

Daerus responded to that with a grunt. Then, as they came in sight of what appeared to be their destination, he stopped and, turning to her, said, "He is the best of good fellows and if you turn up your nose at him, then you are a worse featherhead than Father has always proclaimed you, and I wash my hands of you!"

That made her laugh again. "Well, that is certainly a threat to make me tremble in my boots!" she gasped, but sobered -- with considerable difficulty -- when she saw that he was looking offended. "I do not know what ridiculous scheme you have in your head," she added with fraternally good-natured scorn, "but you *know* that you have never been able to manipulate me into what you had not the temerity to ask for outright. And I have already warned you, Daerus, that I shall leave this place as soon as I may without giving offense."

"We shall see," was all he said, and rather ominously, before ushering her into the room.

Indeed, we shall, she thought very privately as she followed him.

"Lady Dia!" Prince Maermat had risen and come around the table to greet her. "I can see that you have enjoyed a pleasant rest, for you are looking wonderfully refreshed." He bowed.

"Thank you, your Highness," she replied, her eyes brushing his briefly before she sank into a curtsey. "I had a notion that I was looking quite hagged last night, only my brother was too kind to say so," she added with an impish smile.

"Oh, dear," the Prince said with comical dismay, trying to catch her eyes, "you mistake my meaning, my lady! But come, here are my father and sister waiting to greet you."

Again, Dia sank into a curtsey, as the Emperor fixed her with a jaundiced eye and barked, "Well, Dia of Shae, yes? You here, ha!"

The Imperial siblings exchanged a quick glace before Prince Maermat, frowning slightly, said, "Er ... yes, Father. You will recall that Lady Dia joins her excellent brother in attending us for morning audiences."

Emperor Kaerkas responded to this reminder with a grunt. Eyes glittering in a manner that chilled her to the marrow of her bones, he told Dia, "I hope you are properly humbled to be among the favored of Ormaer."

And that, Dia thought ironically, *is certainly the sort of greeting designed to appeal to a proud daughter of Shae.* "Thank you, Sire," she said, wrapping her composure about her shoulders in search of warmth.

"Very well, then," said the Emperor, pushing himself heavily to his feet.

As the small party followed him from the room, Princess Kera fell in beside Dia and smiled at her. "My father was very happy to make your acquaintance, my lady," she said in a caressing voice. "Indeed, he is becoming more and more fond of House Shae."

"How gratifying," Dia replied lightly, still not looking at anyone. In spite of her resolve of the previous evening, she realized that she was going to have to exert considerable force of mind to voluntarily endure another session of mental darkness. "My brother bid me be sure to make a favorable impression upon the Emperor, you know," she went on. "It would appear that I have been agreeable to some purpose. I have nothing now to do but thank him and go back home."

Princess Kera laughed and said, "Your brother warned us that you are a merry soul, my lady. Indeed, he begged us not to take your words too seriously, thinking you might unwittingly offend us with your jests."

"Poor Daerus! I fear I am a sad trial to him," Dia agreed pleasantly.

"Oh, you must not think he does not hold you in affection," said the Princess in apparent distress. "It is merely that he was particularly anxious to keep us from judging you harshly, for I understand that you had never been from home before this trip?" Dia nodded affirmation and her Highness continued, "So, how can you be expected to know how you should go on?"

"How indeed?" Dia remarked thoughtfully. "One would think that the district of Shae was some remote pigsty. How *could* I be expected to know aught of propriety of manner or deportment?"

"Not at all," the Princess insisted. "But you cannot deny, my lady, that at my father's court you are seeing a level of conduct that you are not at all accustomed to."

"And you are quite right," said Dia, seemingly very much struck, "I could never deny *that*!" Without seeming to, she noted the indignant expression on her brother's face with amused interest.

"There!" Princess Kera seemed relieved. "I daresay a touch of court sophistication will do you good and I am sure you will enjoy it excessively. Oh!" she added in her soft voice, as if the idea had just occurred to her, "how would it be if you were to place yourself in my charge while you are here? Surely, that would much relieve your mind."

"Relieve my mind?"

"Why, yes. I expect you must be quite nervous about your first stay at court."

"Indeed?"

"For fear that your inexperience will cause you to embarrass yourself, you know," Princess Kera said, making the matter quite clear.

"I see." The imperial princess was gazing at her earnestly and Dia found herself wondering uncharitably if her Highness' air of ingenuousness was supposed to make these blood insults more palatable. Perhaps she was again being goaded? Dia chose instead to be amused.

"But I can easily guide you so that you will avoid social mishaps, leaving you free to savor the amusements of the palace." The Princess concluded her little speech with something of the air of a successful conjurer.

"And which amusements would those be, your Highness?" Dia asked, her face a picture of innocent inquiry.

The Princess laughed again. "Oh, you are joking me again. Seriously, my lady, what do you say? I would be happy to serve you in this way and," she added with a coquettish glance at Daerus, "it would be as well, I think, were we to become better acquainted."

Dia took another deep, steadying breath, ruthlessly suppressing both her annoyance and her laughter. She was very sure that she was not imagining the sudden, tense silence that awaited her response to that offer. They seemed mighty anxious to adopt her into the family circle, she thought. Given the peculiar behavior of her brother, their very insistence invited her resistance.

Ignoring Daerus altogether, she said serenely, "You are very kind, your Highness, but I am commended by my mother to Lady Tamia's care."

"Indeed?" Princess Kera said, surprised. "Lady Mara knew that the Grand Duchess of Aerandos would be here, then?"

"No, how should she, your Highness?" Dia said calmly. "She merely suggested to me that I might investigate upon my arrival to discover whether the Lady Tamia of Aerandos or the Lady Lena of Gedbaen were in the palace. I gather that they were girls together at court, and my esteemed mother thought that either would serve the purpose admirably, should I find myself in need of an experienced friend."

"How fortunate, then, that Lady Tamia is indeed visiting us at this time," the Princess said woodenly.

Prince Maermat was looking disappointed and her brother's expression was murderous. Dia affected not to see them. "Is it not?" she replied cheerfully. "For I would not wish to impose upon your kindness and my brother, having persuaded me to come here, has wholly abandoned me to pursue his own amusements."

"Oh, if we are to talk of *brothers* ... !" her Highness said, casting a saucy glance at Prince Maermat, which caused that young man to grin, and allowing the matter to drop. Dia, without seeming to, saw the teasing twinkle leave her Highness' glance, to be replaced with a baffled, frustrated expression.

They had by this time arrived in the throne room and proceeded to dispose themselves around the room, Daerus seating Princess Kera while Prince Maermat showed Dia to a chair. That provided the opportunity Dia had been both awaiting and dreading, for while she had thus far avoided allowing any of them to look into her eyes or to touch her, she could not dispense with the protocol of letting the Prince take her hand to guide her to her seat. Dia, beginning to feel that sinking pressure, took yet another deep breath and sank away from it, into herself. As she had hoped, the strange lassitude settled over her but did not consume her, and while she felt remote from the events around her, she did not think she would forget them.

Excellent, she thought, well satisfied even though she felt dreadfully uncomfortable, as if she were covered with the contents of the stable floors. *And now, to work.*

It was a curious process, a bit like closely examining a scabrous but painless rash that had somehow broken out on one's arm. Dia felt/saw the mental intrusion as a blanketing barrier between herself and everything around her. And, she realized now, there was much more to it than the simple languid indifference initially conveyed by its overwhelming darkness. There were subtler influences in it that would have slowly shaped her preferences, without her awareness and against her will, had she found no way to neutralize it.

She sensed a distaste for all the attributes of a purposeful life -- honor, duty, work -- and a mindless, insatiable hunger for the sensual pleasures and for material wealth. As well, she began to understand the shameless debauchery of the denizens of the palace. She candidly admitted to herself that, if she had remained under the influence of this mental fog for long enough, the deadening indifference would have ended in a desperate need to endlessly titillate herself, if only to remain convinced that she was still alive. But if she understood the craving, she also understood, within herself, how ultimately empty such amusements were. A surge of overwhelming pity for these people her brother had styled her 'peers' possessed her. Indeed, she was not even surprised to find the tiny kernel of a suicidal impulse buried deep within the darkness. She would have to handle Daerus with infinite care.

But the question remained: where was it coming from? She would have to find out before she could make any attempt to salvage her brother or even do much to protect herself. She looked around the room at her companions.

To her dismay, but not to her surprise, the peculiarly innocent beauty of Prince Maermat had been replaced -- or perhaps overlaid, instinct told her -- by a sort of arrogant hardness, and the speculative gaze that had become so familiar to her was back. There was, she noted with interest, an additional hint of possessiveness in his eyes as he returned her glance. Princess Kera's insipid girlishness now seemed much less insipid; she now looked upon her world with a cynical, calculating eye. And, yet, they did not really look any different. Dia could not have pointed to any particular feature or act that had changed her impressions of these Imperial siblings. It was almost as if someone or something had already consumed them, even as it had consumed Daerus, and had stamped its mark on their features.

And that left her no closer to discovering who or what was responsible -- and why.

Meanwhile, the Emperor did not seem to have changed at all; his eyes were just as dangerous as they had been when she had first arrived in the imperial breakfast room. He was interviewing a common tradesman, a scribe to judge by the inkstains on his fingers. Dia was a little surprised that she would notice such a detail, groping about in this fog. The tradesman had prostrated himself before the throne, visibly trembling, as the Emperor roared at him, clutching a sheaf of parchment.

"What do you mean, writing such stuff?" the Emperor was demanding.

"If it please yer honor," the poor man said in a voice hardly above a whisper, "I didn't write it, sir. I just copied down what was give me, sir."

"I don't care if you wrote it or not!" declared his Majesty, "You should have returned this commission as soon as you saw it's content. You shall be punished for this outrage! I *shall* have respect!"

The shrill note in the Emperor's last two sentences seemed to confuse the scribe. "Please, yer honor," he said, "I didn't know. I can't read. I just copy."

"That is no excuse! This is **treason**!" Emperor Kaerkas shouted, spraying spittle as he yanked violently on the bellpull beside his throne. "Take this traitor out and hang him," he told the soldiers who answered his summons.

"Please, sir ... " the tradesman pleaded in some bewilderment as the soldiers roughly yanked him to his feet.

"Find his home and burn it to the ground, and hail his family, if he has one, to the slave markets," the Emperor went on with relish. His eyes were alight with cruel anticipation as he issued these orders and seemed to pause to savor the pain he had certainly caused.

For the tradesman's eyes now held panic and terror and despair, as he begged not for his own life but for the safety of his family. "No!" he cried. "My missus don't have nowt to do wi' what I scribe, yer honor! It ain't fair to take her and her babies! *Please* ... !"

Great, wracking sobs and incoherent, panicked entreaties echoed from the cavernous ceiling, but the Emperor, with calculated disinterest, was already instructing his guardsmen to admit his next appointment.

Dia blinked. For an instant, she heard a peculiar shimmering buzz and felt an odd stillness descend on her. Inexplicably, she seemed to see a tiny kernel of light, like a flame applied to a lantern viewed from far away, shining steadily in that inner, sacred core of herself. Without consciously deciding to do so, she found herself focusing all her concentration upon that tiny light, as the room and its occupants faded from her awareness. And she knew, without knowing how she could have known, that something of consequence was about to happen.

Dia ...

Dia immediately recognized her brother's mental touch and realized, as well, that Daerus was not alone. In the instant before her brother's mind had met hers, she felt that same black, bone-deep chill that had assailed her as she had left her rooms before last endmeal. She shivered, wondering absently why that should be.

Yes, Daerus?

I know that you feel this power.

Indeed, she did feel it. The blanketing fog that had enveloped her grew blacker, palpating as if it were a man flexing his muscles. She sharpened her focus on that untouchable inner core of herself, with its small, eternal light, even as she replied, *Of course, I do. It feels perfectly dreadful, dearest. What is it?*

Dreadful? A soundless chuckle tickled her senses. *Oh, yes, I suppose it must seem that way to you, for you have not yet felt the beauty of it.*

Beauty? she injected a note of distaste into her "voice". *Do you find it so, Daerus?*

It is of all things the most wonderful I have ever experienced, sister, he told her persuasively. *It is powerful, irresistibly powerful.*

Is power so sweet to you, then?

Power is everything to such as we, Dia. Why else were we born to the talents we possess?

Why, indeed? she quipped, knowing better. *I confess, I cannot share your enthusiasm for it.*

Why not?

It is cold.

It is clear and stark and beautiful, he told her.

It is dark.

There is peace in the darkness.

It is unclean.

A scornful snort greeted that observation. *Do not be a little fool, Dia,* her brother told her with fraternal brusqueness. *What need have we to care for such things? We are above considerations of what may or may not be unclean.*

I fear I do not have such an exalted opinion of myself, dearest, she said with calm amusement.

She felt him "lean" into her, increasing the pressure that bore down upon her mind. *No, but do you turn away from me so easily?* he asked, wheedling. *We have been together for as long as we have drawn breath; will you not walk with me now?*

As he spoke, it seemed that a thousand memories flooded her mind. Daerus skillfully reminded her of the play, the squabbles, the camaraderie, and, above all, the laughter they had shared all their lives. Without even thinking, she sought to strengthen their mental bond, longing suddenly and passionately for the ease and comfort of their former link. She was so lonely, so very lonely and, while Daerus had been distant and unreachable since she had arrived, he suddenly seemed very close.

Yes! he encouraged her. *Come with me, Dia. Surrender to this power, even as I have. I miss you, too.*

She was sorely tempted, and she knew that he knew it. *But, I detest this darkness of yours,* she told him plaintively, after a long, silent struggle with herself. *It is a vile, revolting, mental muck.*

Do not be missish, Dia. he replied in brisk accents, brushing off her objections as if they were no more significant than a fly. *It is not your style.*

Irritated, she responded in kind. *Well, and if this mire is the price I must pay for the privilege of wielding such power as you offer, I prefer to decline,* she said tartly, as the blackness grew still heavier and she realized she was being goaded again.

You cannot decline, silly girl! Look at how easily I have buried your mind in darkness.

Well, and look at how easily I threw off your darkness after last endmeal, she pointed out, once more calm. *Perhaps it is not so very powerful after all.*

I have been gentle with you, Dia, he told her haughtily. *I do not want to hurt you. But I have chosen my path and I am determined that you shall tread that path with me.*

Why?

Because you must! And with that, his touch was gone.

Once again, she was assailed by a wave of longing for the familiar mental touch of her twin. Could she join him on the path he had chosen? she wondered. Could she willingly wallow in that awful mental slime, simply for the pleasure of the special bond they had once shared? Did she want to? Aye, now, there was a telling question. Her heart called out for her beloved brother, but the fellow she had just spoken with did not seem very like him; his touch was familiar, yet strange. Daerus had said she would soon grow accustomed to the darkness, but she found she had no real wish to become used to this dense mental fog, with its murky, chill indifference.

It seemed that she had a choice to make, and it was of all things the most irritating that she should learn of it when she was not in a position to consider what she had been told. Would she spend her entire stay in this blighted palace wishing for some peace and privacy in which to think? She turned her attention away from her disturbing conversation with Daerus and looked around the throne room again.

Emperor Kaerkas had risen and was stepping down from his throne. " . . . advise them that they are to report to me directly after midmeal," he was instructing a footman. "Come, let us repair to the dining hall." And with that, he strutted toward the door.

Dia got to her feet and, in company with Daerus and the rest of the imperial family, left the throne room in the Emperor's wake. Just outside the door, the party encountered Lord Caelon, in conversation with the same footman the Emperor had just sent on his errand.

"Well met, Caelon of Aerandos," the Emperor hailed the younger man. "I had just sent this fellow to ask your father to report to me after you have had your midmeal, but no doubt you will spare him the trouble. I would have his decision, for the matter becomes urgent."

"Well met, indeed, your Majesty," Lord Caelon replied formally, bowing first to Emperor Kaerkas and then to his son and daughter. "I will be very happy to convey your invitation to my father."

The Emperor gave Lord Caelon a sharp glance for his choice of words and then a curt nod of acknowledgement, before moving on. Lord Caelon, apparently oblivious, stepped up to intercept Dia, who dropped a curtsey and gave him her hand.

"How fortunate that I have found you, my lady," he said, bowing over the hand she had given him.

With that greeting, two things happened. The inner light she had noticed in the throne room brightened and grew -- a little, just a little -- and the cloying mists that had clouded her thoughts and numbed her feelings vanished.

Dia raised smilingly thankful eyes to her unsuspecting rescuer. "Indeed, my lord?" she said quizzically. And, as soon as her mind was her own again, she knew that her choice was already made. Indeed, there was no contest -- but how clever of Daerus and his unseen companion to attempt to pressure her into giving her pledge when she was sunk in that disgusting mental sludge and could not think clearly! She wondered if that had been his idea. *Really,* she thought, both surprised and self-congratulatory, *I am glad I asked this of Lord Caelon. It was a* **very** *good idea.*

She knew he heard her thought, for his eyes suddenly brimmed with suppressed mirth. "I am bid to convey her Grace's compliments and to tell you that she is pining for your company. You recall that you are promised to us for midmeal?"

She had, with some difficulty, retrieved her hand and now cast a surreptitious glance at her brother. He was exchanging a look with his betrothed that was as vexed as it was mystified. With a certain malicious delight, she said, "Yes, of course I remember and was just about to make my excuses to my imperial hosts. I do hope your Highnesses will forgive me," she added, turning to them with a gracious smile once she had taken the arm Lord Caelon offered. *Let them sit and wonder how I have shed their trap so easily*, she thought, knowing but not minding that Caelon of Aerandos could hear every uncharitable word. *No doubt it will keep them out of mischief!*

"You return to us after midmeal?" Daerus asked her, his eyes thunderous.

"I fear not, twin," she told him sweetly, smiling with satisfaction at her brother's silent and bewildered fuming. Never had she derived so much enjoyment from simply refusing an invitation! "I shall be with her Grace for the rest of the day and will likely accompany her down to endmeal. No doubt I shall see you then."

She felt her brother's mind at work before he actually attempted to touch her again. Never had she experienced such a ponderous mental weight, as if he sought to crush her mind and her will to resist, and Dia recalled his previous assertion that he had been gentle with her. Was this his attempt to prove to her how much power he had at his disposal? Did he think to force his stinking darkness upon her here and now? With deliberate calm, she pushed the overpowering touch away, making no effort to be gentle and wondering why the task should be so easily accomplished. *Do not try to bully me, twin,* she told him in tranquil accents. *I will choose my* **own** *path.*

There is only one possible choice, Dia, Daerus told her. *Remember.*

Nonsense! Surreptitiously and, she hoped, unnoticed by Lord Caelon, Dia allowed her fingertip to touch his lordship's wrist as she held her brother's glance with her own. *If one of the choices is darkness, then the other choice must be light.*

And, even as she said it, that inner kernel of light flared unasked into a brilliant flash of bright and cheery warmth. *How intriguing!* As she had previously done with her brother's darkness, she wondered absently why that should be.

Even more intriguing, Daerus flinched away from her. So, Dia noted with interest, did Princess Kera. No, Daerus had **not** been alone, but Dia wondered why he seemed to require assistance to reach out a mere five feet in order to contact her mind. He had never needed such help before. It would appear that this beauteous darkness of which her brother was so enamored was a weakening influence, rather than a strengthening one.

Overall, a productive morning, Dia decided as she sailed away on Lord Caelon's arm. *And instructive. Only now,* she added with a silent sigh, *I must decide whether or not to style my brother my enemy ... and that may prove the most difficult of all!*

CHAPTER SIX

When Dia, accompanied by Lord Caelon, entered the Grand Duchess's sitting room a few moments later, she found that lady bent almost double over a sizable trunk, rummaging about and muttering to herself distractedly. "Oh, no ... no ... it cannot be that I left it at Aerandos ... I was sure ... oh, here it ... no, that's not it ...," her Grace mumbled.

"Oh, Mama," Lord Caelon sang to her agitated Grace, casting a wicked glance at Dia and causing that young lady to choke on a laugh.

"Oh, Caelon," wailed Lady Tamia in tones of the greatest distress, still without emerging from her trunk, "do not be teasing and infuriating. Help me to find it. She will be here at any moment."

"I am afraid she is already here, Mama," his lordship said to his agitated parent.

"Oh!" With somewhat surprising agility that was only slightly marred by the flowing draperies currently fashionable among older ladies, Lady Tamia started, straightened and turned, all in one movement. "Oh, Caelon, you wretch!" she said, recovering quickly with a rueful laugh.

Dia chuckled. "He is very unchivalrous, is he not?"

"I make no doubt that it is entirely my own fault for indulging him shamelessly when he was a child," Lady Tamia owned handsomely.

"If that is so, your Grace, I feel sure you must be right," Dia agreed instantly. "I expect, if my father were here, he would say that Lord Caelon would have benefitted enormously from being spanked as a child -- hard and often."

"As he has perhaps said of his twin children?" asked Lord Caelon, looking sly.

"Caelon!" Lady Tamia said, with a worried glance at her young guest.

But Dia only laughed again. "Never fear, ma'am. My lord is perfectly right, scorch him!" she said in unimpaired good humor.

"Well, but, even so, my dear," Lady Tamia said gravely, "however cleverly he may have guessed the truth, and however much you and your brother may have made nuisances of yourselves as children, it is not at all the thing for him to be *saying* so! Now, what have I said to send the pair of you into whoops?" she asked, bewildered. "I must say, I wonder at Lord Loraed, really I do! To be saying such things of his children, and right in front of them, too! I confess, I am thankful that my lord has never had occasion to speak so ill of his heir."

"At least, not to my face," Lord Caelon added, still grinning.

"There has not been the least need," said a new voice, a deep, rumbling voice that seemed used to commanding attention. "I placed my heir in the ranks of the army and let my drill sergeants teach him the realities of his situation."

Lord Saeros stood just inside the threshold, seeming to fill a great deal of space as he did so. He was an imposing tree trunk of a man, yet he moved quietly and with the precision that came naturally to a lifelong military man. Like his son, everything about him was crisp and soldierly. Dia imagined that he would have as little use for the hedonistic excesses that occupied the minds of the Emperor's courtiers as had her own father; idly, she wondered again what business this no-nonsense gentleman could have with the Kaerkas the Beast.

"And this, I fancy, must be my Lady Dia of Shae," he said, bowing to her with great dignity before strolling toward her in a leisurely fashion. "How do you do, my dear? Her Grace has been rather full of the prospect of entertaining you to midmeal, you know."

"Has she, your Grace?" Dia said, her smile almost shy. This Grand Duke of Aerandos reminded her forcibly of Lord Loraed, and she rather absurdly found herself wanting to win his approval. "I am very happy to meet you, sir."

His Grace paused by Lady Tamia. "Do give over rummaging about the trunks, my lady. Midmeal shall arrive at any time now, and you would not wish to sit down to table with all the dust of Aerandos on your hands," he said, perfectly seriously but with a teasing twinkle in his eye. Dia had a sudden conviction that Lord Caelon very much favored his sire. She looked over at him and was surprised to find herself the object of a sympathetically enquiring gaze.

They are much like my own parents, she told him silently, not knowing quite why she fell impelled to say anything at all. *It must be lovely to be so happily mated.*

But why sound so wistful, my lady? he replied, once more surprising her. *Surely, you expect to be as content in your choice, once you have made it.*

She smiled faintly, but prefaced her response with a sigh. *If I look wistfully, it is because I am surprised to find that I miss Lord Loraed and his lady rather more than I had thought to.* Then, shaking off her brief melancholy, she added. *You are a quick study, my lord. It took Phoebus quite some time to teach Daerus and I to direct our thoughts so precisely.*

I doubt there is any precision involved, my lady ... much as I hate to detract so from myself, he replied somewhat ruefully. *I would imagine I could not speak in this fashion with anyone else. I certainly have never done so before.*

"Well, in that case," Lady Tamia was saying in response her husband's admonition, "I shall just run to my room and wash my hands. I shall return directly." And, with that, she bustled away.

Lord Saeros continued on his languid way across the room toward Dia, as Caelon said to him, "I am instructed to advise you, sir, that his Majesty desires you to attend him directly after midmeal."

"Indeed?" said his Grace, rather absently, taking Dia's hand. "Will you not be seated, my lady?" he asked politely, guiding her toward a chair.

Lord Caelon seemed to think this disinterested reply was amusing, for he grinned, adding, "He would know your decision, he says."

"Yes, I expect he would" said Lord Saeros pensively. Then he went on, to Dia, "You have a great look of your mother about you, my dear, as I expect my lady has already pointed out to you."

Dia could see that Lord Caelon wanted to further discuss his Grace's mysterious business with the Emperor, but was aware of a need for discretion. She could also see that the younger man was hard put to it to keep from bursting into laughter, but what his father was doing that tickled him so she could not guess. To his Grace, she replied with a saucy grin, "Indeed, she has. It is quite gratifying, you know, sir, because I have always thought my mother quite beautiful. I hope I shall not grow quite conceited."

Lord Saeros chuckled. Lord Caelon, apparently unable to contain himself another instant, said, "I beg your pardon, sir, but I was rather wondering myself how you meant to answer his Imperial Majesty."

Lord Saeros bent a sardonic eye upon his heir. "Yes, I expect you were," he said, "although I cannot imagine how it comes about that you thought to beguile our midmeal with such a dreary subject when we are entertaining a guest. I wonder where you can have learned your manners, boy."

This last proved too much for Lord Caelon's self control, and a laugh escaped him. "It would seem that I owe my lady an apology, although," and here he gave her such a wickedly quizzing look that she chuckled, "she already knows me for a churlish knave and surely cannot be surprised."

"To be sure, there is not the least need to beg my pardon, my lord," Dia said, grinning back at him, "and only think how such handsome behavior would spoil your image." Loftily ignoring Lord Caelon's shout of laughter, she added to his Grace, "I am only sorry that my presence prevents you from discussing such an important matter as your business here in the palace. I wonder if I should excuse myself to her Grace so that you can speak freely?"

"Indeed, and you shall do no such thing!" said Lady Tamia, sailing back into the sitting room at that moment. "What have the pair of you been saying to the child that she is ready to fly so soon?" she scolded the two gentlemen impartially.

"Why, nothing, my dear," replied Lord Saeros, mild as ever.

"Indeed?" her Grace retorted with heavy skepticism. "I leave her happily in your company for a mere two minutes, and when I return ... "

"As much as I hesitate to interrupt you, my lady," Lord Saeros interjected, "I wondered if you mean to scold us *very* severely?" Lady Tamia did not immediately reply, merely regarding him with a smoldering, laughing eye. He continued, "If so, do you suppose you might feed us at the same time? For I perceive that our midmeal has arrived."

Instantly distracted, Lady Tamia hurried to the sitting room door and busily directed the Emperor's servants in the disposition of an appetizing meal, talking all the time. Considerably amused by the spousal exchange she had just witnessed, Dia watched her fondly. There was so much love and laughter in this apartment, among this family, that Dia felt both homesick and yet more comfortable than at any other time since she had set forth to join her brother here. She was certainly glad to have met the members of House Aerandos, feeling that they were much more her peers than the minor nobility that made up most of the Emperor's court. (Daerus' comment still rankled; her 'peers' indeed!) But, by the fires of the Phoenix, she would be ever so much happier when she could leave this place and go home!

"Well, my dear," Lady Tamia said, turning to Dia as the servants bowed themselves out of the room, "here is a tidy midmeal, to be sure. Will you take a little wine first?"

Dia accepted the wine with a smile and a mumbled word of thanks.

"I am so very disappointed that I have not been able to find that volume, dear," Lady Tamia went on. "I know that I promised to show it to you, and I am sure I had just been reading from it during the very tedious journey here. I have not the least doubt that I shall find it again just as soon as I no longer want it, for that is always the way of things, is it not?"

Dia grinned. "Indeed, I should not be at all surprised if you locate the wretched book in the instant I leave this room." Then her grin faded as she grew thoughtful. "I confess, I have some passing familiarity with the First Prophesies, you know, your Grace. I have been trying to remember if I have read the passage you mentioned, but I fear I cannot call it to mind just at this present."

"Do you know them?" said her Grace, looking surprised.

"My brother and I were tutored by the archpriest of the Phoenix who serves my father's estate, your Grace," Dia demurely explained, earning her an astonished glance from Lord Caelon and a wide smile from the Duchess.

"Your father keeps to the old ways, then? I have been trying to persuade my lord that we really should have an archpriest of the purple to serve us, but he does not bother his head with such foolishness." Lady Tamia looked over at her spouse with a roguish smile as she spoke.

Lord Saeros smiled back but, refusing the bait, he remained silent.

"But if you know the Prophesies, you must surely have read the passage I have in mind," her Grace continued. "Now let me see ... how did it begin? 'Two children shall be born in the same time ...' No ... that is not quite right ... "

Into the thoughtful pause that followed, as Dia wondered briefly why she could not seem to recall the passage in question -- there was a time when Phoebus had insisted that both she and her brother be able to recite the whole of the First Prophesy from memory -- and awaited her Grace's pleasure, a rolling, booming voice broke the silence.

"Behold!" It was Lord Caelon who spoke -- would he never cease to amaze her? -- his voice unnaturally loud, and with a strangely choral quality that did not sound at all like his usual quizzical tones. "Two children, born of a single Sun in a single House, shall command the Secrets from the instant of their births, for they shall be Our instrument in the confrontation between order and chaos. And when these two children shall come into their own, let this be a sign unto ye that the Gaerud approaches; gird ye well for the first battle of the New Age. Keep truth in thy heart and be steadfast in friendship and enmity, for this battle shall not be fought on any field on this world, but shall instead wage in the minds and hearts of those same children of Our hopes. And if the one does drown in darkness, shall this world perish and be no more. But, if the other does surrender to the light, then shall the fullness of Time be returned to its own and so shall the New Age be born."

Dia could do no more than gape at him. She knew his parents were staring as well. No one said anything.

Then, as he stood gazing into nothing, it seemed to Dia that he slowly became surrounded by a swirling cloud of light that seemed to fill her heart with hope and awe. *Who* **are** *you?* she asked into the silent vaults of her mind as she looked into his face, seeming to see it through a panorama of years, and feeling, without knowing why, that she was seeing her own future.

Lord Caelon, after a few more moments of staring wide-eyed at nothing, blinked. Then he looked at them, amusement slowly replacing bemusement, and said, "Now, why are you all staring at me so?"

No one seemed to feel equal to answering that question. Dia knew that, if the Duchess' suspicions about the Shae twins were correct, it was no matter for wonder that Dia should somehow be reminded of that Prophesy when the time came. But what had Lord Caelon to do with any of this? She supposed it ought not to matter who actually spoke the words; of much greater import was the fact that she should hear them. Yet, she could not rid herself of a strong presentiment that it was as important that she hear them *from* Lord Caelon. She thrust that thought aside, to be considered later, and focused her attention on her present society.

Before anyone spoke, however, a new and much less friendly presence entered the room. Dia heard an angry wailing roar, as from a great distance, and the room was filled with that darkening chill that she was coming to recognize. All three Aerandosians felt it, too, she realized; they were looking around warily, seemingly acutely uncomfortable. Lord Saeros had automatically clapped a hand to his belt knife, Lord Caelon searched the room with narrowed, intent eyes, and Lady Tamia hugged herself and actually shivered. The presence grew stronger, moaning its hate and bearing its waves of cold despair. The room seemed to grow still darker, until Dia could "see" almost nothing. Blinded and feeling almost ill with dread, she unconsciously stepped closer to Lord Caelon. She hardly noticed that he had also taken a step in her direction, as if, all unknowing, they were closing ranks against the malevolent intruder. The enraged howl reached its zenith in a single, shrill scream before it began to fade, as if into some unimaginable distance.

And then, it was gone.

The four of them looked at each other cautiously. Finally, Lady Tamia spoke. "Caelon?" she said, placing a beseeching hand on his arm.

He ignored her, scowling at Dia. "What was it?" he demanded.

Dia shook her head, still bemused. "I do not know, Lord Caelon," she replied shakily. She wondered why he had asked her.

Lady Tamia seemed to wonder the same thing. "Indeed, Caelon, how *could* she know?"

"I have only felt that thing twice," he said angrily, still staring at Dia, "and only in my lady's presence."

Lady Tamia gasped and Lord Saeros glowered at his son. But Dia only smiled. "I could, with perfect truthfulness, say the very same of you, my lord," she told him placidly.

"And that puts you in your place, my boy," said Lord Saeros. Then he turned to Dia. "My compliments, my lady. I beg you will forgive my son, who appears to be quite unnerved. Jesting aside, he is not usually so rag-mannered."

"Indeed, I do not mind, your Grace," said Dia, recovering and grinning with mischief. "I am much more interested in Lord Caelon's hitherto unsuspected reading habits. It would appear that he has been keeping secrets."

"Really, Caelon," agreed Lady Tamia warmly, "I had no notion you were so well acquainted with the First Prophesies! I wonder when you can have had a chance to study them, for I am sure you never asked to borrow mine?"

"Of course I have never read those curst prophesies," replied Lord Caelon furiously, "and I would thank my lady to stop trying to change the subject. I am sure she knows more of that strange visitation than she has seen fit to divulge."

"Enough, Caelon!" said Lord Saeros sternly. "I will not suffer any guest of mine, and particularly a daughter of Shae, to be insulted by your persistent suspicions."

There was a moment of tense silence. Dia wished she were a hundred leagues off, for she knew from experience just how mortifying such a public, parental reprimand could be. Lord Caelon seemed to master his temper with an understandable degree of difficulty before he bowed an apology to her. Dia, feeling uncomfortably that she had disturbed the affectionate tranquility of this little family, nodded her acceptance and was prepared to let the matter drop.

But Lord Caelon had not said all he had to say on the subject. *You are not being very forthcoming, my lady,* he complained to her silently, his mental tone as grim as his expression.

Dia hesitated. *Truly, my lord, there is very little for me to tell you. This evil darkness threatens us both, I think,* she said, as the notion occurred to her.

There was a distinct pause. *I see,* he said, and she could sense that he was little more satisfied with that reply. *I can also see that you and I will need to have a very long talk sometime soon.*

I shall place myself at your disposal, my lord, she retorted primly.

A slightly skeptical laugh echoed in her head, and the sense of his presence was gone.

Midmeal was a rather subdued affair, for the strange visitation and the squabble in its aftermath had cast a pall over the company. Lord Caelon, who seemed to remember nothing of his foray into prophesy, ate in brooding silence and did not appear to see either the oddly smug glance of his mother or the speculative eyes of his sire. Dia thought perhaps they would feel more comfortable discussing the incident among themselves in private, and wondered again if she ought to make some excuse to return to her own rooms. Honesty compelled her to admit to herself that she did not want to leave and, before she could convince herself that it would be the honorable thing to do, the gentlemen had excused themselves and gone off to attend the Emperor.

Once the door had closed gently behind them, Lady Tamia cast a single, uncertain glance at Dia. What she saw evidently satisfied her, for she suddenly grinned, eyes twinkling. "I had feared that you would make some excuse to hurry off to your own chambers, my dear," she said.

Dia smiled. "Not at all," she replied politely. "Rather, I was regretting that I should have disrupted the harmony of your family, however briefly."

"Nonsense, my dear. Surely, you must know that these little family spats are so common as to be almost unnoticeable. I own, I could wish that Saeros -- well, never mind that," she interrupted herself hurriedly. "I had much rather ask you about that peculiar interlude just before midmeal. What did you make of it, my dear? I am very sure that Caelon spoke nothing but the truth when he declared that he had never read the Prophesies."

"From what I have seen of him," Dia replied, laughing lightly, "I am much inclined to agree, your Grace. It would seem, for reasons unknown to us both, that Lord Caelon was chosen to reveal the Words to us at that Time."

"One is lead to infer that the Lord of Chaos was displeased about it, as well," Lady Tamia murmured thoughtfully. Then she glanced at her young guest, her eyes suddenly shrewd and the chattering, fluttery manner she had adopted gone. "I've a notion that there is a great deal going on beneath the surface of this palace, and that there is much you could share with us if you chose," she went on. "Caelon's manners may have left much to be desired, child, but I fancy he had reason to think he could look to you for an explanation."

Dia thought in some amusement that almost no one in this blighted palace was what they seemed.

"I will not press you, my dear," her Grace continued when Dia hesitated, "for the matter seems to be one of some delicacy. Indeed, I ought rather to be wondering how my Caelon comes to be involved in the matter." She paused, watching her young guest. "Is he in danger?" she asked suddenly.

"Oh, I do not think he can be, your Grace," Dia replied, with as much sincerity as she could muster. Merciful Phoenix, what must Lady Tamia be thinking of her?

"Are you?" her Grace asked with uncharacteristic bluntness.

"I do not think so," she replied with almost as much truth. She certainly did not seem to be in any physical danger, in any event.

"Very well, my dear," Lady Tamia said, apparently satisfied. "No doubt we will speak of it another time. I must confess, I have been longing to get you alone since I remembered that passage from the First Prophesies, to ask you if you and your brother are those twin children."

Dia chuckled. "Now, how could I know that, Lady Tamia?" she asked.

The Duchess laughed with her. "Yes, a rather odd question to put to you, now I come to think on it. But *are* you skilled in the Secrets?" After a moment's hesitation, Dia nodded slowly. "I can understand why you would not wish to publish that news abroad and you may rely upon my discretion, my dear. I hope very much that you are and I think you must be. Your twin brother, if you do not mind my saying so, certainly seems to me to be quite as drowned in darkness as any priest could wish. And you ... "

Dia waited.

"Yes, indeed, you must be," Lady Tamia said with slow thoughtfulness, although Dia was convinced that her Grace had caught herself on the brink of unwise speech, "for only consider what has happened just this midmeal. If Caelon has sustained a visitation from the Prophesy, it must certainly be for the purpose of giving instruction to *you*. And shall we ever forget Lord Septha's anger, once you had received that message?" Lady Tamia paused to take Dia's hand in hers. "Remains now only to learn if you are prepared for whatever your task may be. You will not face it alone, you know. I am a true daughter of the Ages and I will stand by you if you find yourself in need of aid."

Dia's eyes widened in unfeigned astonishment. A daughter of the Ages? "It is you?" Lady Tamia merely smiled and did not reply. "It is you! But how does it come about that an archpriestess of the purple is Grand Duchess of Aerandos?"

"I was not yet an archpriestess, to be quite candid," her Grace corrected her, "although I expect I would have been by now. Ageless Phoenix foresaw that I would best serve my Time by leaving the Temple and returning to my family. No doubt He foresaw as well that I should fall in love with Saeros and marry. I never knew why that should be necessary -- until now."

"So you have been protecting your husband and your son from this awful darkness that is everywhere in the palace?" Dia did not even bother to ask if Lady Tamia had perceived that darkness; as a former TimeKeeper, it must be easily apparent to her.

"Well, that is another interesting thing," she said, eyeing Dia consideringly. "I have certainly been able to shield Saeros from the darkness, but for Caelon, my aid was not needed. No, my dear, I do not know why that should be. I own, I was rather hoping you would be able to tell me. Well, never mind. I expect we shall find out all about it in its own time. It bodes well for my ambitions for the upcoming Gaerud." Another of her impish smiles curved the Duchess' lips as she added, "Indeed, I hope very much that I shall be able to participate, for the coming of a New Age does not happen every day."

Dia smiled rather absently, hesitating. When she spoke, it was with some difficulty. "I do not know if Daerus and I are the Chosen of that Prophesy, your Grace. The notion has never occurred to me. I will confess that I am concerned about my brother. He seems ... changed, somehow. He is my twin and we have always been so very close, but now he seems a stranger." Her voice shook as, for the first time, she allowed herself to consider the possibility that Daerus might be lost to her forever. Lady Tamia patted her hand. "I think there is someone or something of great power tampering with his mind. Indeed, I know it, for I have been coming under attack from that same source since I came here." She paused and then shook her head, adding, "It would seem that this mysterious wielder of darkness I have been trying to unmask is none other than Septha Himself but, in truth, I have no notion of what any of this may have to do with the return of the Phoenix."

"Very likely not, for these things never happen in the way one expects," the Duchess said comfortingly. "I was used to think, you know, that Prophesy was designed to make life dreadfully dull, for if one knows the future then there are none of the surprises that often make things interesting. But I have come to see, as I have studied the Gaeruds, that the Prophesies tell what *will* happen but they do not tell *how*. That discovery relieved my mind enormously, you know."

Dia laughed shakily. "Now, I wonder why that should be?" she mused, eager to direct their talk into less personal channels.

"It is because of the Gaeruds, my dear," Lady Tamia explained, her eyes wise. "Septha the Destroyer and Ageless Phoenix always choose instruments of the Gaerud from among the people of this world, you know, and the instruments of the Destroyer are forever cheating. Considering what is at stake, it is really quite shocking!"

"Considering what is at stake, it would be even more shocking if the Destroyer's minions did *not* cheat, would it not?" Dia ventured.

"Perhaps, my dear, but really, for all his faults, Septha *is* a God. You would think he would at least be a *gentleman*. Now," and with that, Lady Tamia briskly changed the subject, "we shall leave such dismal subjects for another time and you shall give me your opinion of Caelon."

Dia blinked. "My opinion of him?" she repeated in some confusion.

"Yes, I know what you are thinking, and it is terrible but true that when a young lady reaches a certain age, everyone she meets will want to talk to her about some young gentleman or another."

For everything she held dear, Dia could not have contained the laugh that escaped her. "I beg your pardon, your Grace," she apologized. "I am very little acquainted with Lord Caelon, but I think I could like him very well. It is a very great pity that he seems predisposed to regard me with suspicion."

"Oh, dear!" said her Grace, looking stricken. "I had wondered if you had taken that amiss but you answered his questions so very calmly that I supposed you never gave the matter a thought. He does have a rather cynical streak, my dear, and I cannot imagine where he came by it. Unless ... Do you suppose it is a result of his military endeavors?"

This was the first time that Dia had heard that army life engendered skepticism in young men, but she did not point that out. "Well, ma'am, as to that I could not say, but I am sure I have only to continue to behave in my usual, irreproachable fashion and Lord Caelon's suspicions will soon be laid to rest," was Dia's cheerful reply.

Lady Tamia giggled. "Yes, and that is precisely the right tone to take with the boy. I must say it is a great relief to know that you have a sense of humor. Otherwise, I would think you must find him quite unbearable."

That set Dia off again but, once she had had her laugh out, she prudently turned their talk to other matters.

Dia's conversation with her Grace was refreshingly merry, at times riotous, and the time seemed to fly. When the gentlemen returned from their imperial audience, Dia excused herself to change for endmeal which, Lady Tamia informed her firmly, she would take with them. "You will be much more comfortable with me, my dear," the Duchess said kindly, "for, if you will forgive me for saying so, your brother does not seem to give much thought to either your safety or your virtue ."

"Indeed, he has proved completely useless, your Grace," said Dia, who was not in the least bit worried about either her safety or her virtue, but had her own reasons for wanting to stay close to the party from Aerandos, "and I shall be thankful for your escort."

"Excellent, my dear," said the Duchess, looking so smug about these arrangements that Dia began to regard her with acute, if good humored, suspicion.

CHAPTER SEVEN

In company with his father, Caelon strode through the palace halls on his way to the throne room. He knew he ought, in truth, to be focused upon the upcoming meeting with Emperor Kaerkas but the strange interlude just before lunch still disturbed him.

He could not tell if Lady Dia were being honest or not when she implied that the dark and deadly chill he had experienced today for the second time was not somehow her doing. Of course, he knew he had no real reason to imagine that hers might be the hand at work. Yet, he could not rid himself of the feeling that it did have very much to do with her. The only question he really needed to answer was whether she was the potential threat or the potential victim.

He could not have explained to anyone, including himself, the peculiar attraction she held for him. Not that she was not worthy of attention, for the lady was remarkably beautiful. But Caelon, no novice to amorous adventures, did not recognize what he was feeling as a prelude to a fit of gallantry. In fact, he would have described it as something much more primitive and primal than that; along the order of instinct rather than attraction. He had a notion, conceived last endmeal and reinforced when he had fetched her to his mother's apartments before midmeal, that presenting himself at her door on a regular basis after she had retired would place a severe strain on his self-control.

Caelon acknowledged to himself that he had somehow encountered something that seemed both powerful and pervasive in the person of Dia of Shae. The fact that he could not satisfactorily explain that something to himself was excessively irksome. And then, there was this ability he had suddenly acquired to listen to the thoughts of another, to carry on a conversation without speaking. Septha take the curst woman, anyway; what had she done to him? He was a soldier, scorch it! Everything he thought he knew about the world he lived in seemed to have been challenged recently, beginning with the strange bond he had unwittingly formed with this daughter of Shae.

Suddenly, he became aware that his father was addressing him. "This is not the time for woolgathering, my boy," Lord Saeros said, regarding his heir with all his usual calm shrewdness. "No doubt you will sort it all out later. For now, I require your attention."

They had reached the massive double doors of the Emperor's throne room and Caelon, as he always did, straightened himself with military discipline at his father's words, and put those puzzles away from his mind.

Lord Saeros had not confided his plans to his son, but Caelon was not particularly surprised by that. Lord Saeros almost never did warn Caelon in advance of what he meant to do. His Grace, when a much younger Caelon had remonstrated with him about that, had informed his son that he would be of little use in the field if he could not accustom himself to decisive action in the face of unexpected events. Caelon could understand the rationale behind this behavior but, he owned privately, he sometimes wished that Lord Saeros were occasionally willing to put aside being a general in favor of simply being a father.

At that moment, the door opened and a herald announced the Grand Duke Saeros of Aerandos and Colonel Lord Caelon of

Aerandos. Those two gentlemen strode into the room, halting when they had reached the foot of the throne, and bowed deeply.

"Ha! Saeros!" uttered his Imperial Majesty.

"Sire," Lord Saeros said, "you wished to see me?"

"I want your decision, Saeros," the Emperor said without preamble.

"I have considered the matter carefully, your Majesty," his Grace told the Emperor, "and I am persuaded that you have no need of the entire army of Aerandos in this part of the Empire. Moreover, while it is plain to me that the imperial corps would benefit from improvements in training, you do not really need my presence here in the palace in order to give the proper orders and see that they are carried out." He smiled ruefully. "It also has come to my notice that certain members of the General Staff have no wish to see me elevated to a position in which I have authority over them."

The Emperor, who seemed to sense that he was about to be thwarted, turned an alarming shade of red. "So," he said ominously, his eyes beginning to bulge, "you say you will withhold both your counsel and your troops from the services of your Emperor when he has need of them?"

"Not at all, your Majesty," Lord Saeros replied smoothly. "It may very well be that the imperial troops would indeed benefit from example. As I say, however, I do not think that you will require the *entire* army of Aerandos."

"And what of you, Saeros?" asked the Emperor broodingly. "Do you mean to leave me with troops but with no leadership? That will not suit the purpose at all." He did not give Lord Saeros time to reply but gestured to a waiting flunky and sent him off to summon General Kraetus.

"By no means, your Imperial Majesty," Lord Saeros answered the Emperor's question. "I expect I can remain here and give the necessary orders at least until I am required to return north by reason of the imminence of HighSun." The Emperor's expression of smug satisfaction faded noticeably when his Grace added, "I cannot think, however, that I need be involved much with the General Staff."

It was unfortunate that, at that moment, the door to the audience chamber opened once again and General Kraetus stepped inside in the wake of the herald preparing to announce him. The General was thus privileged to hear the Emperor's reply perfectly clearly. "Great Chaos, Saeros, how can you mean to leave me saddled with my current staff? All one need do is take a look at the imperial army to realize that they cannot be any but the most complete dolts!"

"General Kraetus," announced the herald morosely.

The General strode forward, his face an impassive mask. "Your Imperial Majesty," he said, bowing.

The Emperor nodded to this greeting shortly. "Ah, Kraetus," Lord Saeros said to the general cordially, affecting not to see the malevolent stare that gentleman was directing at him. "Your arrival is timely. Possibly you can assist me in persuading his Majesty that the General Staff has no need of my advice."

"I am not so quick to contradict my Emperor," the General muttered, much to Caelon's astonishment. "I feel sure he knows better than you or I what is required to improve his army."

That Kaerkas the Beast had never either trained or commanded troops must be obvious to anyone who had listened to his initial proposal, thought Caelon. Yet, Lord Saeros never batted an eyelash. "Your faith in your Emperor is commendable, sir. However," and he turned back to the Emperor, "I must take exception to your assessment of the General Staff, Your Majesty. Indeed, I know them for highly competent military men. They will, if they wish, have the assistance of my sergeants with the day-to-day disciplining of the imperial troops. But they can have no need of my advice and I have no wish to lord it over them so."

"You become womanish in your concern for the sensibilities of my generals, Saeros," said the Emperor blightingly. "I am finding it tiresome."

"Forgive me, my leige," Lord Saeros apologized smoothly. "I have some experience in attempting to direct reluctant troops. It is not an experience I care to repeat if I can avoid it, particularly not with generals."

"And, what is this? A few paltry regiments?" Emperor Kaerkas was asking suddenly, as if he had only just realized what his Grace had said. "Is that the best you can offer to your Emperor? What good do you imagine a few regiments will do?"

"Since their purpose here will be in the nature of aides to the training of your own army, Sire, I would imagine that they will do admirably well," was his Grace's bland reply, which almost caused Caelon to betray himself with a grin. "After all, they will not be required to invade any of our neighbors, so you will not be needing more of them."

Emperor Kaerkas opened his mouth to speak but Prince Maermat, leaving his sister's side with an alacrity that Caelon found excessively interesting, interceded quickly. "Indeed, your plans sound excellently well thought out, your Grace. I must confess, I am relieved that you have discovered a solution to my father's need." Then, he turned to his obviously seething parent. "Of course, we cannot hold Lord Saeros here when he has urgent matters to tend at Aerandos, Father," he said in a peculiar tone of voice that was half soothing and half commanding. "And I feel sure that his Grace can set matters here in motion in enough time to enable him to return to Aerandos before HighSun."

Lord Saeros bowed acknowledgement of the Prince's intervention, before addressing himself to the Emperor. "If my proposal is acceptable to your Majesty, I shall immediately send word for some few regiments to set forth for the palace at once."

Emperor Kaerkas fixed the Grand Duke with a smoldering eye, an expression on his face that would have been called pouting in a less exalted personage. "Very well, Saeros," he said finally. "I shall accept these few regiments -- for the moment. For the rest of it, while we await the arrival of these few soldiers from the north, you shall attend me at all meetings of the General Staff. Is that clear?"

"Certainly, Sire," said his Grace. Only Caelon was aware of the faint sigh that accompanied Lord Saeros' words.

"And I shall expect you to do more than sit mute and worry yourself about the wounded sentiments of my generals," added the Emperor.

"As you wish, Sire," said his Grace with a bow that concluded the audience.

Once they had left the audience chamber, Caelon turned a wryly amused eye upon his father. "One wonders just how he will attempt to inviegle you into bringing the rest of our forces south, for it is quite plain that he had set his heart on acquiring our entire army for his personal use."

"Indeed," Lord Saeros replied, still in that bland tone, "it will be interesting to observe his method." He smiled faintly when Caelon snorted cynically. "Never underestimate the value in learning the way your adversary's mind works."

Caelon digested that in silence for a few moments. "Do you count the Emperor your adversary, then?" he asked, speaking too softly to be overheard.

"Not at all, my dear boy," Lord Saeros replied instantly, "although I have a notion that he counts me as his. No, it is merely that I have something he seems to want. You will note that he did not order me to hand the army over to him, even though, as my Emperor, he might be forgiven for attempting to do so. It would appear that he -- or someone -- perceives the need to handle me carefully."

"Yes," Caelon agreed thoughtfully, "the tone Maermat takes with his father does cause one to wonder which of them is running the Empire."

"Why, I can say quite truthfully that I feel some sympathy for the Emperor, to be saddled with an impudent heir," his Grace said, loftily ignoring Caelon's chuckle. "So you made note of young Maermat's manner as well?"

"How could one escape noting it?"

Lord Saeros replied with a satisfied grunt before returning to the subject at hand. "So far, we have seen that care of me involves flattery and appeals to my ego -- weaknesses which his Highness assumes I am prey to, but which, sadly for him, I am not. I shall shortly provide an opportunity for all parties involved see whether Prince Maermat considers it worth his while to handle you as carefully as they have tried to handle me. Then, we shall see what he imagines *your* weaknesses to be."

"I could venture a few guesses on that score. And why are we so interested in what they imagine our weaknesses to be?" Caelon asked, intrigued as always by the complex mind of his father.

"Because, my boy, they make assumptions about our weaknesses based upon their own," Lord Saeros told him promptly, amusement lighting his eyes, "as surely you have already surmised."

"And how do propose to provide this opportunity, sir? Will you, in fact, be removing from the scene?" Caelon asked, noting but not commenting on the oblique reprimand. "It seems strangely unlike you."

Lord Saeros chuckled but did not reply, saying instead, "As to that, I am not wholly convinced that care of me is what is intended."

"Indeed, sir?" Caelon asked.

"Well, it certainly has not escaped *my* attention," Lord Saeros said pointedly, "that twice now my Emperor has created an occasion to inform the head of his General Staff that he is incompetent and I am not. It is not the way I would choose to introduce anyone to someone he is then expected to work with."

"Yes, sir," Caelon said meekly, "I confess I was surprised at his Majesty's lack of discretion -- and even more surprised at General Kraetus' lack of protest."

"Kraetus does not protest *openly*," corrected his Grace. "Unless I much mistake the matter ...

"Impossible," Caelon interjected with grinning impudence.

"I shall soon be made to feel his displeasure," his Grace went on, ignoring the interruption.

At that, Caelon frowned. "It is to be hoped that his displeasure does not take too violent a form," he said thoughtfully.

"It is even more to be hoped that that is not precisely what his Majesty intends," said Lord Saeros calmly.

"Indeed," Caelon agreed emphatically, wondering once again what, exactly, Lord Saeros was thinking. "Wither away, sir?" he then asked when he realized that his father was not immediately returning to their rooms.

"We shall see about sending one of my men off with a message for Colonel Braeden and then we shall explore whichever of the splendid amusements the palace has to offer at this time of day catches our fancy."

At that, Caelon frankly laughed. "What amusements does this palace *ever* have to offer, sir?"

"Come, my boy, surely we will be able to find something with which to occupy ourselves."

"Why do we not simply return to my mother?"

"Because I have no wish to interrupt her visit with her young friend," Lord Saeros said, again with that faint smile. "Really, lad, do you want to spend the next few hours listening to my lady giggling? Now, pull yourself together. It will never do for the men to witness Saeros' heir grinning like a moonling."

When the gentlemen finally returned to Lady Tamia's sitting room, she informed them cordially that Lady Dia would be returning to join them for endmeal. Caelon took this news in very good part, even though he was thoroughly familiar with the glint in his mother's eye. He accepted her efforts at matchmaking much as he accepted everything else about her and was only left to wonder if my lady was a party to this plot. He rather fancied it would be very unlike her, and found himself looking forward to some very good sport.

Lady Dia rather quickly fell in with her Grace's notion that she should spend most of her time with the House of Aerandos and, from then on, arrived in his mother's sitting room just before each midmeal. As often as not, Caelon did not see her then, for he was much involved in attending the Grand Duke at seemingly constant meetings of the Imperial General Staff. Not much was accomplished at these meetings; the generals could not seem to agree on even the necessity of establishing a regular training routine. Caelon wondered how Kaerkas had managed to saddle himself with a pack of commanders who were so concerned with their own personal power and proximity to the throne that none of them seemed able to focus upon the requirements of maintaining an effective fighting force. He would have found the frequent gatherings unbearably tedious if it were not for his ever-wayward sense of humor, for the speed with which Kaerkas' generals found reasons to reject even the mildest and most insignificant of suggestions from Lord Saeros tickled him.

He did, however, regularly act as Lady Dia's escort to endmeal, staying by her until she had been safely escorted to her rooms and had shared a handclasp with him. What benefit she derived from their frequent, tactile contact she never said. Caelon could easily feel strange bond produced when their hands met, and very pleasant he found it, but to Lady Dia it must have been vastly more important than a means of simply tickling her senses. He would have been hard put to it to have described her response to his touch: a profound relief, a relaxing of an almost unconscious tension, a release from an unnamed fear, and something else to which he could not have put a name. Whatever was happening between them, she seemed to need it and to be genuinely grateful for it. And, as much from innate kindness as from the dictates of his pledged honor, Caelon made it his business to somehow touch her hand every time he saw her, anywhere in the palace.

In time, of course, the Emperor's court began to notice the very particular attentions that Lord Caelon of Aerandos was paying to Lady Dia of Shae. Rumor was rife, whispers abounded, and stares accompanied them whenever they appeared together in the public parts of the building. To Caelon's amused interest, Lady Dia greeted the gossip with a rather contradictory mixture of mortification and indifference. While she was clearly not enjoying the notoriety she was acquiring, neither did she at any time even hint that she wished to dispense with their frequent handclasps.

Among the many eyes turned in his direction were those of Prince Maermat, Princess Kera and Lord Daerus of Shae. Unlike the courtiers, however, Caelon perceived that these onlookers were not idly curious but seriously concerned and more than a little hostile to his attentions to Lady Dia. While Lord Daerus' antagonism toward a gentleman whose gallantry had made his sister the talk of the palace was understandable, Caelon was at something of a loss to account for the interest of the Imperial siblings. It was not until he had had an opportunity to observe, unnoticed, Prince Maermat trying unsuccessfully and rather laboriously to get up a flirtation with the lady that he understood and, from the moment he made that discovery, his enjoyment of his situation was assured. With a sad want of chivalry, he soon began to imbue the act of bowing over Lady Dia's hand with as much innuendo as one could with so commonplace a gesture.

Lady Dia was, of course, inspired to protest the extravagance with which he greeted her. "Does it not bother you to be the object of so much curiosity, my lord?" she asked him in exasperation as he escorted her to midmeal, which he occasionally did.

"I think you do yourself an injustice, my lady," he told her, a teasing gleam in his eyes. "Surely, the fixed glances you have noticed are admiration rather than speculation."

"I pray you will not talk such nonsense, my lord," she said briskly after a pregnant pause. He wondered, as he often did, whether she was *really* debating the relative merits of offering violence to his person, or whether those vivid images in her mind were purely for his edification. "And I very much wish that you would restrain yourself when next we meet. *You* may be enjoying the scrutiny but, frankly, I am not."

"Really, my lady," he protested, "how *could* you imagine that I would do anything so ungallant as to suggest to all the interested spectators that I am less than enthralled with you?"

He watched her sternly suppress laughter. "It would serve you very well indeed if I did marry you, my lord," she told him smolderingly.

Such a caveat very naturally made Caelon laugh heartily. "What a dreadful thing to threaten a man with!" he said, when he could speak at all. "Really, my lady, I am sur ...," his voice trailed off as he stared down the corridor.

His father had come down the hall toward them, stopped at his mother's sitting room door, and had then paused as he made note of their approach. At this time of year, as HighSun steadily approached, the halls of the palace were never well lit. Now, however, the ever-present shadows seemed full of menace. Lady Dia seemed to sense it as well, for her eyes were narrowed suspiciously and darting about the shadows.

Abruptly, several things seemed to happen at once. Shadows began to move, resolving themselves into four men brandishing swords and menacingly approaching Lord Saeros. Almost instantly, even as Caelon started forward wondering furiously what they could do with belt daggers against four swords, two of them fell, one with a jewelled dagger hilt protruding from his forehead and the other from a dagger in the side of his neck.

"Caelon!" he heard Lady Dia call to him urgently. He glanced toward her. Something was hurling out of the shadows toward him and, when he instinctively put out an arm to protect himself, found that his hand closed on the sword she had expertly tossed him. Now properly armed, he closed the distance between himself and his father's attackers and engaged one of them. My lady, meanwhile, had scooped up the other discarded sword and circled around to confront the last ruffian herself.

It was all over in moments. The fellow Caelon faced was a competent enough swordsman but Caelon, a professional soldier with a great deal of incentive, easily outmatched him. He dispatched the ambusher quickly, eager to go to Lady Dia's aid, and whirled in time to see her wrench her blade from her adversary's chest.

My lady stared down at the crumpled, bloody bodies for a moment. Then she tossed her borrowed blade down before the man she had just felled, making of it a gesture of purest contempt, before turning icy grey eyes toward him. *I hate assassins*, she told him silently.

You have had much experience of them? he asked her.

Not until now, she replied.

Caelon turned to his father. "Are you well, sir?" he asked in some concern.

"Very well, I thank you," Lord Saeros replied, thoughtfully eyeing the corpses littering the hallway. "Accept my compliments; your arrival was fortuitous. And my thanks to you, as well, my lady," he addressed himself to Lady Dia, who was retrieving her daggers. "I had not realized that young ladies still trained in the warlike arts."

That made her grin. "Many of them do not, your Grace," she replied. Then she shrugged. "I do not like this new fashion of selecting a champion; I find it to my advantage to fight my own battles. Unlike the cur who hired this lot," she added, her grin fading.

"Indeed," agreed Lord Saeros impassively, his eyes twinkling.

The unhappiness of most of the imperial generals with the addition of His Grace of Aerandos to their number was suddenly no longer amusing. That they did not dare take their plaint to their Emperor was not entirely unexpected. But, Caelon had assumed that those gentlemen would indulge in the usual political maneuvering in order to have Lord Saeros removed from his advisory position; in spite of his recent conversation with his father, it had not seriously occurred to him that they might elect to simply have him murdered. "So it begins," he murmurred, fixing his sire with a fierce gaze.

"Aye, so it does," Lord Saeros agreed again.

Lady Dia looked from one of them to the other, opened her mouth to speak and then apparently changed her mind. Finally, she said, "It would appear that you both have some notion of who might be behind this attack, and why. I have no wish to pry, your Grace, but clearly you would do well to look to your defenses. Calm acceptance is surely better than panic, but I hope you will not take this incident lightly."

"You are very right, my lady, but there is no need to disturb yourself," he Grace told her kindly.

"Yes, Father," said Caelon, with determined patience, "it is all very well to tell us not to concern ourselves about it but, if we had not happened along at just that moment, you would likely not have survived this encounter."

"Very likely not," and with that, his Grace fixed both young people with a stern eye. "I wish you will tell me why the pair of you must needs instruct me in the obvious? Lady Dia, I make allowance for your slight acquaintance with me but you, my lad, really ought to know better."

Caelon, his concern causing him to rapidly lose patience with his tight-lipped sire, was about to reply until he saw my lady flush scarlet. "I beg your pardon, your Grace," she muttered, mortification in her tone.

"Never mind, my dear," said Lord Saeros, taking her hand and patting it soothingly, "come along inside now. I expect her Grace is wondering what has become of us. You, no doubt, would like a chance to wash your hands before midmeal and," here, his Grace paused to glance with faint disapproval at the blood-spattered hall, "I really must ring for a servant to tidy this corridor. Shall we ... ?"

CHAPTER EIGHT

As the season wore on and the sun inexorably climbed higher in the sky, Dia continued to divide her time between Ormaer and Aerandos. Her schedule suited her well enough and she derived a certain malicious enjoyment from watching her brother all but gnash his teeth in frustration. All his attempts to intervene in her growing relationship with and affection for Aerandos had met with failure as, for the first time in his life, Daerus found himself coming into conflict with the obstinacy their parents knew so well.

Dia could not tell if she was growing used to the terrible darkness that had seemed so frighteningly irresistible when she had first encountered it, or if the antidote she had found had caused it to grow less effective every time she grasped Lord Caelon's hand. However it may have been, she could still see and feel that ever-present darkness that surrounded the imperial court, but it no longer had the ability to smother her senses.

In some ways, she was sorry for it. Uncomfortable that mental fog may have been, but it would have been a splendid buffer against the frustrated or even worried stares and whispered conversations between her brother and his beloved. It might even have rendered Prince Maermat's tediously heavy-handed wooing rather more bearable. She could not tell whether the Prince was in earnest or merely attempting alleviate boredom. She conceived a notion that his Imperial Highness was, in fact, a rather shy young man whose position had forced him to conceal or conquer his self-consciousness as best he could. He generally managed to do so quite effectively, but idle flirtations, or even the earnest courtship of a young lady, still seemed to betray him into awkwardness. Indeed, she felt rather sorry for him, but still she found his attentions wearisome and wished he would find another object for his gallantry.

"Tell me, my lady," he said to her one morning, "are you at all ambitious?"

"Ambitious?" she repeated in some surprise. "How so, your Highness?"

"Do you aspire to hold a great position in the Empire?"

She stared at him for a full minute, deliberately calming herself before answering. "I am a daughter of Shae, your Highness," she said with quiet pride. "I do not think I need aspire any higher than that."

"Oh, of course, of course," he acknowledged hurriedly, nodding. "And, yet, do you not think that a daughter of Shae would be more than fitting to be a wife of Ormaer?"

"Certainly, Highness," she replied, placidly, "but I am not on the hunt for a husband."

"Nonsense, my lady," Prince Maermat argued. "Somehow I cannot see you dwindling into spinsterhood, hanging on your brother's sleeve."

"Very likely not," she said, unable to contain her amusement. "Poor Daerus! In any event, I am sure that my parents and my brother share the hope that I shall meet many suitable gentlemen among his Majesty's court and shall receive an acceptable offer from among them."

"And do you expect such an offer?"

Again, she fixed him with a level stare. Imperial prince or no, the fellow was mightily impertinent. "Really, Prince Maermat, you take an inordinate interest in my matrimonial prospects!" she finally protested.

"I take an interest in everything about you, my lady," he replied meaningfully, his speculative gaze holding hers.

"How very dull that must be for you!" Dia said cheerfully, hoping to douse some of his ardor. His Highness, in Dia's opinion, had all the subtlety of an enraged bull.

She said as much to her brother some days later, as they walked together toward the Emperor's audience chamber, adding, "I have no notion of what he may mean by such oppressive gallantry, but I do wish he would stop."

"Why should he?" Daerus asked her. "Just think what a splendid Empress you would make! I feel certain that you would be gratified by occupying such a high station. And," he added with considerable asperity, "I was being perfectly serious, so you need not stand about chortling in that ill-bred way!"

"Daerus, I refuse to argue with you," Dia managed to say, still laughing. "Only know that I have no wish to be further embarrassed by his Highness, and not the least ambition to be an Empress. One of us marrying into the imperial family is quite enough."

"No ambition to be an Empress?" he repeated in the greatest astonishment. "What can you mean?"

"Well, what do you suppose me to mean, Daerus?" she asked, still amused. "Can it be that you are surprised to discover that I have no imperial aspirations?" Then, curious, she asked, "I can accept that you have been changed by your sojourn at court, but must it follow that you no longer remember the character of your twin?"

"No, of course not," he said -- a little too quickly, she thought. "But you are Shae, Dia. You cannot wed a *nobody.* Or do you mean to be wed, then, into Aerandos?" he went on, suddenly suspicious. "Is that why you are so assiduous in your attentions to Lady Tamia?"

"In the expectation of receiving an offer from her?" asked Dia, lifting a brow. "I fear that would not be at all the thing, you know."

"Dia ... !"

"I *like* her, dear. Indeed, I like all of House Aerandos that I have met so far. Lady Tamia and her lord remind me forcibly of my own parents, you know." She sighed wistfully. "*How* pleased I shall be to see them again!"

Into the brief silence that followed that nostalgic remark -- to which, she noted with interest, he made no sort of reply -- Daerus asked in a determinedly casual tone, "By the by, *are* you anticipating an offer from Caelon of Aerandos?" Dia found it excessively curious that Daerus seemed to be growing ... really, there was no other word for it but *nervous* ... about that possibility.

She sighed wearily. "No."

"There has been a great deal of talk, you know, my dear."

"It is not like you to listen to the gossip-mongers, my dear."

"You are certainly spending a great deal of time with Lord Caelon."

"I am spending a great deal of time with his mother, Daerus."

His mother, her Grace of Aerandos, was making no attempt to hide from the world her delight at the prospect of Dia as a marriage-daughter. *(Really,* she thought, *is there no one in the capital who is not preoccupied with who I may take to husband?)* Dia knew of that lady's scheming and so, judging from the cynical smile with which he sometimes observed their chats, did Lord Caelon. That was certainly bad enough, but Dia had a notion that his lordship thought her in league with his mother, and that vexed her almost beyond bearing. She had not spoken of it to him; the subject was a matter of considerable embarrassment to her and she dreaded broaching it because she knew, if he did harbor such doubts, that she had no way to counter them. Still, if she could not defend herself against unvoiced suspicions, she could take great care to do nothing to lend weight to them.

Such a course of action was not easiest to accomplish when the entire palace seemed rife with conjecture about the pair. Dia, in a fair-minded spirit, acknowledged that the speculation was undoubtedly fed by his lordship's habit of pausing at her door just before retiring to his chambers for his rest. Lord Caelon had scrupulously kept his word to her, shaking her hand whenever he met her in the palace, and appearing at her door after she had left the endmeal frolic to share a handclasp. He had not questioned her about this ritual, for which she was thankful. She knew that he felt the same power she did in the contact, and she was certain she would be unable to explain it to his satisfaction. Indeed, each time she felt the strangely compelling power that fortified her and strengthened the growing bond between them, she found herself unable even to explain the matter to herself. Yet, when she considered how little she had told him of her situation, she realized that she owed him a long explanation.

Meanwhile, Dia had long since suspected that her brother's frequent goading had come about because losing her temper would somehow make her more vulnerable to the power of the darkness. Her counter-strategy was very simple; she took a page from dear Phoebus' book and strove to remain calm whatever the provocation. She had no way of knowing whether or not Daerus had guessed that his clumsiness had betrayed him, but she did notice that eventually he stopped baiting her. Dia, not for an instant imagining that would be the end of it, now awaited his next move.

He did not realize it but her twin was running out of time. Dia had every intention of bringing her visit to a close within the next few wakings, before the sun had climbed high enough to make travel impossible. And why, it suddenly occurred to her to wonder, was it so important to ensnare *her*? Daerus had given her only the rather implausible explanation that, as his twin, she had always been with him and must remain with him as he walked his dark path. When she had expressed her dissatisfaction with that rationale, he had refused to explain further. Odd, that. Well, she had grown perfectly willing to allow Septha and His instruments to dip their evil fingers into the mind of her twin, if only they would leave her alone.

She shook her head at her own thoughts. In truth, Dia was a little ashamed of herself, for honesty compelled her to admit that she had not tried very hard to get through to Daerus. She could offer in her own defense that she had been busily trying to preserve her own mind and had little leisure to try to reclaim his. Besides, how was she to free him of the darkness when he seemed so enamored of it? He would fight her every inch of the way. But the heart of the matter lay in the fact that she found she did not much care for this new Daerus. So very detestable was she finding him that she had almost forgotten that the man she now knew as Daerus was not really her beloved brother.

Seated at endmeal beside Lord Caelon, she glanced across the table at the heir to Shae and became aware of a sudden overwhelming sadness. He did not even *look* quite like Daerus anymore.

"Someday, you will have to tell me what I have done to earn your brother's disapprobation," Lord Caelon said in her ear.

"What can you mean, my lord?" she asked him. "I did not even know that you were acquainted with him."

"I have not been formally presented to him," Lord Caelon agreed, "but that has not prevented him from directing some very formidable stares my way. Perhaps I should hasten to assure him that my intentions toward his sister are completely honorable?"

Dia smiled faintly. "I am afraid he would not be pleased with you, no matter what your intentions might be," she said ruefully.

"He objects to my attentions to you?"

"He has lost his mind and has taken to talking such complete nonsense that it is not worth repeating."

"I see." Lord Caelon looked down at her with that quizzing smile in his blue eyes. "Do you know, I do not think I should care to figure in your memory as the cause of a permanent breach with your twin -- no matter how much entertainment I may be deriving from needling the crown prince."

That confession made her laugh. "What a handsome admission for you to make, my lord!" Then she sobered. "There is no need for you to fret on that score. You have never even seen my brother."

"Indeed! How peculiar that everyone at court seems to believe the young gentleman currently scowling at you so disapprovingly is Lord Daerus of Shae."

"I ... No, he ... " Impulsively, Dia reached out and grasp his hand, having made a sudden decision. "May I beg your aid for just a moment, my lord?"

"My dear Lady Dia, surely you must know that you may command me in anything!"

"Oh, stop that!" She looked away from him and took a deep, calming breath. "I fear you may find this just a bit uncomfortable, my lord."

"I have met the Throk on the fields of Aerand and lived to tell the tale, my lady. You do not frighten me so easily."

Fleetingly, Dia wondered if Lord Caelon ever took anything seriously.

She would have to be quick about this, she realized. Daerus, as she knew him now, was not alone; instinct told her that he was never left alone. She hoped her contact with Lord Caelon would protect her, for she knew that she would be at least somewhat vulnerable during the sort of penetrating mind-touch she had in mind. Carefully, she prepared her defenses and reached out to touch the thoughts of her dinner companion.

I do apologize for this, my lord, she told him with silent sincerity. *It will not be pleasant.*

Not waiting for his reply, she stabbed in her brother's direction with their joined minds, moving as quick as thought. As she had expected, she encountered a formidable barrier of dank darkness before she even reached him and, without slowing down, she stabbed through it with everything she could muster. Then she was penetrating her brother's once familiar mind, and she had to clench her teeth together to keep from retching. To her, it felt exactly like plunging her arm into a stable midden. Daerus' mind bore a heavy, dense cloak of sticky, cold blackness, rancid and poisonous, that seemed to go on forever.

And then, huddled miserable and alone deep in the core of his mind, she finally found the twin brother she had known and loved all her life.

And, as always, he recognized her touch immediately. *Dia! Take care! It is not safe for you to touch me in this way ...*

Daerus! she cried out in relief, sensing his fear for her and all his terrible longing. *Tell me what to do! How am I to free you of all this blackness?*

Surrender to the light!

What?

Surrender to the light... And then he pushed her away, urging her wordlessly to escape from his prison. With a suddenness that bespoke a determined mental wrench, he was gone.

As briefly as she had touched her brother's mind, she was not quite quick enough. She felt the first few tendrils of the same disgusting mental sludge that had overcome Daerus slowly entering her thoughts. Lord Caelon seemed to feel it too, for she felt his shoulders stiffen and sensed his indignation through their mind-link. Very suddenly her mind was filled with a blazing, blinding light, and the dark mire withered and died. She quickly reestablished her defenses.

Then she turned her head to glance at Lord Caelon and found him already regarding her pensively. "I have the oddest feeling ... ," he began slowly.

"Yes?"

"... that I should like, above all things, to excuse myself and go bathe."

She grinned. "I did warn you, my lord."

"So you did," he replied cordially. "I see now what you meant when you said that I had never met your brother," he went on, sobering. "Can nothing be done for him?"

"I am not sure." A number of thoughts crowded her mind just then. Surrender to the light, Daerus had pleaded with her. That was what the Prophesy had said, as well. Surrender to the light? *How* was she to surrender? To what light? Daerus had not wanted her to do anything for *him,* she realized. Why? How could her surrender to this mysterious light free her brother? What did that mental mire in which he was trapped have to do with her?

Dia mentally shook herself and returned her attention to her companion. She found him watching her with a faint smile. "Tell me," he asked in an innocent manner, "does your brother's plight have anything at all to do with the service you asked me to perform for you when first we met?"

Touche, she thought. "It has everything to do with it, my lord," she replied after a moment's hesitation, an inexplicable discomfort making her sound prim.

He nodded in a satisfied fashion. "I had wondered what that might be about," he said thoughtfully. "It did not seem likely that it was some sort of feminine ploy, for it has not escaped my attention that my mother's plotting is embarrassing you to death."

Blushing, she laughed, saying "Oh, but ... ,"

"And, while it seemed that *something* was happening whenever we shook hands," my lord continued as if she had not spoken, "I could not fathom what it might be or what benefit you derived from it." He paused to look enquiringly at her.

Dia still felt some heat in her cheeks but she had recovered enough to reply with some composure. "As to that, my lord, I am not entirely certain what it might be. All I do know is that I, too, had succumbed, just as Daerus did, to that stinking darkness and that as soon as you took my hand, my mind cleared." Another thought occurred to her. "How did you do that? Just now, I mean," she demanded, rather incoherently.

He did not pretend any lack of understanding. "Did *I* do that? I had thought it must be you, and was lost in admiration of the skills you seemed to possess that your brother apparently does not."

She shook her head, too deep in thought to defend her absent sibling. "Indeed, it was not I. Can you recall what you were thinking just at that instant?"

He was still smiling down at her. "Is it so very important?"

"Yes ... yes, it must be! Do please think, my lord!" Dia was remembering her brother's injunction.

"Well, I will," he promised, "but we will have to continue this conversation later."

Dia saw that the dining party was rising from the table at the Emperor's cue and was preparing to return to the salon. She wanted to scream with vexation; she had been right on the brink of it, she was certain of that. What perfectly dreadful timing! She would have to take care not to let this day end without learning from him how he had accomplished what neither she nor her brother, both fully trained by Phoebus, had been able to do.

Once again, she found herself wishing she could speak with her tutor. She sighed, allowing Lord Caelon to lead her from the dining hall.

Perhaps, if she could understand how Lord Caelon had commanded the blazing, brilliant power that had vanquished the dark might of her enemies, she *could* help her brother. Was that what Daerus had meant by "surrender"? Perhaps that is how one learns control over it, by submitting to it? Lord Caelon might be able to help her with that, since he had apparently commanded the power of the light without effort. Indeed, she thought ruefully, he seemed to command powers he did not even believe in.

Dia paid little heed to her surroundings and her thoughts continued to race. She almost did not hear Lord Caelon's softly spoken words.

"I might easily walk you into a wall, for all the heed you are paying to where you are going," he said cheerfully. "I perceive you cannot set this matter aside, so perhaps I can be of some assistance."

"Your aid would be most welcome, sir," she replied, adopting what she hoped was an air of hesitant appeal. "I did not like to ask it of you, for you seemed to hold poor Daerus in the greatest aversion . . . "

"Yes," he agreed readily, his smiling eyes advising her that he was not fooled by her manner in the least, "but, as you have pointed out to me, I am not acquainted with your brother and, after the experiences of the last half hour, I am much inclined to believe you. So. You are wondering how best to help the fellow, are you not?"

They had reached the periphery of the crowd and Dia cast a nervous glance around to make sure they were not overheard. "I suppose I am. For the most part, I was trying to determine how it comes about that you so easily vanquish a power that neither of us seem able to defend ourselves against, for all our training."

"I have not the most distant guess how I am doing it, if that is what I have been doing," he told her unhelpfully. "And, while I can see how that would help *you,* I am not certain the knowledge would be of any use to your brother."

"Possibly not, but it might help me to decipher his cryptic instructions. 'Surrender to the light' does not really tell me very much."

"No, I suppose it does not. And I am afraid I can be of little help to you there, either."

"Why, how is this?" she asked, rallying him. "I received much the same instructions from you."

"I beg your pardon?"

She looked at him curiously. "Do you have no recollection of quoting the First Prophesies for us, that first time I joined your mother for midmeal?"

The expression on his face was one of determined forbearance. "No, my lady," he said patiently but with a directness that was almost rude, "I do not. Although I suppose I must bring myself to believe I did so, since my mother has also questioned me along these lines. And while I gather from her that the incident has something to do with this Gaerud of yours, I fear it would be a waste of time to rehash the incident." Dia perceived that Lord Caelon most assuredly did *not* want to discuss the matter, and she wondered briefly what he feared. She was still curious about it, but decided not to pursue it.

"So," his lordship was saying, "let us pursue another avenue of investigation, my lady. Did you not tell me that your brother had summoned you here?" Dia nodded confirmation and he went on, "Do you know why?"

"He did not give me a reason when first he did ask," she replied thoughtfully. "That was the last time he seemed as he had always been. By the time I had arrived here, he is as you see him now. He said that he wished to take the Princess Kera to wife and that he would present me to the Emperor in furtherance of his suit."

"And did that not strike you as odd?"

She smiled at the question, remembering the protests she made at the time. "Decidedly odd, my lord, for what should I have to say to his Majesty's approval of Daerus as marriage-son? And yet, if that was not my brother's purpose in asking me to come here, what can it have been?"

"To own the truth, I have no notion of what may have occurred to inspire your brother to invite you here," Lord Caelon said. "Whatever it may have been, it seems that once he knew you were coming, he fell pray to whatever ails him now. I find that very interesting."

"You think he was tricked into luring me here?"

"It certainly seems that way to me."

"But why?"

"A home question, my lady. What were you most likely to do, once you arrived and found your twin enmeshed in someone's toils?" he asked her, beginning to smile.

"I suppose," she said slowly, "I would do what I have done. Try to learn what has happened to him and how best to help him."

"And he has told you that, in order to do that, you will have to 'surrender to the light.' Logic suggests that they will wish to keep you from surrendering to this light of which your brother speaks and that that was their purpose all along." Lord Caelon was smiling broadly by this time.

Dia wondered what he was finding so amusing. "It does?"

"Of course! If you do as your brother has asked, if you find this light of his and submit to it, then they lose." She was still unsure of his meaning and that must have shown on her face, for Lord Caelon continued to patiently explain. "Lord Daerus was bait, my lady. We know that this unseen enemy of yours -- of ours, I suppose" he amended with a wry smile, "is seeking to put you under their power in the same way they have enslaved your brother. I would wager that they could only do that if you were here, where they are. So, they persuaded him to send for you and then, once you were on your way, they imprisoned him in order to keep you here. They have used him to get to you."

"But why?" she asked again. "Why me?"

"I haven't the vaguest notion," Lord Caelon replied with unabated good humor. "But it does seem that you, not your brother, are the key to this business -- whatever it may be."

"I see," Dia said slowly, frowning again. "You have given me much to ponder, my lord. I th ... "

"Hail and well met, my lord, my lady," said Prince Maermat, abruptly joining them.

"How do you do, Highness?" Lord Caelon welcomed him so heartily that Dia looked at him sharply.

Her own greeting to the Prince was much more restrained but he did not appear to notice.

"I have been searching for you, my lady," his Imperial Highness went on. "We are making up a game of *thannaer* and wondered if you would join us."

Even as he spoke, Dia felt the blackness descending upon her like the falling of a curtain. Her mind lurched out, instinctively reaching for Lord Caelon. *Do you feel it?* she asked him.

I do not feel it of myself, he said, *but I can feel what is directed at you. It would seem to confirm our theory that you are the target of whatever your enemies have in mind.*

"We?" she was asking Prince Maermat.

"Your brother and my sister mean to play," he replied, even as the pressure against her mind grew heavier. "Lady Petra and Lord Taedal join us as well. What do you say, my lady? There are places for you and even for Lord Caelon if he should also wish to play."

It would seem that any touch from you preserves me, my lord, Dia told her escort, *even a mind-touch. I wish I had known this sooner.*

Do you, my lady? I am not sorry for the frequent priviledge of taking your hand, he retorted, suiting action to words. "Do you join their party, my lady?" he asked aloud.

Dia noted but did not comment upon the measuring glint that came into the Prince's eyes as he observed that seemingly possessive gesture. Nor did she reply to Lord Caelon directly. Well aware that he could feel her amusement, she said to Prince Maermat, "I am sorry, your Highness, but I do not care for cards." And still the pressure of the darkness grew even heavier.

"Why, how is this?" asked a gay feminine voice. Princess Kera, on Daerus' arm, joined them. "Daerus was certain that you would find a game diverting, and surely your twin brother would know your favorite amusements."

"Indeed," Dia agreed, fixing Daerus with a considering eye, "one would have thought so."

"Come, Dia, you were used not to be so missish," her brother chided her. "I cannot imagine what has come over you since you came to Ormaerand."

That reprimand made her grin. "I might say the same of you, my dear," she told him sweetly, "but I shall not." Thinking quickly, and loftily ignoring Lord Caelon's fit of coughing, she continued, "In any event, I shall be returning to Shae presently, and I have no wish to return to Mama with gaming on my conscience."

A moment of shocked silence greeted this remark. Indeed, the company looked as perfectly appalled as if Dia had just announced her intention to appear for next endmeal completely naked. Except poor Lord Caelon, who continued coughing in such a distressing fashion that the Princess Kera glanced at him briefly and in some alarm.

Finally, Prince Maermat broke the silence. "You are returning to Shae?" he asked, his speculative gaze intent.

"Why, yes, your Highness," Dia said cordially. "I shall have to leave soon, you know, before HighSun makes travel quite unsuitable."

"Surely you do not intend to leave us so soon!" Princess Kera protested, worriedly glancing toward her brother.

"We shall speak of this later, sister," was all Daerus had to say.

"If you wish," Dia replied serenely. "And now, if you will all excuse me, I really must make my way to Lady Tamia's side. No doubt she will be wishing to retire by now."

"Allow me to escort you, my lady," Lord Caelon wheezed, having almost completely recovered by this time, and placed the hand he still held on his arm. Together, they left the little knot of people behind. "And what of this sudden announcement of your departure, Lady Dia?" he asked her as soon as they were out of earshot. "Do you really mean to abandon your brother so callously?"

"I very much doubt that I shall be permitted to do so, my lord," she replied, still very calm. "For so long as I remained here, trying to help Daerus, they need do nothing other than continue with their attempts to ensnare me with their darkness -- and that cannot be very difficult for them, for their darkness is everywhere," she added wearily. "But, if I am about to bring my visit to a close, they shall have to do *something*, and I am very curious to know what that something will be."

"You play a dangerous game, my lady," Lord Caelon said seriously after a moment's consideration. "If they find they cannot control your mind as they have your brother's, they may decide to put a period to your existence instead."

"I do not think so, my lord," she disagreed. "If their only purpose is to prevent me from some act which they fear, then the simplest way to accomplish that would be for me to die. Yet, they have not tried to kill me. No, for some reason, they need me and I am very curious to know why. Perhaps, if I push them a little, I shall find out."

CHAPTER NINE

"Come in, Daerus."

So certain had Dia been that she would be gratified by a visit from her brother that she had not even begun to prepare for bed when Lord Caelon had delivered her to her room. Instead, she had spent that time in peaceful meditation, furnishing herself with the core of a calm she knew she would need. By the time she recognized his altered aura outside her bedroom door, she was ready for him.

Daerus did not await a second invitation, but let himself into her sitting room without ceremony and fixed her with a brooding stare. Dia placidly returned his gaze and waited.

"Why are you leaving?" he asked her abruptly.

She smiled. "Why should I stay? I do not *live* here, you know."

"Are you *trying* to offend the imperial family?"

"Not at all, and I know of no reason why they should be offended."

"Oh, come now, Dia!" he said, distracted. "Almost no one

leaves the Emperor's court so soon! He is sure to be offended and my chance to be wed to Kera will be lost!"

At that, she laughed aloud. "How can you be so absurd, Daerus? It has been obvious to everyone at court since before ever I arrived that his Majesty quite dotes upon you. Indeed, I fancy you had no need of my aid, no matter what you may say to the contrary. No, Daerus, do not start to rant at me, if you please. I have met the Emperor and his family, and have thoroughly charmed them all. What reason have I for prolonging my visit?"

He was shaking his head. "What I do not understand," he said in bewilderment, "is why you would want to leave. Do you not find the palace comfortable? Is not the company far more congenial than any to be found at Shae at this season?"

"My tastes do not run in that direction, Daerus, and you should know that," she replied gently. "I have told you many times that I will not stay here any longer than I must, so I cannot conceive why you should be so surprised. Moreover, if I do not go soon, I will be stranded here for the better part of half the year."

"And what of Maermat?" Daerus went on, ignoring her protests. "Have you given any thought to his reaction to this news?"

"No," she said.

He frowned. "Why not?"

"Why should I?" Dia asked. "Surely, his Highness must be quite used to bidding his father's guests farewell."

"Come now, Dia," he said impatiently, "you know perfectly well that you are more than just another imperial guest in his eyes."

Dia regarded her brother calmly for a few moments, wondering if his keepers had given him permission to be more forthcoming than he had been so far. "I fear I know nothing of the sort. Do not say that the fellow has developed a passion for me?" she asked in mild amusement.

"Is that so difficult to believe?"

"Frankly, yes." She waited but he did not speak. So, she added, "Daerus, do you tell me that your Prince Maermat intends to offer for my hand?"

"His Highness has not confided in me," Daerus said, repressively if unconvincingly, "but I should not be at all surprised if that was indeed his intention. It should be obvious that he is quite smitten with you."

"It is not obvious to me," Dia stated. "In any event, since I have no wish to be wed to Maermat, I shall hope that you are quite mistaken and that I shall be spared the embarrassment of having to refuse him."

"Refuse him?" asked Daerus incredulously. "Are you mad?"

"Me?"

"The most advantageous offer any female in the entire Empire could wish, and you would refuse it?" he raged at her. "Have you any idea how many ladies at court would give *anything* to be wed to Kaerkas' heir?"

"No, but I very much wish that his Highness would offer for one of them, instead," Dia said, still serene. She paused, fixing him with an interested gaze. "Just as a matter of some curiosity, I gather that you favor the Prince's suit?"

"Well, of course I do!" he told her.

"And it does not appear to you to matter whether or not I hold him in the greatest aversion," she observed. "Or does it?"

Daerus did not reply, merely bending a look of brooding disapproval upon her.

"The Daerus I once knew would never have urged me into a marriage simply for the sake of power or position," Dia said, softly pensive.

"The Daerus you once knew," he mimicked with a sneer, "was an ignorant bumpkin who knew little of the ways of the world."

"Perhaps," she said thoughtfully, "but that fellow was also my brother and I loved him dearly. I shall miss him."

"Treasure your memories, my dear. That naive, stupid fellow is quite dead."

Dia looked at him with a laugh in her eyes, knowing that he lied and that he knew she knew it. "How unfortunate! But that is neither here nor there," she went on, not giving him a chance to reply. "You give me to understand that you desire that I respond favorably to Maermat's suit, and no matter that I hold him in the greatest aversion?"

Once again, for a moment, he did not reply. Patiently, Dia

waited as he brooded in silence. Then, finally, he said, "You *must* wed him."

"Must I?"

"Yes, hang it all, Dia!"

"Why?"

"Think of all the people you will disappoint if you do not!" he replied, answering her question obliquely. "If you think my father will be glad to know that you turned down the opportunity to be the future Empress, you must be all about in your head. And my mother! Not to mention the whole of the imperial family. Do you care to distress them all so needlessly?"

"You have not answered my question, you know," Dia said, still very, very calm. "Why *must* I be wed to Maermat?"

Again, there was a moment of tense silence. "Is it not enough that I wish it?" he asked her in some desperation. "Once, you would not have refused me this favor."

"Once, you would not have asked it," she retorted instantly. "Now, do please answer me. Why must I be wed to Maermat? What will happen if I am not?"

"You force my hand," he told her reluctantly, his eyes growing as hard as granite. "Understand this, Dia, you *shall* be wed to Maermat, if not willingly, then unwillingly. I had hoped that you would come to your senses in this matter, and so be spared a great deal of pain and humiliation. If you will not, then so be it; I have done what I could. You may refuse his *honorable* offer, if you are feeling so capricious, but in the end, you will find yourself with no other choice."

Dia chuckled. "Really, Daerus, such theatrics! Truly, I am not so unreasonable as you seem to think, my dear. But if I am to mortgage my future and my happiness in this fashion, then you will at least have to give me a reason for it." She paused but he did not reply. "Since you seem unwilling to do so, you cannot be too surprised to find me intractable."

There was a long pregnant silence. "You know *nothing* of the power you so disdain," he finally said in a hoarse, tortured voice, "and, as you will learn to your sorrow, *you cannot escape it!*"

"And, still, he has not answered my question," she mused sadly. "Or perhaps he has? Never mind, then, since you are reluctant to answer that question, let us try you another. I make no doubt that this proposed espousal to Maermat has to do with that cold, beauteous darkness of yours, is that not so?" When he did not reply, contenting himself with staring at her warily, she added, "Come, twin, do not be coy. That is what you meant when you spoke just now of the power I so disdain."

Still, he hesitated for a moment before finally nodding an affirmation.

Dia smiled then. "You say I cannot escape it," she told him gently, "but it must surely be obvious to you that I *have* escaped it."

"What can you mean?" he asked, sounding so shocked that she might easily have laughed aloud.

"Can it be you have not noticed that I have thrown off that blanket of darkness and have not succumbed to it again?" she asked him placidly. "I rather fancy that 'escape' does not even come into it, Daerus. I have made my *choice.* I choose to eschew that revolting darkness and you cannot force me to choose differently."

Her brother's scowl grew blacker and blacker throughout this speech and, when it was done, she saw his hands bunch themselves into fists. That amused her, and she smiled faintly but her gaze remained steady. "You would be among the Chosen of Lord Septha, and you presume to refuse Him?" he asked, outraged.

"Most assuredly, dearest," Dia replied readily.

Daerus continued to stare at her, breathing heavily, looking angry, offended, even shocked, and quite obviously bereft of speech. Then, as if he must put some distance between himself and his sister, he flung himself to the door, wrenched it open and almost fell into Lord Caelon's arms. "Your pardon, sir," Daerus said stiffly.

"Indeed, I beg *your* pardon, sir," Lord Caelon replied promptly, smiling.

"Tell me, Daerus, have you been presented to his lordship?" Dia asked him, the picture of innocence.

"I have not," replied her brother with an ill-grace.

"Really, Daerus, how remiss! You must certainly pay your respects to Lord Saeros and Lady Tamia of Aerandos, for Lady Tamia is a particular friend of Mama's and she would be so disappointed if you did not." *Indeed,* she thought to herself, *I am beginning to sound like Lady Tamia, chattering on like this.* "Allow me to present Lord Caelon, heir to Aerandos. This is my brother, my lord, Daerus of Shae."

"I am very happy to make your acquaintance at last, my lord," Lord Caelon said, apparently taking his cue from Dia and holding out his hand.

Daerus stared at that hand as if it were a poisonous snake, and it seemed for a moment that he would commit the terrible solecism of refusing to take it. Finally, he reached out, moving as if he were about to plunge his arm into a fire, and executed the expected handclasp. Dia, an interested spectator, saw Daerus turn pasty white and wince when Lord Caelon's hand closed around his. Really, the lad looked quite ill!

Hurriedly, Daerus excused himself and rushed off toward his own apartments. Lord Caelon looked after him for a moment before he turned quizzical eyes upon her. "I do hope he makes it back to his rooms before he faints!" he said.

Dia gazed pensively after her brother's rapidly retreating form. "I must admit, I had wondered what the result would be, if I could contrive to place him in a position in which he would have to grasp your hand." Then she smiled at him. "I am surprised to see you again, my lord. You are taking very good care of me, you know."

He laughed at that. "Dear me! I am now wholly at a disadvantage, for in fact, I have come to you in the hope that you will indulge me with a few explanations."

In reply, she held open her door, wordlessly inviting him inside. As she did so, she reflected ruefully that this new development would certainly give the palace rumor-mongers much to occupy them.

Lord Caelon seemed to have had the same thought. "Are you sure you want to encourage the speculations that have been distressing you so, my lady?"

"To be honest with you, I do not care one whit for these silly people and what they may have to say of what I do. There are much more important matters to occupy my thoughts."

"So I perceive. It begins?"

"Indeed." She crossed the room to resume her seat.

"And what have you learned?"

"I am informed that I am required to be wed to Prince Maermat."

Lord Caelon greeted this news in silence for a moment, absently refusing her gestured invitation to seat himself. She got the distinct impression that he was disturbed. "You will accept?"

"I had rather be wed to a toad," she assured him promptly.

He chuckled. "I would think your brother's reaction to such sentiments rather defies description. Maermat is the premiere catch in the Empire, you know. Your parents may not be pleased with your choice."

Dia shook her head. "My father has little use for Emperor Kaerkas, although he is very careful to speak of him with respect. Papa will not reproach me for my decision."

"You are fortunate, then, in your family."

"Very true, my lord, but I do not think you came here to discuss my family with me," she said smoothly.

"Well, only insomuch as they affect your present predicament," he replied with a grin. "Your brother thinks to somehow force you into this marriage?"

Dia nodded.

"I wonder why."

"So did I. I did ask him, but he would not answer. Or at least," she corrected herself thoughtfully, "he did not answer directly."

"I see. And what was his indirect answer?" his lordship asked.

"I gather that Lord Septha is unwilling to allow me the privilege of my choice," she replied, wondering if she would be obliged to argue with him about the identity of their adversary.

To her surprise, however, he did not comment on her theological assumptions. "One is forced to wonder whether this proposed match is the means to an end or the end itself," he pondered, beginning to pace the floor.

She frowned thoughtfully. "Do you know, I cannot tell. Certainly, Prince Maermat has been very particular in his attentions all along, but I am not sure if his purpose has been to keep me here, basking in his favor," and Lord Caelon laughed at her sarcasm, "or if he has been in earnest in trying to persuade me to favor his suit. But why would the God of Chaos need me to wed the prince?"

"I should have thought the answer to that question would be obvious," Lord Caelon said. "He does not want you to wed someone else."

"Oh, goodness, surely this elaborate scheme does not have so simple an aim!" Dia protested with sudden impatience. "They could have let me remain at Shae and accomplished the very same thing. What possible difference could it make who I take to husband or even if I remain unwed? That cannot be it!"

"That must be it, my lady. Either that," Lord Caelon added, smiling, "or it is their intent to imprison you here without seeming to."

That gave her a moment's pause. "Frankly, that makes a great deal more sense. After all, they cannot fling me into a dungeon. I fancy my father would have something to say to that."

"And not just your father. Should the Emperor treat the child of any of the Great Houses so, he would find himself embroiled in a civil war without delay, for you may be very sure that Aerandos, Tamaer and Gedbaen would stand with Shae, even if Ormaer cannot be expected to stand against an Emperor of their own House."

"I wonder if they will care?" Dia said slowly, still frowning. "Septha the Destroyer is aptly named, you know. His purpose is always the same: war, famine, anarchy, chaos. His minions here in the palace may be working toward those aims without even realizing it." She looked at him very seriously. "I do apologize, my lord. I fancy that this must all sound like perfect nonsense to you ..."

To her astonishment, Lord Caelon actually flushed. "No, my lady, do not apologize. I find myself forced by circumstance to revise some long held opinions. There was a time," he added with a wry smile, "not so long ago, in fact, when I would have said that anyone who claimed to be able to hear the thoughts of another was either dreadfully untruthful or a raving lunatic."

"Oh dear!" Dia laughed.

"Now I am forced to conclude either that *I* am a raving lunatic or I was mistaken." He grew serious, adding, "In the wake of everything else that has transpired, I perceive that I must have some small part to play in this matter."

Unbidden, she heard Lord Caelon's transformed voice saying, *"But if the other should surrender to the light ... ."* Aloud, she said, smiling impishly, "I shall hope you will not find that inconvenient, my lord."

"I am apt to find it very inconvenient," he retorted, "for although I would readily lend you my aid, I have not the smallest notion of what is required of me, or even what our goals are. I am a soldier, my lady. I am not comfortable without a battle plan."

"I can certainly understand that," she said feelingly. "Well, I will tell you want I can, as best I can recall from my studies with Phoebus." She paused, steepling her hands in front of her face thoughtfully. "It were best, I think, not to bombard you with an entire theology at this time, however."

Laughter suddenly lit Lord Caelon's eyes, banishing embarrassment. "I would tend to agree with that."

She smiled absently at his remark, still reviewing her lessons in her mind. "Very well then. Since you require a battle plan, the best I can do is to tell you of the battle." She raised her eyes to his. "The Ages always end in the same way. Septha the Destroyer is said to await the final death of each Phoenix, for in the Interval between the death of one and the rise of another, He gains His chance to achieve a place in this world. If He succeeds in making that place for himself, He is then in a position to engage Ancient Phoenix in battle for what is said to be His lost place among the Gods of this world."

"The Gaerud." Lord Caelon's guess was not really a question.

"Indeed, my lord," Dia responded. "Right now, this world is in terrible peril, for never before has there been such a long Interval between the death of one Phoenix and the emergence of the next."

"The length of the Interval affects the pitch of the battle?" he asked her, his expression intent.

"Well, the longer that Septha abides in this world and poisons our minds and hearts ... "

"In much the way that seems to have happened in this palace," interjected Lord Caelon.

"Indeed, my lord, in the entire city and much of the lands in the district of Ormaer," she agreed. "As more time elapses, Septha feels his strength as the number of His followers grows greater. His instruments acquire Secrets and spells of their own, even as the TimeKeepers' Secrets grow feeble and useless until the emergence of the next Phoenix."

"Hold a moment, my lady," Lord Caelon said. "Septha's followers? I fear I have noticed no mass conversion, nor anyone proposing to build temples to His worship. What can you mean?"

"Do you imagine the worship of a God or Goddess depends upon building temples and constructing dogma? Septha acquires His following through the lives of the people of this world, even as does Ancient Phoenix. Under the gentle hand of the Phoenix, we live in peace and order. Septha brings chaos and destruction."

Lord Caelon nodded his comprehension. "So, the longer this world must await the Phoenix, the stronger Septha's power grows."

"That is the heart of the matter, my lord," she confirmed. "In the transition between Ages past, it was enough for the new Phoenix to wave His hand to banish Septha once more. It has been so long now that our Phoenix is like to have quite a fight on His hands, when finally He does appear."

"If a fight is the final order of business, then perhaps I am well-chosen after all," Lord Caelon said, sounding so satisfied with this arrangement that Dia laughed. "The only question to answer now is still the first: what must be done to clear the way for the return of the Phoenix?"

"'Surrender to the light,' Lord Caelon. That is the only instruction we have received," she said ruefully. Then she frowned. "You know, that is really rather odd. The instruction for me is not to avoid the darkness. Nor is it to live with the light, or something to that effect."

"Yes," Lord Caelon said slowly, his brow furrowed in concentration. "You are charged with the act of surrender, rather than passively accepting this light."

"So, while Daerus has already fulfilled his part of that prophesy -- for he has surely drowned in darkness -- it is not going to be enough for me to resist his schemes. I must find this light of which the Phoenix spoke and submit myself to it." She paused again, and then sighed. "How very difficult this is! I *wish* I could speak with Phoebus!"

Lord Caelon regarded her with an uncharacteristic diffidence in his expression, clearing his throat to attract her attention. She raised her eyebrows questioningly, and he said, "If this Prophesy is, in truth, a prophesy, it is destined to happen, is it not?"

Dia nodded, her eyes narrowing as she tried to anticipate the direction of his thoughts.

"If it is destined to happen," he went on, even more diffidently, "then you have no need of deciphering those cryptic instructions, have you? All you will have to do is avoid interfering with it."

She stared at him in astonishment for a moment before breaking into reluctant laughter. "Oh dear!" she gasped finally when she could. "You are perfectly right, of course you are! For now, all I need do is to keep Daerus and his friends from succeeding in their attempts to prevent me from performing my task. The rest will follow as naturally as the Great Dark follows High Sun." She shook her head. "I think I have been overly concerned because *they* seem to know what my task is, even if I do not. Unless ... "

"Unless?"

"Unless they have no more notion than do we but they believe they can control me by marrying me to Maermat," she said, thinking aloud.

"There is no way for us to know, my lady, nor is it really necessary for us to know. For now, we must simply wait. I shall allow myself to be guided by you, for I am even more in the dark about this business than you are. But I mean to do what I can to help."

Unexpectedly, Dia felt the sting of tears in her eyes. She could not have said why, but she found it profoundly moving that Lord Caelon, self-proclaimed unbeliever that he was, should utter so simple and sincere an expression of pure faith.

"Now, what have I said to distress you, my lady?" he asked, watching her.

She shook her head slowly. "Why are you doing this, Lord Caelon?" she asked in her turn, blinking the moisture from her eyes.

"Why am I doing what?"

"Why are you so willing to come to my aid in this pass?"

He smiled. "To own the truth, I do not really know. Perhaps it is because you are worth the effort, daughter of Shae."

It was not until he spoke that she realized she was hoping for something more personal, but she nodded an acknowledgement of that reminder with quiet dignity, rising from her chair. It had long been established among the Great Houses of the Empire that they would stand together when any one of their members was being threatened or improperly importuned.

"Or," Lord Caelon continued, "perhaps it is because it disturbs me to witness such fear and dismay in a gently-bred young lady -- however valiantly she tries to hide it. I am a soldier of Aerandos, my lady; my instinct is to protect and to defend."

Much to her chagrin, Dia blushed. "Thank you, my lord."

With no further conversation, she escorted him to her door.

Just before he left her, Lord Caelon said, "Remains now only to discover your brother's next move. I wonder how he will try to force you into betrothal with Maermat."

"No doubt we shall find out soon enough," she replied placidly.

Upon her next waking, Dia rose and unenthusiastically prepared herself for what had become her routine session with the Emperor and his children, fully expecting another harangue from Daerus on the way. Thus, she was somewhat surprised when Daerus did not come to her rooms as usual, apparently deciding to exclude her from the imperial audience chamber. She wondered in considerable amusement if her twin actually thought such an act would be punishment enough to persuade her to change her mind.

Not long before midmeal, however, she answered a knock on her door and found herself face to face with the detestable Lord Oshaed, accompanied by two ceremonial guards. "Your business, sir?" she asked him frostily.

"One hopes that you are well, my lady," he said with his usual leer, "and are not too exhausted from your romping last night."

Dia, eying the fellow like the insect that he was, considered and discarded various likely responses before settling on one of them. "Jealous, my lord?" she asked gently, with the faintest of smiles.

It was a bow drawn at a venture, but when Lord Oshaed's leer was abruptly replaced by a ferocious scowl and a dull red flush, she realized that this wrinkled little man's preoccupation had its roots in what others enjoyed that he could not. From the direction of the guards, she heard a muffled snort. Even more gently, she added, "Was there anything else you wanted, my lord?"

Through clenched teeth, he retreated into formula, "His Imperial Majesty commands my lady's presence in his audience chamber."

Still with that faint smile, she curtseyed and said, "Thank you, my lord."

Lord Oshaed turned and stalked off down the corridor. The two guards followed, one of them being so impertinent as to wink at her before he left.

Dia beguiled the short walk to the imperial audience chamber wondering why she had not been summoned directly after firstmeal, as had been her brother's custom. Surely, the day's audiences must be almost over. Immediately upon entering the imperial presence, however, Dia knew that something was in the wind. Instead of occupying unobtrusive seats along the walls, her brother and the Prince and Princess were ranged in statuesque formality around the Emperor's chair. The scene at once registered in her mind as of a pack of hungry jackals poised for an attack, for there was that in their postures that suggested decisive divisions into "us" and "them". She saw at once that she had not been invited to accompany the imperial family during the Emperor's audiences; she had been summoned to an audience herself.

"Lady Dia of Shae," the herald announced her and withdrew.

"My lady," the Emperor nodded at her.

Dia sank gracefully into a deep curtsey. "Your Imperial Majesty," she responded with equal formality. As she rose, she noted the almost identical expressions of smug triumph on the faces of Daerus, Princess Kera, and even the amorous Prince Maermat. They looked very much as if they considered this particularly battle already fought and won. Quite unconsciously, Dia's back stiffened.

"As you may know," the Emperor began, "your good brother had gratified Us by aspiring to the hand of the Imperial Princess Kera. Shae is an excellent House and We are pleased to bestow her on so worthy a gentleman."

Dia smiled calmly. "The House of Shae is honored, Sire, and I am sure I wish them very happy," she replied, still very formal.

"Since Our daughter is so admirably settled, We have turned Our attention to Our heir. We are sure you will agree that it is even more crucial that he be wed suitably and that Our line be continued," his Majesty continued.

Dia nodded and waited.

"We have decided that he too shall be connected by marriage to the most excellent House of Shae. Therefore, it is Our decree that you, Lady Dia, shall be wed to the Prince Maermat immediately."

There was a long silence, during which Dia felt the oppressive darkness that permeated the palace grow thicker and heavier around her. Silently, she cursed her own arrogance. It had never occurred to her that Daerus might take this matter to the Emperor. Yet, she saw now that she should have known what his next move would be.

An imperial command, and what was she to do? Sternly, she reminded herself that her first task was to hold panic at bay. Her determination hardened as she recalled that she did, after all, have options, and she silently vowed once more that she would *not* be wed to Maermat, even if it meant she had to escape Ormaeranda altogether and live in exile in nearby Lemantia or out in the islands of Akkam to the west. If to force her into marriage with Maermat of Ormaer was the Destroyer's means of strengthening His position for the upcoming Gaerud, he would find that he had chosen the wrong vessel.

Then, suddenly, she began to feel a warm glow, deep inside her, that pushed away the darkness that was bearing down on her and the chill fear that had frozen her tongue. The glow expanded, enfolding her in such a comforting warmth that her entire body stilled with an absolute calm such as she had never experienced. With no conscious notion of having formed the words in her mind, or of having ordered her tongue to utter them, she said, "I am very sorry, your Majesty, but I am afraid that that is quite impossible."

CHAPTER TEN

" . . . and so, of course, his Majesty asked me at once whatever I could mean by such a statement," Lady Dia was recounting to an audience of interested Aerandosians, kneading her hands anxiously. Caelon watched her with interest, rather amused that the normally self-possessed Lady Dia should be reduced to the nervousness of a kitten and wondering what under the sun could have happened.

Neither he nor his parents had been a bit surprised to see her when he had opened his mother's sitting room door and invited her inside. After all, she usually arrived shortly before midmeal to enliven his mother's day with her company. Today, however, she had hurled herself into his mother's sitting room as if all the demons of Chaos were chasing her and, instead of settling down to chat, she had said in some agitation that she had done something dreadful and wished to beg their pardon. Thus far, the nature of her crime had wholly escaped Caelon, for the girl seemed to be taking the devil of a long time getting to the point.

"So, I told him . . . I told him . . . ," and Lady Dia faltered to a stop.

After a seemingly interminable wait, during which it became apparent that her ladyship could not bring herself to continue, his mother prompted gently, "You told him . . . ?"

She took a deep breath. "I told him that I could not honorably accept the Prince's offer b-because I was already p-promised . . . ," her eyes fell away from Lady Tamia's and, crimson cheeked, she continued in a mortified whisper, " . . . to Lord Caelon."

For an astonished moment, no one spoke. Caelon exchanged a glance with his parents and then, as one, they fell into gusts of merriment. Lady Dia raised startled eyes to gaze at them all and, sadly, her obvious bewilderment made the laugh all the more.

"Well, young lady," his father said when he could command his voice again, "you have certainly shown that you know how to keep your wits about you in an emergency."

"You do not mind this subterfuge?" she asked anxiously, directing the question impartially at the three of them.

"Mind? My dear child, I would willingly commit a far worse crime than this to preserve a daughter of Mara's from having her hand forced in this fashion!" his mother declared. She suddenly giggled, adding, "Your mama would be so proud of you!"

Lady Dia paled, her eyes dilating. "Oh, dear! Mama!"

That made his parents laugh again. Caelon, managing to keep from grinning, chimed in, "Well, really, I find all this mirth unseemly! Here am I being entrapped into marriage by this designing female, and you two can do nothing but laugh!"

Lady Dia stared at him in considerable dismay. His parents, who knew him rather better than did my lady, very naturally laughed again, until his father grinned at him and said, "You know, you could do much worse, lad."

"Oh, you two are perfectly dreadful," Lady Tamia declared, trying unsuccessfully to contain her mirth. "Here is poor Lady Dia, almost ready to sink from the mortification of having been forced into this prevarication (and doubtless terrified that we will think ill of her), and all you can think of to do by way of reassurance is to tease her in this terribly unkind way!"

"How can you say so, my lady?" protested Lord Saeros, eyes twinkling. "I am sure I would never behave so callously toward Lady Dia. I was teasing *Caelon*!"

"Odious wretch!" retorted the Dutchess with a fond smile. Then she looked at Lady Dia. "So, what had his Majesty to say to your mendacious tale?"

Her ladyship reddened once more. "He has said that he will take up the matter with Lord Saeros and Lord Caelon presently," she told them, still looking terribly embarrassed.

Lord Saeros looked at her with shrewd eyes. "And you hurried off to your alleged groom to beg him not to give you away. Is that it?" he asked her gently.

Lady Dia, once more kneading her hands, nodded miserably. "Really, I am so sorry, I would never have embroiled any of you in this, but truly, I did not know what else to do. My father is not here and Daerus . . . ," here, she hesitated.

"Daerus," Caelon completed the sentence for her, "is unlikely to be of any more use in this case than he has been since you arrived. In fact," he added, thinking aloud, "I shouldn't wonder at it if this whole thing was his idea."

Lady Dia ducked her head, looking so ashamed that he found himself wishing he had left that thought unsaid.

Lady Tamia, also noting her distress, said, "Oh, surely not! Your brother might wish for you to wed into the imperial family as he intends to do, but he could not be pleased to think that you are forced to wed against your will!"

To Caelon's complete astonishment, Lady Dia's only response to this protest was the single tear which escaped her control and slid down her cheek. Her hands worked even faster, until he wondered if she would tear her own skin in her agitation.

Naturally, that was entirely too much for his mother. She leapt at once to her feet to enfold the girl in a tender embrace, crooning and fussing over her comfortingly. But Caelon could see, by the stiffness with which she returned Lady Tamia's embrace and the muscles rippling along her jaw, that her ladyship was not so much hurt by her brother's betrayal as she was enraged at his machinations. He would have given a great deal to have been present at their next private interview.

Meanwhile, Lord Saeros cast an appraising eye over his son. "The question now," that gentleman said, "is whether or not you mean to expose my lady as an undutiful fraud."

"It is a very lowering reflection," Caelon said mournfully, to no one in particular, "that my own father thinks his only son a dastardly villain. Of course, I will maintain the fiction. I am a gentleman, sir, and I shall always lend my aid to a damsel in distress, whether I save her from a ferocious dragon or a boring bridegroom."

"Well, you may laugh at all this, my dear," Lady Tamia said regretfully to her husband -- a gracious permission of which Lord Saeros seemed to be taking full advantage -- "but I for one will be honest with you and admit that I wish my lady's tale were indeed true."

Lady Dia, listening to this confession, blushed a fiery red and looked more mortified than ever.

"Why, how shocking," Caelon said in wholly feigned amazement. Then, he grinned again. "Really, Mama, there was no need for you to make such a disclosure. You have been as subtle in your matchmaking as an axe to the head."

"Now, stop it, young man," Lady Tamia said, unruffled. "Here is poor Saeros, guffawing and wheezing in the most distressing fashion, and just think how dreadful if he should take a fit of choking and die of laughter. We will discuss this matter calmly just as soon as my lord has composed himself."

"What is there to discuss, ma'am?" Caelon asked his mother.

"Do you still mean to leave the palace, my dear?" she asked Lady Dia by way of an answer.

"Indeed, your Grace, I shall be gone from here before ever firstmeal is served," Lady Dia informed them fervently. "I must advise my father of all that has come to pass. Daerus will wed where he chooses, but I rather fancy Papa will have some words for my dear brother about his duty to compel the respect due his sister."

Caelon grinned. She spoke with a certain vindictive pleasure that made perfect sense to him. Really, the boy deserved to be horsewhipped -- or he would, if he were not bound in that accursed mental slime. Recalling their conversation when first she had announced her intention to return to Shae, he now wondered what next their enemies would do to prevent it, for they had certainly given Lady Dia good reason to want to leave the palace as soon as possible.

"You are going to have to accompany her, you know, Caelon," Lord Saeros interrupted his thoughts.

"Indeed?" Lady Dia asked in some surprise. "May I know why?"

"If we are going to maintain this fiction long enough for the Grand Dukes to respond, it would look odd for your prospective bridegroom to permit you to set out alone, my lady," Lord Saeros explained.

"Respond?"

"Whether or not you and my son are to be wed is beside the point," his Grace continued severely. "It is quite intolerable that you should have been put in a position in which you had to fabricate such a tale in order to avoid a distasteful marriage of the Emperor's choosing. His Majesty cannot simply dispose of the children of the Great Houses as if they were his chattels, and he seems in need of being reminded of this."

Caelon looked at his father sardonically. "Just how long is that going to take, sir?" he asked politely. "Shall I, in fact, be required to wed my lady in order to give you enough time to prepare this response?"

"I think not," Lord Saeros said blandly, "but how ungallant of you to display your distaste for the notion so plainly. I have already given you my opinion that you might do much worse." Caelon grinned at that reproach as his father continued. "Loraed's prompt reaction cannot be in doubt. Gaeron of Tamaer can also be counted on for swift action, for he has three daughters and will no doubt be quite dismayed by his Majesty's behavior."

"And Permaedon of Gedbaen is your marriage-brother," Caelon interjected, still grinning, "and will do as he is told."

"Sisters do have their uses," Lord Saeros remarked blandly.

Two pairs of unfriendly, feminine eyes fixed themselves upon him.

Dia sat in the bathtub that had been prepared in her sitting room, trying to soak the accumulated tensions of recent events from her tired body, and considered Colonel Lord Caelon

Aerandos. He had certainly seemed to take the whole betrothal charade in much better part than she had expected, for she had feared he would take this as some sort of ploy to entrap him into a match. She would have liked to have explained to him that the deception had not been entirely her idea, but since she could not have said from where those unbidden words had come, she knew that such an explanation was unlikely to mend matters. She sighed and found herself wishing, not for the first time, that she could have met the Grand Duke Saeros of Aerandos and his delightful family under different circumstances.

Turning her thoughts to her much more immediate problems, she wondered once again how Daerus and his imperial fiancee would now contrive to get her wed to Prince Maermat. Perhaps they would give up on that idea, if they could decide upon some other course of action by which they could hope would control her. If she could imagine what they hoped to achieve by such a match, she could also perceive certain disadvantages to them, for Dia would be no docile, dutiful bride and her position within the imperial family would be likely to give her a much better vantage point from which to combat the evil darkness that had consumed her brother and was threatening her.

And yet, even with those advantages, she felt a growing conviction that she would very soon have to leave this place. Not just yet, for there was still a piece of the puzzle missing, but very soon. She smiled ruefully to herself. From her point of view, the puzzle was still a puzzle and all of it was missing. Once again, she was visited by the rather odd notion that she was being fed minute bits of information, little flashes of insight that would prompt her to act but would give her no extras in the way of explanation or instruction. She recalled that comforting warmth and light that had overwhelmed her in the throne room during her interview with Emperor Kaerkas. In its way, it was every bit as powerful and irresistible as the cloying darkness which Septha the Destroyer spun, but Dia did not fear its power. She could not have said why she felt so certain that the warm brilliance was no threat, even when it was every bit as controlling as the darkness, and it occurred to her that she was operating on hunches and guesses and gut instincts that reduced to a more profound sort of faith than any she had ever had to summon to her aid before.

Suddenly, there was a loud knock at her sitting room door. Dia, stepping from the bath and wrapping a large toweling sheet around her body, reached out with her mind and encountered her brother's familiar presence. "Go away, Daerus," she called to him. "I am indisposed."

Much to Dia's annoyance, her brother's reply to that denial was to open the door without further ceremony. She opened her mouth to scold him but the words died on her lips as her eyes met his. His smile was distinctly unpleasant and the only word she could think of to describe the way he looked at her was *evil.* Unaccountably, her heart gave a frightened thump.

More to dispel that ridiculous knot of fear -- *Whatever they have done to him, this is still Daerus,* she told herself sternly -- than from any real desire to exchange in bantering converse with him, she said with a resigned sigh, "Can you never rid yourself of this habit of bursting into my chambers whenever you have news? Really, Daerus, only think what Mama would say to such incivility!"

To her surprise, the wicked light faded from his eyes and he blinked in some bewilderment. "Mama?" he said stupidly.

"Yes, Mama," she said, taking a free corner of the towel and beginning to pat herself dry with it. "You *do* remember her, I trust?" Deliberately, she kept her tone casual and offhand as, without betraying her interest, she watched his reactions.

"Yes, of course I remember her!" he said impatiently, sounding just as he might have a week before he left home. "What has she to say to anything?"

Dia grinned. "What, indeed? Poor Mama! Papa would not thank you for speaking so disrespectfully of her."

"Dia ... !"

"And how often has she had to remind you that," and here, Dia's voice took on the sing-song quality of one reciting an oft-heard refrain, "no matter that she is your sister, my dear, Dia is still a lady, and you must not go about bursting into her rooms as if they were your own."

Oh, how he fought against the smile that was curving his lips! "I am afraid I have lost count," he said. Then he sighed. "Poor Mama! It is as well that she can have no notion of what her children get up to when they are from home."

She chuckled, longing with all her heart to prolong this interlude with her twin, for he seemed suddenly so much more like the brother she knew. "For that matter, it is as well that she can have no notion of how often we find ourselves saying, 'Poor Mama!' about one thing or another."

A reluctant laugh greeted this sally. Again, Daerus sighed and the wistful sorrow in his eyes touched her to the heart. "Indeed," he agreed. "I wish ... well, never mind. I am sorry, Dia." And then, so slowly that she knew he was fighting against it, the eyes that held hers lost all their warmth and laughter until, finally, her beloved twin was once more hidden from her sight.

Affecting not to notice the change and deliberately misunderstanding him, she said cheerfully, "And so you should be, but never mind. Tell me what has occurred to send you barrelling into my chambers in such a bang. Has the Emperor dropped down dead? Is the palace on fire? What's afoot?"

He shook his head, and Dia saw with some misgiving that the evil leer was back. "Nothing so earth-shattering, my dear." Then he turned his head to speak over his shoulder. "Come in, your Highness."

Dia frowned as her brother opened the door further to admit Prince Maermat. *What* were they about? The prince strolled into the center of the room, his gaze frankly sensual. Defiantly, she straightened as her temper heated. How dared they ... !

"I shall myself attend to the meddler Aerandos," Daerus was saying to Prince Maermat.

Dia saw that he fully intended to leave her alone with the prince and her eyes widened. "Daerus, have you utterly taken leave of your senses?"

He looked back at her over his shoulder. "Not at all," he said, smiling. "I did try to warn you, Dia."

And, with that, he stepped into the corridor and quietly closed the door behind him.

Prince Maermat, still smiling, began to walk toward her and she stood her ground. She did not attempt to deny to herself that she was very much afraid, but she preferred to focus upon the fact that she was also growing angrier by the minute. Clearly, she had underestimated the depths to which her foes would stoop in order to assure her cooperation. Daerus had warned her that she would be given no choice in the matter, but it had never occurred to her that the Prince might try to force himself upon her. No doubt they were trying to frighten her into capitulation.

"What are you about, your Highness," she asked primly, and with a degree of formality that she privately acknowledged was rather ridiculous under the circumstances.

The Prince stopped. "I am securing my own," he replied, his smile widening as if he agreed.

"Securing your own?"

The smug smile he wore never wavered. "Your brother has already explained matters to you, my lady. You will be *mine* whether you would or no." He seemed very sure of himself.

"And is this your notion of persuasion, then?" she asked suddenly scornful. "I am Shae. You are Ormaer. Do you truly think I would stoop to wed one with so little notion of the honor of his House?"

At that, Prince Maermat frankly laughed. It was not a pleasant sound. "What do you think I care for that?" he asked her. "The chosen of Dark Septha have no need to concern themselves with petty notions of honor." Once again, he started toward her. "Come, my lady, let us have done with this missishness. If you will but cooperate, you may find that you enjoy the experience prodigiously."

Dia's flesh crawled at the thought. Indeed, somehow, she still could not bring herself to believe that Maermat truly intended to ravish her. "And if I refuse?" she demanded with a prideful tilt to her chin and a considering expression in her eyes.

He eyed her up and down in something very like contempt. "It will be no particular trouble for me to take you," he told her. "I'd had some hope that, in this situation, you might bow to the inevitable and make this a pleasant interlude for us both."

"I had rather by far that you killed me, sir," she said, her voice flat with hostility. "You may very well overpower me, but I will never submit to you and yours."

"Ah, no, I cannot." he told her. "There are rules, you know. You may choose to kill yourself when, once I have done with you, you discover yourself to be with child," he added indifferently, closing the distance between them. "Or you may choose to go on living, to give birth to the ultimate instrument of Chaos. It really does not matter, my lady. Whatever you choose, the end will be the same and Great Septha will finally regain his place in this world." He paused for a moment, his eyes travelling over her face in such a way that, for a moment, she could almost have believed this man genuinely might have cared for her. "I will confess, though, that I rather think I should like to father a child of you, my lovely Dia," he told her gently.

That insolently spoken familiarity was completely lost on Dia. As the sense of his words penetrated her shock and anger, she began to see that Maermat had nothing to lose in this pass. And now, as she realized that bedding her was not a means to an end, but the end itself, she began to be truly afraid.

The Prince lifted a hand to caress her cheek but Dia struck it away angrily. His eyes hardened, but the smile he wore did not falter, and those eyes continued to hold hers as he unexpectedly reached out to rip the towel away from her clutching hands as if he would strip her of the honorable pretensions to which she had clung. Then he grasped her shoulders and drew her resisting body against his with a jerk, to caress her neck with cold lips. Dia felt certain that her soul froze at the touch of his mouth on her skin. She instinctively cringed away from him and, aware that he was done with talking, she gave a tremendous heave to free herself.

There she stood, naked, and no longer tall and proud as a daughter of Shae but crouched into a fighting posture that dared him to try his might against her. He laughed lightly. "And still you resist me, foolish Dia? Observe how useless such defiance is." She felt him release a spell, felt the strength slowly draining from her limbs and felt her fear as quickly escalating to panic. Struggling now against his magic as well as the arms that encircled her once more, she silently screamed, *Caelon!*

It was only because she continued her seemingly hopeless struggle against his Secrets that she gained a reprieve when, quite by accident, her knee violently connected with her assailant's crotch. Distracted by pain, Prince Maermat's spell dissolved in his curses and Dia, once more in command of her body, wrenched herself free of his embrace. But before she could make any further move, Prince Maermat, still snarling incoherently in pain, fetched her a stunning backhanded slap that sent her hurtling halfway across the room to crash into the table that held her daggers.

Dia's cheek throbbed where he had hit her and her vision was blurred as a result of rapping her head on the furniture. Frantically, struggling to retain consciousness, she made a desperate grab for the table. It matter not to her in that moment whether she used them on herself or her attacker, but she had to get to her daggers. She *could* not black out now! *Caelon!* she called again, putting all the fervent urgency she felt into that silent shout.

Each of her hands closed on the hilts of her daggers and, sensing that Maermat was coming up behind her, she tried to spin to face him. As quick as she was, she was not quite quick enough. As she was in the act of turning, he grasped her left wrist and levered her arm up so that her fist was raised toward the ceiling. She struggled to get free of his grip for a moment but, realizing that leverage was working against her, she slashed out with her other hand instead and Maermat, in the act of dodging her blade, loosed the wrist he held. Then, she felt his mind at work again, felt the peculiar inrushing sense of gathering strength and knew that he was preparing to release his spell once more. She could not fight him if he were going to use Dark Secrets to rob her limbs of the will to resist. Her arm whipped out like a bolt of lightening as she sent one of her daggers spinning through the air, directly toward the Imperial heir's head.

With a startled shout, Maermat dodged. The knife whistled past his ear but she had at least distracted him, and thankfully felt his spell dissipate. She would have to stay on the offensive, she realized, keeping him off balance so that he would not have the focus he would need in order to use magic against her. She did not have leisure to attend either the fluttering in her belly or her thundering heartbeat, and was aware of nothing but her own desperate determination. She also saw with considerable misgiving that her resistance, her willingness to resort to violence and his own extreme confidence in his ability to overcome that resistance were combining with the spectacle of her nudity to enflame him even more. He was thinking very loudly. Vile images of his imagined eventual conquest flickered across her mind, both revolting and terrifying her, and *where was Caelon?*

Meanwhile, she saw that she now had only one dagger, while the other was stuck in the wall behind the Prince. Before it occurred to him to turn and arm himself with it, she rushed him, the dagger in her had flashing dangerously. For a moment, it seemed she saw an opening but Maermat was not to be bested so easily. He danced clear, sidestepping her attach and slipping around her to the other side of the room.

But it seemed he had seen his own dilemma: he would have to stay far enough out of reach to avoid her blades, yet not so far as to give her room for a clean cast. She could not tell if Daerus had, indeed, warned him of her skill with knife and javelin, or if the sound of her dagger whistling past his head had given him pause. Whatever he might have been thinking, his awareness of his own physical danger now that she was armed served the purpose of giving him other things to ponder than the Dark Secrets he would use against her.

Before she could get to the dagger protruding from the wall, Maermat rushed her, as aware as she that she was twice as dangerous armed with two daggers than she was with but one. She danced back, her blade flickering while with her other hand, she groped behind her in search of a dagger hilt. It was awkward, as well, for she could not look away from his attempts to grasp the hand that wielded the knife. Dia began to wonder despairingly just how long she would be able to keep this up.

And then, just as his hand closed on her wrist, a very welcome voice barked out, "Maermat!" Caelon of Aerandos stood in the doorway, his aura brilliant, his expression thunderous.

Starting with surprise, the Prince released her and backed away. Rendered almost faint with relief, Dia sagged back against the wall, letting her arms fall to her sides, although her hand still convulsively clutched her dagger. As reaction set in and she began to tremble violently, she slowly slid down the wall to the floor, hugging her knees into her chest.

Caelon had been striding down the halls of the imperial palace, when he realized that he was being watched. That cold menace was back, oozing waves of hatred that were laced with a peculiar sort of puzzlement, as if there was something about Caelon that it could not understand. Much more to the point from

Caelon's perspective, there were human watchers awaiting him in the shadows ahead. Very well, then. Caelon gave no outward sign as he passed them, reaching surreptitiously for the short-bladed sword he now wore concealed among his clothes.

He had just walked past yet another darkly shadowed embrasure when they leapt at him in the same instant that he heard Lady Dia call him, her voice in his mind so full of furious and desperate terror that he felt his guts congeal with fear. What in Chaos was happening?

Caelon's sense of self-preservation was well-honed in any event but the added impetus of her ladyship's cry lent strength and speed to his arm. Even as he spun to face his attackers, ducking under the sword stroke he felt more than saw, he ripped out his sword and plunged it straight into one fellow's chest. Before he could recover from the thrust, another sword whistled toward him out of the darkness. Cursing the shadows of the hallway, he pulled his shoulder back and the blow, which would have caught him across the chest, slashed instead across his arm. It was not a serious wound; he hardly felt it and at least it was not his sword arm.

But, if the lighting was causing Caelon some trouble, it was not helping his attackers, either, he realized as he ducked into the shadows from which the fellows had just emerged. He had an urge to even the odds; slowly and silently, he pulled his dagger.

"Chaos and confustication!" exclaimed a rough sounding voice. "He's gorn and disappear't!"

"He has done nothing of the sort," snapped another voice, a voice with which Caelon was wholly familiar. "He has not gone far. Find him!" Caelon discarded his initial assumption that this attack had to do with his father's position on the General Staff. But why would Daerus of Shae make an attempt on his life?

Caelon! As if in answer to that question, Lady Dia's voice echoed in the vaults of his mind once more, lending even more urgency to his taut nerves. The outrage that had been in her voice before was gone now, leaving only despair and a terrible fear.

He could not have known what was happening, but the thought that she was somehow in danger and needed him, and that her brother was apparently determined to keep him from coming to her aid, roused in him an outrage of his own. His anger grew, his vision cleared and he found suddenly that the darkness had been swept aside, seemingly by his own fury. He loosed the dagger in his hand.

Lord Daerus' hireling doubled over with a grunt, clutching the dagger that protruded from his lower chest. Coughing blood, he crumpled and fell.

But Caelon had forgotten him almost as soon as he had thrown his dagger. Now, he faced Daerus of Shae. Looking into the boy's cold grey eyes, Caelon thought again of the young man's obvious intent to keep him from helping my lady. The thought brought with it another wave of unmitigated rage.

Lord Daerus screamed with a gut-wrenching agony and stumbled away from him. He screamed again and fled back into the shadows and down the hall . Caelon did not pause to wonder why. Without any further waste of time, he turned and sprinted the short distance to my lady's chambers.

The scene that had met his eyes had required no explanation and he was engulfed in a fury that owed something of its power to the fearful knowledge that he had almost been too late. When he had promised Lady Dia that he would help her, would champion her cause, he'd had no notion of the depths to which her enemies would sink to ensnare her as they had her brother. Now, more than ever, Caelon renewed a private resolve. Whatever else happened, he *would* not fail her.

"I think you forget yourself, sir," he now said icily.

Prince Maermat, who had automatically straightened to attention when Lord Caelon had snapped out his name so commandingly (for, after all, his lordship had spoken to the Emperor's heir in much the same way he would have spoken to the rawest recruit to the Grand Duke Saeros' army), cast his speculative gaze at Lord Caelon consideringly.

"Do not," Caelon advised him quietly, still seething.

"My lord?" asked Prince Maermat.

"Do not seek to convince me that you are an invited guest in my lady's chambers," Caelon readily supplied. He then opened the door behind him a little wider, indicating with that gesture that his Highness should take himself off.

In a voice he hardly recognized, so harsh and trembling with emotion, Lady Dia endorsed that silent suggestion. "Get out!" she said emphatically.

The Prince once more looked from one of them to the other. Then, appearing neither embarrassed nor remorseful, he shrugged and strolled toward the door. As he reached it, however, he paused and turned back to Dia. "Very well, my lady," he said to her, supreme arrogance in every line of his body, "I am willing to allow you this small victory. Do you use the time to consider the matter well and remember, for I *will* not be denied!"

Caelon swung the door closed directly into the imperial heir's face.

He stared at that closed door for several moments, frowning thoughtfully. It would seem he had been quite right, both in believing that wedding her to Maermat was an end in itself and in cautioning Lady Dia about the dangers of the game she played. Being right was little consolation in that moment, he found. Why would it be so crucial for Dia to take Maermat to husband that they would try to ravish her into it? For his part, he would have thought such a course of action to be fraught with all sorts of dangers for them, not the least of which was his very strong conviction that he would not wish to take any woman to wife who had good reason to plot to murder him in his sleep.

Setting such speculations aside, he turned back to Dia and found her still seated in a trembling little ball on the floor, staring at him in shock. "Where is Daerus?" she asked him tonelessly.

"I could not say," he replied, keeping his counsel. She did not need to hear of how her brother had tried to aid her ravisher. "As well you were planning to quit this place as soon as your eyes open, my lady. If he will stoop to this, there is no knowing what Maermat will be trying next."

Caelon was trying very hard to behave normally, but he was contending with such a confused tidal wave of emotions that he found himself pacing the floor to walk them off. He wanted Prince Maermat to return so that he could thrash the fellow soundly. He wanted to throttle Lord Daerus, as well, for doing nothing to help his sister and everything to injure her. He wanted to comfort Lady Dia, to somehow wipe the shock and terror out of her eyes. He hoped he never saw such an expression in a woman's eyes again as long as he lived. And, suddenly, without warning, he felt an overwhelming wave of desire rise in him, almost drowning all else, and filling him with self-disgust. It caused him to bend and scoop up her towel, tossing it at her and snapping irritably, "For the love of Chaos, ma'am, cover yourself!"

He regretted the words as soon as they left his lips. Lady Dia's stricken gaze flew to his for an instant. Judging from her expression, he might just as well have struck her. Then she dropped her eyes and flushed scarlet as she tried to get the towel around her body with violently trembling hands.

Cursing himself fluently, Caelon strode into her bedchamber to snatch a blanket from the bed. He then knelt beside her and wrapped her in the blanket, saying gently, "I am sorry, my lady. After what you have just been through, I should not speak to you so."

She drew a shuddering breath, and the last vestiges of anger and defiance faded from her face as tears streamed down her cheeks. Then, as if his words had caused a dam to burst, she began to cry -- great, heaving, wracking sobs that tore themselves from her throat so painfully that his own throat closed in sympathy. He enfolded her in a tender embrace and let her weep into his chest, easily ignoring the inappropriate clamoring of his body in his compassion for her ordeal.

Finally, her sobs quieted and she slumped, exhausted but trusting, against his shoulder. He picked her up and carried her into her bedchamber to lay her upon the bed. Kneeling by the bed to bring his head level with hers, he asked, "Are you hurt, my lady?"

Mutely, she shook her head, still apparently unable to bring herself to look at him. He traced the bruise forming on her cheek with a gentle finger, wondering absently if she would tell him if she *were* hurt. He knew he should go; she was neither ill nor injured, so his presence was not really needed. Yet he felt a curious reluctance to leave her, telling himself without conviction that she had sustained a severe shock and needed his support until she had recovered. More than anything, he was aware of an irresistible need to look into her eyes, to see that the shame and pain he had seen earlier were gone.

"Come, Dia," he said to her, very softly, "look at me."

For another long moment, she kept her eyes lowered, seeming to struggle with herself. Then, finally, she slowly raised them to gaze at him. The shadow of hurt was still there and Caelon knew suddenly that it would be a very long time indeed before she fully recovered. "It's over, Dia," he told her, hardly knowing what he said. "You are safe now."

She continued to stare at him gravely before one hand timidly emerged from the blankets wrapped around her to grip his. Her eyes widened. Caelon felt it, too; a warm, comforting light that seemed to come from nowhere to close around the two of them as if it would sheathe them both in a protective cocoon of peace. Again, he was swamped by a wave of passion that he considered wholly inappropriate. He fought against it, unwilling to betray the absolute trust he saw in her gaze, but it was much stronger this time.

Abruptly, he became aware that she was in his mind once more, with an immediacy and intimacy that they had not before experienced in their mental joinings, and that mental touch was his undoing. "Dia . . . ," he heard himself say, experiencing a reluctance which she did not seem to share. Now, her eyes glowed joyously, tenderly, relieved.

Then, another voice spoke to him, a voice he did not recognize, that was deep and resonant and seemed to carry all the echoes of all the endless corridors of eternity. *Surrender, Caelon,* it said. *Surrender to the light.*

He had no very clear recollection of how it came about, but the next thing he knew, he was naked in her bed and everywhere his skin touched hers burned with holy fire. There was no drawing back nor hesitation on her part and, when his body joined with hers, it felt so profoundly right that it seemed to Caelon as if he had somehow become a part of that very first perfect moment of creation so long lost in the misty realms of antiquity. Their minds still linked, he experienced her pleasure as well as his own, causing this encounter to reach a zenith of intensity such as he had never known, and his release, when it came, was so total and complete that he felt he had poured his entire soul into her body to do with what she would.

Finally, exhausted, he slept.

CHAPTER ELEVEN

Danger!

Dia's eyes snapped open. She was suddenly and completely awake, memories flooding her of both the crown prince's frightening attack and the glorious interlude with Caelon that had followed. Indeed, that remembered pleasure was so vivid that her body was enveloped in a languid sensuality that was not usual for her, even as her mind was preternaturally alert. It was difficult to make herself move, but her mind knew, if her body did not, that she had to get away from here *now*.

The delicious languor faded from her limbs as, once again, the sense of a vivid danger, drawing ever closer, invaded her senses and dispelled pleasant memories. Dia did not question the impulse. She simply rolled out of her bed and dressed herself quickly in her cool, travel clothes. As the unseen threat seemed to grow stronger, she began to get frightened and her fingers shook as she fumbled with her clothes, haste making her clumsy. Within minutes, she was hurrying out of her room, moving as silently as possible and keeping to the shadows. Yet, the shadows did not seem to offer friendly concealment; they were cold, threatening, and she looked around nervously as she crept through the corridors of the imperial palace.

Why was she skulking about the palace in this absurd fashion, anyway? she asked herself in some irritation, trying to dispel the peculiar notion that she had somehow left the ordinary world behind in favor of an enchanted world full of unknown wonders and unseen horrors. She had done nothing wrong! The law allowed a woman the right to refuse her favors to any she chose, and the crown prince was not above the law. There was no cause for her to steal away like a common criminal from the gutters. She was a daughter of Shae, scorch it!

Still, she crept on, impelled by that sense of approaching danger. *Being a daughter of Shae did not stop that disgusting Prince Maermat from trying to ravish me*, she told herself ruefully. Nor was it likely to mean much to the headsman's blade, if the Emperor took it into his head to declare that she either be wed to his son or be outlaw. Better to be safely away from here. She would contact Caelon once she was within the stables. He would be looking for her.

Dia stealthily let herself out into the palace courtyard and, after peering around carefully, made her way across to the stalls. The sun had been climbing steadily in the eastern sky during her stay in Ormaerand, and the air inside the sheltered stableyard was still and terribly warm. She would have to make sure she brought adequate water supplies for the journey, still trying to think pragmatically, even if she was sneaking away as inconspicuously as possible. She hoped there was a well inside the stable complex, so that she could get the water she needed while staying out of sight. She wondered if she dared to wake any of the servants who had accompanied her up from Shae. *Better not*, she decided. *There isn't time.*

She stepped into the dim stables and stopped short, her jaw dropping in amazement. The figure standing before her was carefully shrouded in a white robe with the cowl turned up to conceal his face, but the familiarity of his presence left her in no doubt of his identity. Relief flooded her. "*Phoebus!*"

Phoebus, archpriest of the Phoenix, appeared to be a man of middle years although Dia knew that he had been in service to the Grand Dukes of Shae for some six or seven generations. The archpriests did not possess the Phoenix Gift, but among the Talents of those who rose to the purple in the service of the Phoenix was the Secret of holding Time at bay. Phoebus was only as tall as Dia but the white and purple robes of his station gave his lean body the appearance of great height. Overall, he gave one an impression of quiet, of stillness and of repose.

The priest unhurriedly lifted a hand to push back the hood of his robe. He gave her a keen glance and then, to complete her astonishment, he dropped lightly to one knee before her. "My lady," he said, bowing his head.

She had never seen Phoebus bow to anyone and she was profoundly embarrassed to be greeted with such reverence. "Please, good Phoebus, do get up!" she implored him. "I do not deserve such homage, I assure you."

Rising easily to his feet, Phoebus smiled his faint smile but did not reply. Instead, he said, "Do you feel well, my lady?"

"Yes, yes, of course I am well," she said hurriedly, staring at him. "How do you come to be here?"

"The Phoenix comes, my lady," he told her, and his smile widened. "I have some small part to play in the dawning of the New Age."

"As do I?"

At that, Phoebus actually chuckled. "Just so, my lady. But come, we must leave this place before you are discovered here."

"Oh!" She glanced back toward the castle and hesitated. "But what of Lord Caelon? He was to accompany me and . . . "

The priests shook his head. "Lord Caelon does not travel with us at this time," he said with finality, "but will travel in another fashion to meet us at another time." She looked at him doubtfully, unable to make sense of his words and, for some peculiar reason, reluctant to leave his lordship at the palace without her. Phoebus, seeing her reluctance, said again, "Come, my lady. We must not tarry here. Will you not trust me?"

Of course, she knew that she could trust Phoebus as she had once trusted Daerus. Indeed, she thought with wry amusement, she had been pursuing ends and means that she did not understand ever since she had arrived at the palace. Why should she cavil now? The sudden twinkle in her mentor's eye told her that he had heard her impious thought, and she grinned. Still, and in spite of her momentary levity, the sense of danger had not lessened, and Dia was assailed once more by its urgency. She turned away from her old friend and began to saddle her horse.

Colonel Lord Caelon of Aerandos stalked down the corridor, on his way to his mother's rooms. That he was angry would have been obvious to anyone observing the absent scowl he wore as he walked. He had encountered none of the Emperor's guests, for which he was thankful. He was in no mood to endure the sly winks and twitters with which he was likely to be greeted by his peers, who, he privately snarled to himself, had minds like cesspools.

If the truth were known, Caelon was angry with himself. He did not like being manipulated, and his loss of control infuriated him. Not that my lady had complained; she had seemed positively eager for his embrace. That did not excuse him, however. No doubt her ladyship would, if taxed with her unmaidenly behavior, spout some nonsense of prophesy and surrender and such. Well, if that was what she needed to believe in order to live with herself, so be it. Caelon preferred to assume that he was responsible for his behavior, even when his behavior left a great deal to be desired. He also chose to disregard the voice that had commanded him and overcome his will to resist. No doubt that irresistible command had been nothing more than the demands of his own lust.

In fact, Dia's obvious trust in him made his capitulation to his appetites that much more dastardly. His feelings for her were both new to him and more complex than he could easily evaluate. In a more orderly universe, he would have taken the time to decide what those feelings really were and then, if it had seemed appropriate, he would have very properly offered to make her his lady. Even if he had decided that he did not care for her, he would still have been inclined to treat her with respect. She was, after all, a daughter of Shae.

Caelon had not been suffering from any of this doubt or dismay when he had awakened to find her sleeping beside him. He had lay there for a few moments, simply watching her and remembering. She had spoiled him for anyone else, he had thought ruefully. Coupling alone was pleasant enough, but when combined with the mind-touch he had shared with Dia, the act transcended love and lust and every other emotion for which he had a name. His body remembered, as well, and had awakened, clamoring for more. He wanted to reach for her, to rouse her to repeat that incredible act of union. But he did not. Instead, he contented himself with gently pushing aside a stray tendril of her soft, dark hair with infinite care. Then he rose, dressed and quietly made his way back to his own quarters. He would be escorting her back to her home; he had plenty of time.

Once he had refreshed himself with a wash and fresh clothing, he decided, he would make his way to his mother's sitting room to take his leave of his parents. He was certain they would already be awake; even in the timeless time since the days had become years, his father kept military hours and could be counted upon to be up and about when all others were still abed.

While he had busied himself with the first part of this program, he considered the tidings that he had been taking to her rooms when he had been waylaid by Lord Daerus and his ambushers. He considered her likely reaction to the news that she had gained a reprieve in the matter of the Emperor's insistence that she be immediately wed to Prince Maermat. Not that His Imperial Majesty had made any promise not to pursue the matter; in fact, Emperor Kaerkas had never spoken of it.

Caelon and his father had reported to the imperial conference room for their usual meeting with the General Staff after midmeal. They had both had a notion that the Emperor would want to try to pressure Caelon into releasing Lady Dia from their fictitious betrothal. Instead, Emperor Kaerkas greeted them in a businesslike fashion, expressed the hope that they had enjoyed a hearty midmeal repast and, then, launched his firestorm.

"Gentlemen," said His Majesty when the generals were all gathered as usual, "I have been giving some thought to the matter of the spiritual doings of the Empire."

Everyone stared. No one spoke.

"I will declare this evening before endmeal the institution of a new religion to replace what was lost when the sorcerer Phoenix was killed," Emperor Kaerkas continued, remaking history, as rulers are sometimes apt to do. Each of the generals, including Lord Saeros, was pinned briefly by a beetling imperial stare. "I fully expect considerable resistance to the idea of a new religion for Ormaeranda, particularly from the uncouth peasants in the hinterlands, and I shall require the assistance of all the armies of Ormaeranda to quell any unrest and to compel the observances of respect and worship of our new God."

Another member of the General Staff, a General Lord Baenar of the Duchy of Gedbaen, asked rather diffidently, "If you will forgive me, your Imperial Majesty, exactly Who is our new God?"

Emperor Kaerkas stared frowningly for a moment before he replied, "Why, Ormaeranda will be dedicated to the glorification of Lord Septha, of course!" He paused, seeming to wait for protests. The silence was deafening. His Majesty continued. "Saeros, you are to pull the armies of Aerandos away from the northern border and position them about the northern quadrant of the empire. You will be responsible for the area north of the Aerie Wood. General Kraetus, I want you to place the Third, Fourth and Seventh Infantry units in the foothills of the Tamaer Mountains and I want extra men ... "

His Imperial Majesty was abruptly interrupted. Without ceremony, the door opened and in walked a young woman. She wore a deeply cowled, white woolen robe with a bleached rope belt. Her feet and head were bare and she carried no weapon and no purse. Her manner was deferential but determined. She seemed neither afraid nor cowed, and she walked in unannounced.

When she reached the conference table, she bowed deeply but she was very obviously angry. And then she spoke. "For five wakings have I awaited word from thee, Emperor of Ormaeranda. My sisters can wait no longer. Wilt thou hear me?"

"Hear you!!???" the Emperor all but screamed. "How dare you simply walk into this meeting, uninvited and unannounced! Did I not advise you ... "

"Indeed, Emperor of Ormaeranda, thou didst instruct me upon my arrival some five endmeals ago that thou wouldst hear my urgent message as soon as thou didst have some leisure," she agreed readily, her eyes as hard as steel. "If it was thine intent to ignore we who have commended ourselves to thy care, it would have been as well if thou hadst the temerity to own it when first I did arrive."

Dear, me, thought Caelon, thoroughly enjoying the scene and wondering what was afoot.

"Since it is plain that thou wouldst prefer to ignore thine obligations, I but thought to present our plight directly to thy generals. Mayhap, as military men, they will comprehend the urgency of the matter as clearly thou dost not." The Emperor was yanking the bell pull, obviously intending to summon servants or guardsmen to expel this determined woman. She ignored him, turning her attention to the men sitting around the table. "Gentlemen, the matter is simple. The Throk, evidently despairing in their hopes that the Long Interval had dulled the wits of the armies of Aerandos, have left their usual points of attack and have, instead, come east and south, and now threaten the eastern border of Lemantia."

Both Caelon and his father sat straighter in their seats upon hearing this news. Lemantia was a tiny nation, a matriarchal theocracy without a standing army. Infinitely vulnerable, Lemantia had always looked to its powerful neighbor for protection. In practice, however, Lemantia had actually been protected and defended by Aerandos, and the heirs to Aerandos had always been instructed, from early in their military careers, in their obligation to the preservation of Lemantia.

The messenger, observing the alert attention of the gentlemen from Aerandos, had nodded in satisfaction. She then said, "No doubt, General Lord Aerandos, thou dost well perceive the implications of this new threat to Lemantia."

"It is of no moment, ma'am, what you imagine Aerandos to perceive!" the Emperor said, regaining control of the conversation. "I have other uses for the forces of Aerandos at this time; they are not free to come to your aid and, indeed, I do not see that the matter is of any consequence."

"Art thou then ready to proclaim to The Chosen, and to the world as well, that thou art without honor, Kaerkas of Ormaeranda?" she asked him.

"Honor be ashes!" exclaimed the Emperor. "The armies of

Ormaeranda are available only in the service of my God; they will aid you only if you forsake your Goddess and bow down to worship Him."

The woman stared at him for a moment. Then her face blanched. "Forsake Divine Istha to worship Septha the Destroyer?" she whispered, appalled.

"That is my price," said Emperor Kaerkas.

She said nothing. She cast a brief, worried glance at Lord Saeros. Caelon could not know what she saw in the thoughtful face his father wore as he observed this scene, but it seemed to reassure her. And then, for the first time since she had entered the room, she had looked at him and her eyes widened briefly. Only for a fleeting moment did their eyes meet but that was long enough for Caelon to realize that he had somehow been ... there was no other word for it ... he had been recognized. *Now, what's afoot?* he wondered.

Her gaze swept the rest of the men sitting at the table. Then she turned and swept from the room.

But, as he watched her retreating back moving toward the door, for the second time in his life, he heard a woman's voice in his mind. *Have a care, Caelon of Aerandos.*

And then, she was gone.

Caelon wondered now whether he would not be better employed riding north to direct their forces in the relief of Lemantia. He did not for one instant imagine that Lord Saeros would simply leave the tiny nation to its own devices, regardless of what plans his Imperial Majesty might have made for their army. He would see my lady on her way first. She had a sizable retinue; she would be safe once she was away from here. Still, Caelon decided, he would see what plans Lord Saeros might have made for his heir.

His ablutions completed, Caelon's thoughts turned back to the Crown Prince and his iniquitous attack on Lady Dia. He was puzzled by it; what would the rape of the lady have accomplished? It seemed that their object cannot even have been marriage, for a lady so abused had often been known to take her own life rather than be forced to take her ravisher to husband. Lord Daerus and Prince Maermat seemed willing to take that chance. Did they perhaps believe that Lady Dia would not do such a thing as to take her own life? Or did they care? What could their object be, that it could be accomplished simply by bedding her?

He had been flinging a few items into a saddlebag but, as his thoughts progressed, his hand slowed. Indeed, he realized, what *could* their object be other than to get her with child? Once again, he grew outraged at the thought that Prince Maermat and Lord Daerus would be willing to use my lady so callously. She was not a chambermaid or a whore, or even a brood sow. She was a daughter of Shae. She deserved to be treated better.

And at that moment, Caelon, himself born to one of the Great Houses of the Empire, realized the enormity of his weakness. Lady Dia was *not* a chambermaid or a whore. She was a daughter of Shae, and she had a right to be treated with respect by both the Crown Prince of Ormaer and the Lord Caelon of Aerandos. He should have resisted base impulse and left her untouched -- no matter that their joining had felt as if it were so *right* as to have been fated since the beginning of time, a niggling little voice in the back of his mind reminded him.

Caelon continued to wrestle with his conscience, torn between his lack of real remorse for his behavior -- how could he be sorry he had laid with her when it had been such an extraordinary interlude of multi-layered intimacy? -- and his awareness of the constraints of his and Dia's heritage. So involved was he in this self-castigation that he did not see the young man standing partly concealed in the shadows of the corridor until he had nearly walked into him. A sneer curved Caelon's lips. "You are abroad early, Lord Daerus," he said in greeting. This young man was surely the last person he wanted to see at this moment!

"I have something I must attend to," Lord Daerus replied hoarsely. Caelon looked at him sharply. Dia's twin brother was looking terrible; his eyes were puffy and bloodshot and haunted. He looked as if he had been through a terrifying experience and Caelon, recalling his brief encounter with the imprisoned reality of Daerus of Shae instead of recalling his most recent encounter with the fellow, felt himself relax slightly with remembered sympathy.

And that slight relaxing proved to be Caelon's undoing. When Lord Daerus moved suddenly, Caelon thought only that his lordship would pass on his way to complete his errand, and so he courteously stepped aside with a polite nod.

Instead of going on his way, however, Lord Daerus thrust the small, light sword he had been holding in the shadows straight into Caelon's chest, puncturing heart and lung. Pain seared Caelon's suddenly shallow breathing; he stared in shock at the man who had just killed him. Lord Daerus' face twisted with some intense emotion -- perhaps it was grief or remorse, perhaps it was grotesque triumph, Caelon did not have the time to decide. His knees buckled and he began to fall. As the blackness slowly crept across his sight, his last thought was of Dia, of the fact that he would never again clasp her hand, and of the fact that he had failed her.

CHAPTER TWELVE

Dia had just finished tightening the cinch on her saddle when she felt Caelon die. His mental touch weakened with alarming rapidity and then, abruptly, it was gone, leaving her feeling empty, incomplete and far more alone than she had when she had closed off her mind to her twin. For an instant, everything within her stopped -- her blood, her breath, her heart, her mind. She had had no notion of the power of the bond they had formed with a handshake and infinitely strengthened with their recent, shared passion. Now, she understood, and it seemed to her that she knew how it must feel to have a limb amputated. For the rest of her life, she would remember that moment of indescribable loss.

Uncomprehendingly, she stared at Phoebus. What had he said? "Lord Caelon does not travel with us at this time, but will travel in another fashion to meet us at another time." And suddenly, she was certain that Phoebus *knew*, had known all along, that poor Caelon was doomed. "Why?" she grated out around the lump in her throat. "Why could you not have told me? We could have gotten him out in time."

"Lord Caelon fulfills his destiny," Phoebus told her imperturbably, "as does your brother, as do you."

"My brother? What has he to say to this?" The priest held her gaze but did not reply. As unmistakably as if he had spoken the words, Dia had her answer. She drew a ragged, shuddering breath. "Do you say that *Daerus* has murdered him?"

Phoebus still did not reply, wordlessly handing her up into the saddle.

"Why did you lie to me, Phoebus?" Dia managed to say. Gods, the pain was terrible! "Could you not have prepared me for this?"

Her old tutor gazed at her sympathetically. "I doubt that anything could have prepared you for this, my lady. Come," and he took the reigns and guided her stallion out of the stables.

Dia rode slumped in the saddle, torn between grief and fury, neither knowing nor caring where the priest led her. Her tears streamed unheeded down her cheeks but her thoughts burned like acid. *As soon as I have surrendered to the light and welcomed Caelon into my bed, he was fated to be slain? Why? What is the point? Was it my destiny then to come to this wretched place and, by enlisting his aid, cause the death of my lover at the hands of my twin? Of what earthly use is any of this in the dawning of a New Age?*

"By the by," Phoebus interrupted her roiling thoughts, "I did not lie to you, my lady."

Incredulously, Dia stared at the back of his head. She could not have forced any words past her raw throat, but let her thought challenge such an absurd claim. *He will not be there waiting for us, Phoebus,* she said accusingly. *He is dead.*

That is not quite what I said, my lady. And does not the Phoenix wield his power over death? Phoebus reminded her.

Caelon *is to be reborn as the Phoenix?* Dia asked incredulously. Her feelings about that possibility were jumbled and she had no wish to pause to analyze them just then. *How exquisitely funny! He does not even believe -- and I am coming to have some sympathy with him.*

The archpriest was silent for a moment and Dia, who had made no effort to keep the bitterness out of her voice, felt a little ashamed of herself. *All will become clear in time, my lady,* he said at last. *One wonders what has become of the faith you once professed to have?*

I have borne a great deal since I went from home, Phoebus, she told him wearily.

So. Then, all that you have believed since childhood is set aside for bitterness and doubt at the first true test?

Another wave of pain rose to engulf her. Caelon and Daerus had been reduced to "tests"? *Have I not reason to be bitter, after all that I have lost?*

Perhaps, child, but if your faith is so easily vanquished, you had as well hand this world into the keeping of Dark Septha without further delay.

I have passed your tests, Phoebus! Why must you reproach me still?

On the contrary, my lady, if they cause you to turn your heart from Revered Phoenix, then you have **not** *passed them,* Phoebus chided her gently. *And, in that case, the death of Lord Caelon and your brother's blackened soul are indeed without meaning.*

Dia was silenced and the tears had their way with her again. She closed her eyes and let them flow unheeded. She had managed not to interfere with the fulfillment of destiny, but she could not have pretended to be glad that it was so. *If the triumph of the Phoenix must rest upon my ability to endure these sacrifices willingly and cheerfully,* she thought, *then I have surely failed and Chaos will abound.* In that instant, she could not make herself care. Daerus had been right about one thing, at least; their lives in the neighborhood of Shae had in no wise prepared them for the Emperor's court. Disillusionment was always painful, she bitterly supposed.

Shortly after they had set out, she heard her brother calling faintly but she did not answer. Nothing that he said to her could undo what he had done. Nothing that he said could matter. Nothing mattered.

As well that you do not answer, was Phoebus' approving comment, *and never mind the reason. Daerus seeks you out at the bidding of his Master. If He finds you, He will immediately have you killed.*

That did not really matter, either. She did not have the will to defend her life and she did not have the energy to wonder why

Lord Septha should suddenly wish for her death. Let Phoebus concern himself with such irrelevancies; Dia wanted nothing other than to be left alone.

After an unknown period of time, Phoebus stopped her mount and now busied himself with some chore or other. She felt too depleted and bereft to care, and offered no resistance when, moments later, he helped her down from her horse. "We will go no further today, my lady," Phoebus said solicitously. "You are tired and must rest."

She drank the warm, sweet concoction from the cup he handed her without comment. She *was* tired, she conceded privately. Indeed, she thought, she had never been so exhausted in her life. Certainly, she was much too tired to think clearly. Without protest, she lay down with her head on the saddlebags her escort had provided as a pillow. As Phoebus gently covered her with a blanket, she realized groggily that her exhaustion had seemed to come on her awfully suddenly, after all, and she wondered what the wily priest had put in that drink.

Phoebus' sly chuckle sounded very far away in her head. Vaguely comforted, she slept.

When she woke, she felt much rested but her heart was heavy indeed. She ate what Phoebus gave her and recommenced their journey without comment. She had nothing to say. Her anger had dissipated, but pain still gripped her, and apathy had laid its cold hand on her spirits. She stared dully at nothing, her eyes fixed on a point between her horse's ears and her mind as blank as she could keep it.

She could not have said how long she rode in that abyss of dispair, eating what Phoebus provided for her, sleeping in dreamless exhaustion at his bidding and travelling on with him when she woke. She let Phoebus lead her where he would, plodding along with the reins in his hands. The TimeKeepers did not ride. Phoebus had told her once, long ago, that to artificially shorten distance was an act of disrespect to the amount of real time needed to cover that distance. When the TimeKeepers were in a hurry, they used time windows, which allowed them to go to any single instant in time as that instant occurred wherever they needed to go. The more skilled among them -- and, certainly, the archpriests -- could even travel back and forth in time, within the confines of their particular Age. Of course, time windows were one of the many Secrets of the TimeKeepers that had begun to fail after the death of the last Phoenix.

And, still, Phoebus elected to walk. Dia wonder what the point of that gesture could be. It seemed wholly futile to her.

It was the weather -- or lack of weather -- that finally reached her in that bleak place in which her mind dwelt. Suddenly, for no apparent reason, it occurred to her that she had been out of doors all this time with a bare head, and had not suffered so much as a peeling nose. In fact, she realized in some astonishment, she did not even feel heat. Dia's eyes suddenly came back into sharp focus and she looked around.

The world was grey. That was the first thing she noticed. Not precisely colorless but dim, as if they sky was overcast. Everything around them was perfectly still and quiet. Not even the air was moving; at a season of the year when the hot, dusty winds out of the north should have been growing ever more forceful, there was not even the hint of a breeze. Dia somehow got the distinct notion that she, Phoebus and her stallion were the only things in the entire world that were moving. Something was wrong.

The next thing she noticed was that she did not recognize anything around her. How long had she been woolgathering? "We should be home soon, should we not, good Phoebus?" she asked, her voice sounding dusty with disuse.

"We do not return to Shae, my lady," Phoebus said, as calm as always.

A frown slowly gathered on Dia's brow. "Indeed?" She looked around again, taking careful note of her surroundings. They were in the foothills of some mountains, and behind them were the sere plains they had just crossed. The trail they followed wound up into the hills, surrounded on either side by tough, scrubby thorn bushes that were already starting to look parched, and a few tall, majestic oaks with their roots so deeply buried in the soil that they had survived two years of peculiar weather with vigor. Trying to recall the geography of the region around the capital, she said, "Wither away, Phoebus?"

"I am taking you to the Temple of the Fires, my lady," he replied. "You will be safe there."

"You may as well tell me the rest of it, Phoebus," Dia said, her voice studiously reasonable. "How does it come about that I have been traveling all this time with no protection from High Sun and have not fainted or died of it?"

"It seems that we are outside time, my lady."

Shock held Dia speechless for several moments. "Outside time?" she repeated faintly.

"Why, yes, my lady," the priest assured her, so sedate that he sounded smug to her. "I believe we stepped into this particular unmoving instant shortly after we left the city."

Dia digested that piece of information in silence. Finally, she said, "You have unsuspected talents, good Phoebus. I had thought your Secrets were of no use to you without the Phoenix to lend them potency."

"I am touched by your confidence in me, my lady," said Phoebus, "but I did not do this."

"Come, Phoebus," said Dia impatiently, "do not be modest. It certainly was not I; it must have been you!"

Phoebus merely shook his head. She could not see his face but she was almost sure he was smiling his sly smile. There was no need for Phoebus to be coy. Indeed, she found it quite annoying. Dia sighed in some irritation, but decided not to persue the matter.

Instead, she returned to his earlier words. "How long must I remain in hiding at the Temple?"

"We are outside of time, Lady Dia," Phoebus said, and Dia very definitely heard a note of amusement in his voice, "so it does not matter how long we stay here. I did not cast this spell and, to be completely frank with you, I would not have the least notion of how to reverse it."

"So, we are to remain in this limbo until whoever put us here decides to let us go back?"

"So it would seem."

"You do not seem particularly worried about it."

"I am not worried about it."

She closed her eyes and sighed with determined patience. "I suppose I should envy such placid acceptance," she said. "I find I do not care to be in this place in which I did not enter willingly and have no way of leaving. Particularly when I do not know who brought me here and why."

"I expect you will discover why soon enough. As for who ... do you bend your mind to the problem," he advised her. "It will give you something to occupy your thoughts during the journey."

Dia cast a smoldering glance at the back of the priest's head and colored her thoughts with vividly gruesome images of the many possible ways to torture an archpriest of the Phoenix.

Phoebus chuckled. "Really, my lady, how macabre!"

"Come, good Phoebus, can you not tell me what task I have been brought here to perform?" she demanded.

Phoebus stopped and turned to face her. His glance on her face was penetrating. "Do you not listen to your body, my lady?" he asked, sounding genuinely curious. "Can you not hear what it is telling you?"

Great Phoenix, grant me patience, she thought irritably. *Is the fellow incapable of answering a simple question in a direct fashion?* "My body has been telling me nothing except that I am excessively tired, good Phoebus," she said.

"You have also grown quite clumsy, you know," Phoebus pointed out. "I very much doubt if you could manage to hit the side of a tree at ten paces with those much-vaunted daggers of yours. As well, you are become uncommonly irritable, my dear Lady Dia." As he spoke, he had walked back to stand by her side, still gazing up into her face, and Dia idly wondered why he should be looking so joyous. "And your thoughts tend to wander," he added, smiling faintly.

"You are taking a very long time to get to the point, my dear Phoebus," she told him severely.

"Very well, my lady," he said with a chuckle. "We journey to the Temple to care for your health."

"But . . . "

"We will remain there until you give birth to the child you now carry."

Dia stared. "*Ch-child?*" A dozen different feelings swept through her heart in that instant. Instinctively, she placed a protective had low on her belly.

"Indeed, my lady," confirmed the imperturbable Phoebus. "And now, what would your ladyship like for endmeal?"

CHAPTER THIRTEEN

Their journey consumed what seemed, as best as Dia could tell, to be two months and they were, without question, the two longest, most uncomfortable months she could remember. She spent most of her waking hours in the saddle and their pace was a sedate walk, which conserved the stamina of her mount but also slowed their pace to what seemed a crawl. When she was not riding, she found herself sitting or attempting to sleep on the stony ground and Dia was certain that her unfortunate body memorized each rock, pebble and clump of dirt on which it rested. It seemed she was always tired now and wanted nothing more than to stop, find a pillowed surface and sleep for about a year.

She could not know if it was due to the peculiar time in which they travelled, but her pregnancy seemed to be speeding along much more rapidly than normal. Within a few days, her belly began to swell, and it continued to grow so quickly that, for a few days, Dia grew almost afraid of it all -- and, particularly, of her baby. Phoebus had to speak with her sternly about that.

She grew ungainly and awkward and, as she did, her temper grew more and more uncertain. At one moment, she was filled with tender joy at the thought of the child she and Caelon had created and which now rested under her heart. The next moment, she was frightened of the awesome responsibility of mothering a child without his father's support. She felt she was somehow being used by the faceless, heartless, unseen thing called "destiny," and was filled with an impotent rage at the injustice of her lack of viable options. And, of course, her grief at Caelon's death was too new and raw to have run its course; she sometimes sat her mount and quietly cried her sorrow for that loss.

Phoebus accepted her rapid changes of mood as calmly as he accepted everything else, simply making sure she ate well and rested often. Dia complained about that, too; they would never reach their destination if he insisted on coddling her in this absurd manner. His reply was invariably the same, that they had as much time as they needed and speed was far less important than her well-being. His serenely meticulous care should have been a comfort, but Dia found it another source of irritation.

The notion of bearing a child seemed so unreal to Dia that she was startled when the baby began to move. Tentatively, she placed a shy hand on her belly; the baby promptly kicked her palm. It suddenly occurred to her that there was a living creature inside her body, and that she was really going to have to go through with this. Her lack of experience filled her with sudden alarm. She had no young matrons among her acquaintance, had never even attended a birthing, and so had no idea of what to expect. Knowing that Phoebus would have little comfort to offer, she brooded about that privately, wishing with all her heart that someone else could have been chosen for whatever further tasks awaited her.

"When we have arrived," Phoebus suddenly told her, "I shall place you in the care of the priestess Phoenedra. She will attend you during the birth of the child."

"And what does a priestess of the Phoenix know of childbirth?" Dia asked.

"She has studied midwifery, my lady. She, too, has been carefully prepared for what the New Age requires of her."

"How very interesting," Dia replied ironically. "*I* know

nothing of the requirements of the new age; indeed, I do not even know what this child has to do with the New Age. It seems that everyone involved in this particular event has been carefully prepared, except the mother-to-be."

"Really, my lady, what further preparation do you require?" the priest asked reasonably. "Were you wed and expecting your first child, you would have no more schooling than you have had already. You have nothing more to do than what will come to you naturally."

"Were I wed and expecting my first child, no doubt my mother would have had much in the way of advice, and the benefit of her own experience, to offer," Dia retorted. "And I should not have had to spend the whole of my pregnancy in this curst saddle!"

Phoebus chuckled. "Patience, my lady. We should arrive at the Temple tomorrow. Perhaps it is unduly sanguine of me, but I fancy your confinement should begin shortly after that."

That prediction effectively silenced her. *Tomorrow?* Suddenly, her saddle began to look much more attractive as she contemplated what lay ahead. Dia fervently hoped that this Phoenedra knew what she was about.

They were well up into the mountains of southeast Ormaeranda now, in the Grand Duchy of Tamaer, and the steep trail made the going slow indeed. Were it not for the dreadful concerns weighing upon her, Dia might have enjoyed this leg of the journey, for they rode along a path that traced the meandering of a dried out streambed through a pleasant forest of pine. As it was, when she was not involved in any of her other emotional upheavals, she spent much of the time before their arrival at the Temple speculating on what had happened to her since she had arrived at the Emperor's palace and what any of it might have to do with the emergence of a new Phoenix.

Casting her mind back over her studies, she realized that the past would be of no use to her in predicting the nature of the battle in the imminent Gaerud. Indeed, she could not even say for certain who the instruments of the conflict would be. Would she be one of them? Would her child? Was that why Phoebus was taking such good care of her, so that she could raise the child who would be the champion of the New Age? Phoebus had certainly ensured that she and her brother were well-taught in the nature of the Phoenix and his TimeKeepers. Dia thought that she would be very well suited to such a task.

But no, she realized, that could not be it. The passage from the First Prophesies was very clear about one thing; she and her brother would herald in the New Age through the choices they would make. He had chosen the darkness, as was foretold. Had she surrendered to the light? She had thought, as she lay in Caelon's arms, that that was precisely what she had done. And yet, that tender interlude had resulted in nothing except his murder and her pregnancy. There must be more, even if she could not fathom what it might be just then; she had a very strong feeling that her task would not end with the birth of Caelon's son.

Now, how do I know that this child is male? she thought, a bit surprised at the strength of her certainty. Since the child would never know his father, she rather hoped that she was wrong even as that deep inner core of her being with which she had recently become so well acquainted assured her that she was not. The boy would need a father. Dia sighed.

She had not wanted to think about Caelon just then but, as soon as his name entered her thoughts, she was suddenly seized by a curious compulsion to return to the scene of his murder. *Oh,* she told herself, *that is quite insane!* And yet, with every second that passed, her conviction grew. "Phoebus," she said tentatively.

"Yes, my lady?"

"I have just had the most curious notion ... "

"Oh?"

Dia hesitated. *He will think I have quite lost my mind, and I will no doubt agree completely.* Finally, in a rush, she said, "I want to go back."

As usual, Phoebus received this proposal calmly. He came back to stand at her knee, gazing up at her inquiringly. "Go back? To where would you return, my lady?" he asked. In fact, Dia noted with some curiosity, he did not even seem particularly surprised.

"To the Emperor's palace," she said slowly, "at the moment of Caelon's death."

"May I ask why?"

"We have to bring him with us," she said with finality, hoping he would ask her no more questions, for she would not have answers.

"I see," said the priest. He stared at Coer's hocks for a few moments, deep in thought. Then he raised speculative eyes to meet her gaze. "That will require a time window, my lady," he told her.

Dia frowned. Yes, of course Phoebus was quite right. It *would* require a time window, and the TimeKeepers lost their ability to control their time windows during the Interval, making them dangerous and unreliable. "Do you think you will be able to open a time window when Ageless Phoenix still has not returned?" she asked doubtfully.

"I do not think I would be able to do so," he said slowly.

She nodded. "No, of course not," she sighed. "We shall have to leave him then." She would not confide in the archpriest just how much the notion disturbed her.

"No, my lady," Phoebus disagreed.

"No?"

"I have often reminded you to trust your instincts, Lady Dia," he reminded her gently. "You are quite right, we will need to return for Lord Caelon and without delay."

"But how ... ?"

"I suspect that, while *I* cannot open a time window, it is very likely that *you* can," was his surprising answer.

"Me?"

"Do you make the attempt, my lady, and we will see what transpires," Phoebus counselled her. "If it is meant for you to do this, then I think you will find yourself able to accomplish it without assistance."

She looked down at her gravid belly. "I may have some trouble dragging a corpse through a time window, good Phoebus."

He nodded. "Never fear, my lady, I shall accompany you."

Phoebus helped her down from the saddle and tied the reins to a low-hanging branch. "Do you remember your lessons, Lady Dia?" he asked her.

She did, and with a clarity that should have surprised her but somehow did not. Vividly, she recalled even that she had not believed Phoebus when, as a child of some twelve summers, he had informed her that she was possessed of the Talent that could reach into time, across space. She had listened to his patient instruction even as she had been privately convinced that she could do no such thing.

Now, still doubtful, she focused her thoughts on the moment to which she would return. That part of the process was not at all difficult for her, for she remembered vividly that awful emptiness when she had felt Caelon die. "Very well," she told her mentor, "I have the moment firmly in mind."

"Splendid. Now that you have the time, you must find the place," he instructed.

Dia nodded. Diving further into her perception of that moment was sheer torture, like walking into fire, but she searched her sense of his death and constructed a picture of his bloody body sprawled on the floor in one of the corridors of Kaerkas' palace. She had no notion of which corridor it might be, but that did not matter. The bond she had formed with him would serve her well; she would open the time window to take her to his body, wherever it might be.

"Now, my lady, find the emptiness between where you stand now and the time and place you wish to travel to, and expand that emptiness until you can step through it." Phoebus' voice sounded curiously distant, so intent was she on the picture she had constructed in her mind.

Find the emptiness? That, too, should be a simple matter. The emptiness she felt between the time Caelon's touch had lived in her mind and the time it had died was gigantic, and the time window she managed to open was large enough to have accommodated her stallion -- with her on his back. She opened her eyes and stared at the yawning blackness before her with something like awe.

"I did it," she breathed.

"Indeed," Phoebus agreed, "very well done, my lady."

The sense of danger swept back to her through the open time window like a warm, humid wind, and Dia responded to it once more. She entered the time window with Phoebus at her heels, stepping back into moving time and finding, when she emerged in the Emperor's palace, that the child she carried was once more a tiny seed, deep in her body. *Well, that is certainly much more comfortable,* she thought absently.

Then her eyes fell on Caelon's body, taking in the deep wound in his chest that had spilled out his life, and she drew a deep, shuddering breath. Phoebus stepped out from behind her and stooped to grasp his shoulders. *We must hurry, my lady,* he urged her.

Dia hardly heard him. Again, she felt that searing pain, made all the more terrible by this confrontation with the sight of the crumpled, bloody body that had, in life, roused her to that unforgettable height of passion. Her eyes and throat burned anew with grief and anger.

"Dia!"

She raised her eyes then, and found herself face-to-face with her twin. Hatred flared in her heart, and that must have shown on her face, because he winced away from her briefly. "Do not look at me so contemptuously, Dia," he said raggedly. "Had you but cooperated, this need not have come to pass."

Dia sucked in a burning breath. "You would have some difficulty convincing me that this *needed* to come to pass in any event," she told him. Then she saw his hand tighten on the sword he held, which was still dripping Caelon's blood to the stone floor. "Do not," she added in a deadly and peculiarly augmented voice.

He seeks to delay you, my lady, Phoebus told her silently.

Why?

He awaits the arrival of his cohorts.

Why?

That is unclear. They will either strike you down or prevent us from removing Lord Caelon's body from this place.

No, they will **not***!*

The rapid mental exchange did not appear to impinge upon Daerus' awareness, she saw as she continued to stare at him. Then, to his palpable dismay, she bent to Caelon's body. "Convey my apologies to your friends, Daerus," she said sardonically over her shoulder. "I fear I will be unable to remain here to greet them."

Although she did not bother to keep an eye on him, she felt him beginning to move. Before she could decide how to react, before she had even glanced back up at him, there was a flash of that mysterious, brilliant light. The small sword fell from her brother's hand as, with a hoarse cry, he stumbled back several steps.

"I do not fear your darkness, Daerus," she said, briefly lifting her eyes to meet his startled glare.

With Phoebus, she dragged the still-warm corpse back through the time window. Once she was back in her own, timeless present, she was once more heavy with child. The energy of her anger lent her strength, but the task of moving Caelon's body rapidly winded her. "Stay a moment, good Phoebus," she panted.

"You must close it, my lady," he said after a quick glance to assure himself that the corpse was clear of the time window, "else we will soon be followed."

She nodded, still gasping for breath. Then she concentrated and the gaping portal began to shrink rapidly. As it was closing, she heard running feet and her brother's voice saying, "It's still open ... ."

"Excellent," another voice that sounded to her like Prince Maermat replied. "It cannot be completed without Aerandos, even if she *has* managed ... wait! Wha--"

And then, the voices and the window were gone. "It seems we were just in time, my old friend," Dia said thoughtfully.

"Indeed," Phoebus agreed. "Now, how shall we carry him?"

The wrapped Caelon's body and, after a great deal of pushing, pulling and heaving, managed to hoist it up into her saddle. Phoebus would not let her help him much, admonishing her to have a thought for her child. Dia, who was quickly exhausted, tended to agree and, since she had tacitly elected to walk for the remainder of this trip, decided to conserve her strength.

Once they had rested briefly, they resumed their journey and Dia, who had been pondering that strange fragment of conversation she had overheard, said, "It seems that, even in death, Caelon's task is not yet done."

Phoebus did not reply.

"Is it possible that those bitter words of mine were, in fact, truth? *Is* Caelon to be the new Phoenix?" she asked.

Phoebus remained silent.

"Phoebus," Dia said, resisting the impulse to grit her teeth, "do you not know or do you refuse to reply?"

"Can you give me a reason why you need these questions answered *now*?" Phoebus asked her, his manner faintly apologetic.

"I am constrained by my vows to tell you nothing other than what you need to know to perform your tasks, you know."

"I have my answer, I suppose. You would not refuse to tell me if it were not so." Dia grinned and then sighed dramatically. "This New Age is asking much of us, old friend."

"I know, my dear Lady Dia," Phoebus said with a gentle smile, "and it demands more of you than of any other."

"I hope all this will be worth it," she murmured.

"I expect it will be," was the bland reply.

They stopped to rest in a small, rocky canyon that had been cut through the mountains by one of the many streams that fed into the Tamaer River back on the plains they had left behind. Dia felt particularly exhausted and wondered if she would ever be hale again. She deliberately avoided looking toward her horse and its grisly burden as she waddled over to one of the steep rock walls nearby and sank to the ground with a weary sigh. Phoebus busied himself with the fire and his cookpot and Dia, too tired for coherent thought, simply stared at the bend in the streambed that hid the rest of the canyon from her sight. Her companion prepared their meal and Dia simply sat and stared, wholly without consciousness, at a slowly gathering darkness that reminded her of the thunderstorms that had sometimes boiled across the Shae estate from the Sea of Akkam before the end of the Time. The darkness grew gradually, slowly clouding her sight until she could not see what she was looking at. Still, she said nothing in her trance-like fatigue. Vaguely, she noticed that she was getting chilly.

A hand touched her arm and the darkness, which had grown so slowly and imperceptibly that she was hardly aware of it, vanished. Dia blinked and turned startled eyes to Phoebus. He held a steaming cup. "Drink this, my lady," he instructed.

She accepted the cup with a muttered word of thanks, saying nothing of the odd interlude. She felt strangely disoriented. It seemed as if she stood outside herself with nothing solid upon which to place her feet. The sensation was both calming and uncomfortable.

Once she had composed herself for sleep upon the pallet Phoebus constructed for her comfort, the dreams began. Dia seemed to see herself stretched upon an altar, covered with blood.

A great, hideous beast stood over her, roaring and snarling as she labored to produce the child she carried. It had dry, scaly skin that was as black as coal and two long, curving fangs that dripped a venom which seared everything it touched. It had two massive, arched horns atop its head and, impaled upon one of these, was her old friend Phoebus. Dimly, she could see dead Caelon, his skeletal face a cruel caricature of the vitality he had had in life, feebly swinging a sword at the monster's face in a weak effort to protect her.

With a sudden, negligent move, the beast struck Caelon's pale shade away from it almost contemptuously. And then it spoke. "You cannot escape; you cannot resist the might of great Septha," it rasped in the most horrid voice Dia had ever heard, a voice that filled her with cold fear. Then, it roared in the greatest rage: "*No!* The child dies."

Dia struggled against the crushing weight that bore down upon her as Septha the Destroyer stalked her labors. She must protect her baby, she told herself frantically, but she could not save him if she could not even bear him. Cruel laughter punctuated her efforts and she whimpered her fear and helplessness. The weight was growing heavier and blackness was creeping across her face, drowning her ...

And then she became aware of a gentle hand shaking her shoulder. She clawed her way out of sleep and opened her eyes to meet Phoebus' concerned gaze. She stared at him blankly for a moment and then she began to cry.

The priest enfolded her in an embrace. "A nightmare, my lady?" he asked her gently.

She nodded, still weeping.

Phoebus said nothing more, merely holding her and stroking her hair soothingly. Yet, she felt his support and drew strength from it, to still the deep foreboding produced by the vivid nightmare. Finally, warmed by her old tutor's comforting, she fell asleep once more.

There were no more nightmares. After a long and restful, dreamless sleep, Dia woke, ate and proclaimed herself ready to continue on their journey. They followed the canyon for perhaps another half mile to a steep rock path, walking at a sedate pace that

Dia did not find too taxing for her unwieldy gait. At the top of the rise, the path continued atop the side of a deep ravine curving around the rock slope of a tall mountain. It continued to climb, but much more gently now, and Dia was hardly winded by the time they came upon a small thicket of pine saplings and scrubby thorn bushes. Perhaps, she thought hopefully, they would reach the Temple today.

She had become convinced that she had felt so compelled to return for Caelon's body because he was destined to be reborn as the next Phoenix, and she was anxious to reach their destination. She had noticed that the corpse had not stiffened and grayed in death but remained as warm and flaccid as it had been in the instant to which she had returned to retrieve him. She took that to be a good sign, for some part of her heart could not accept the notion that he was lost to her forever. Certainly, as the Phoenix, he would no longer be available to her as either friend or lover, and she would miss that, but at least he would not be dead. In some measure, such a rebirth would assuage her guilt. She had not absolved herself of responsibility and Daerus' words to that effect had flicked her on the raw. She would not have thrown in her lot with the servants of Septha in any event, but that did not alter the fact that Caelon would not now lie dead if she had not entangled him in her affairs. For Dia, this journey, with herself on foot and carrying his child, had become a pilgrimage of penance.

After they had rested and eaten -- still in silence, for neither Dia nor Phoebus had said a single word since they had set out -- they walked for another hour or so before they rounded a curve in the path and abruptly found themselves at the entrance of a rock bowl that had been scooped out of the side of the mountain, giving the natural construction the appearance of an amphitheater. Nestled in that amphitheater as if it sat in the lap of the mountain was a large, graceful building with soaring spires, much intricately carved decoration, and many colored windows. The two of them stood side by side for a few moments, simply staring.

Then Phoebus turned his head toward his companion. "Be welcome to the Temple of the Fires, my lady," he said softly, his voice filled with all the joy of the weary traveller who finally comes home.

CHAPTER FOURTEEN

Dia and her companion arrived at the Temple to be greeted by a woman who appeared to be of middle years, garbed in the purple-trimmed white of an archpriestess of the Phoenix. She stood in the precise center of the shallow steps leading to the door of the Temple and hailed them as soon as they were within hearing.

"Be welcome to the house of Ancient Phoenix," she proclaimed in ritual greeting.

"May your Time be rich in the bounty of His peace," Phoebus responded, closing the distance between them.

"And may the blessings of Order mark your days," the priestess said.

Then, in a gesture that apparently completed the ritual, they faced each other squarely and each held up a hand, palm to palm, an inch apart. Once the ritual greeting was over, the inhuman calm seemed to slide from her face as she turned to survey her other guest. "Be welcome, my lady," she said, a warm smile lighting her eyes.

"Thank you," Dia said absently. Something seemed wrong here. "Do you have any grooms here, ma'am? If not, I can see to Coer once we have removed his sad burden, if you will direct me to the stables ... "

"Indeed, my lady, and I shall do no such thing!" The priestess seemed shocked at the suggestion. "Phoebus and I will tend to Lord Caelon; you will come inside to the rooms that have been prepared for you. I have not the least doubt that a warm bath and a mattress will be most welcome."

Somehow, the thought of being treated so royally by the TimeKeepers made her feel disconcertingly blasphemous. Why were they being so deferential toward her? she wondered, mentally squirming as she recalled how Phoebus had knelt to greet her. How long ago that seemed! "Oh, no! Truly, it will be only the work of a moment ... "

"I am sorry, my lady, but I cannot permit you to risk your child with such exertion. I do assure you that my old friend and I are quite equal to the task, which," she added, eyeing Dia's protruding stomach, "if you will forgive me for saying so, you do not appear to be."

Dia could not help laughing. Phoebus, smiling his sly smile, said, "This is Phoenedra, my lady. I believe I spoke of her when we were journeying here."

"Why, so you did, good Phoebus," Dia replied with a wholly feigned look of innocent astonishment. She then looked around a little uncomfortably, still unable to quite pinpoint the vague discomfort she felt -- almost as if she were being watched. Until she saw that she was.

He appeared to be a peasant, dressed in a tunic of rough burlap and linen breeches, and he was watering a donkey at a silent, unmoving stream at the edge of the clearing. He seemed to be staring at her with the blank gaze of one who looked but did not see. Neither he nor his beast moved or uttered the slightest sound.

Of course! The Temple and its occupants stood outside time, just as she and Phoebus did. "How do you come to be here?" she asked in an awed whisper.

"We were placed here," Phoenedra said gently, "by the last Phoenix just before his final death. Have you never wondered what had become of the Temple of the Fires, such that no man or beast has been able to find it these two years? We have been here, outside time, waiting."

"Here? Why?"

"Because, my lady, this is the instant that marks the beginning of the Gaerud," the priestess explained. "There are certain things -- and people -- which must be in place at that instant. We will see to that here, in this now." She opened the Temple doors and gestured her inside. "Come, let us get you settled."

Dia automatically followed as her mind reeled. "But ... then, how do we come to be here, in this instant?"

"You were brought here, my lady."

"By whom? Phoebus?"

Phoenedra smiled her warm smile. "Ah, no, dear Lady Dia. Neither Phoebus nor I have that kind of power."

"Then ... ?"

"I could not really say, my lady," she confessed placidly. "It may be that the Phoenix, in His wisdom, placed some sort of portal in a particular place at this particular instant, knowing that circumstance would bring you to pass through it at just that moment. It may even be that the *new* Phoenix is responsible for your presence in this unmoving instant."

Dia was silent for a moment, digesting that possibility. "But, if that is so," she mused, "then He is already here."

"Well," Phoenedra temporized, "He is here -- in spirit, if not in the flesh. He is always here, you know; the spirit of the Phoenix never really leaves us, even during an Interval as lengthy as this one has been." Again, she smiled her gentle smile, adding, "I know some of what is to come, my lady, but certainly not all, and I make no claim to even begin to understand the powers wielded by the Master. I do not even know exactly when your own child shall arrive."

Dia, who had long since arrived at that point in her pregnancy at which she felt she'd never be either comfortable or energetic again, hoped she would not have too long to wait.

She was to be granted her wish. She had retired to a wonderfully soft bed, after a private endmeal served to her in her quarters by an attentive Phoenedra, feeling very much at ease and more peaceful than at any other time since she had left her home. Perhaps something of the spirit of the late Phoenix remained in the atmosphere of the Temple. As she drifted off to sleep, Dia decided that, if she was to be deprived of her mother's support during the birth of her first child, she was thankful to be so protected by the hand of the Phoenix.

She slowly swam back to consciousness some indeterminable time later, for no reason that she could immediately perceive. She lay there, sorting through her senses and trying to decide what had awakened her. Something had, she knew, yet she could find nothing to account for it. She drifted back to sleep.

She was to repeat this pattern of sleep disruption three more times before she finally realized that what was troubling her repose was pain. Pain? She sat up suddenly, remembering Phoebus' prediction and trying to quell the nervous fluttering of her stomach. *Oh, stop being so silly,* she admonished herself sternly. *Ladies have babies all the time.* She lay back down and, breathing deeply, tried to relax.

Phoenedra, she called, once she had schooled herself to some measure of calm.

Yes, my lady? the priestess answered almost immediately.

I think . . .

The time approaches?

Another spasm rippled across her belly, causing Dia to inhale sharply. *Indeed, I fancy the time may arrive precipitously.*

Very well, my lady, came the placid response and Dia, insensibly, was reassured.

It was not very long before relaxation was completely impossible for her. Just as her pregnancy itself had seemed to be peculiarly accelerated, so her confinement seemed likely to be rapid and intense. She completely lost track of time as the contortions of her womb racked her with pain. No one had ever told her that this process was so very uncomfortable!

Phoenedra had arrived promptly and lent her support but, as she pointed out to Dia at one point during the process, "Until the young gentleman is ready to make his appearance, I can do little except to offer my support."

Dia had to bite back a sarcastic response. While she

appreciated the justice of Phoenedra's remark, she was in no mood for either logic or justice, her temper decidedly frayed as her body labored to produce her child.

She soon had little leisure for even temper, however, and coherent thought was beyond her. Her contractions continued, growing stronger and stronger still, and she surrendered, perforce, to that curious phenomenon when a woman's body is no longer her own but merely an instrument of creation. Even when it seemed to her that this task was more than her body could perform, she continued to obey the demands of the process, pushing with as much strength as she could muster when it seemed she must, resting whenever she could. Finally, just as Dia decided that she *could* not do this and that her body would simply have to burst in order to free itself of this child, a warm weight seemed to flow away from her and the pressures and pains abruptly eased. A few minor twinges remained, just enough to assure her that she was not wholly numb, but the relief was tremendous. Tiredly, she sighed.

Phoenedra spent a few moments cleaning her up and helping her get comfortable before she brought her child to receive her greetings. Dia gently gathered the baby in her arms, thinking of Caelon and how proud he would be. The infant stared solemnly at her, his face puffy from his arduous journey, and Dia returned his regard gravely. "Welcome, little one," she whispered to him.

Moving slowly, she offered her newborn a breast and he latched on readily, a look of peaceful contentment coming over his small face and a tiny fist wrapped around one of her fingers. Before long, as Dia watched him with a sort of tender fascination, he fell asleep. She might have stayed just as she was indefinitely -- just at that moment, she felt she could have spent years patiently watching him and wondering at what she and Caelon had wrought -- but Phoenedra suggested that she put the baby down and get some sleep.

Once she had put the baby in the cradle Phoenedra had provided, Dia realized how exhausted she was. She crawled into her bed and, within minutes, fell asleep.

Lord Septha was back. Dia knew that because she could hear him roaring and snarling. He seemed to be looking for something and Dia, cradling her infant son in her arms, trembled with fear as she hid. She wished she could see; it was so very dark that she did not even know where she was. How was she to escape and carry her son to safety? The need to escape gnawed at her urgently, until she felt she could wait no longer. She leaped to her feet and began to run. The blackness was everywhere. Before her, a plain of darkness spread from horizon to horizon under a black sky. Behind her, dread Septha gave chase, bellowing in triumph.

Dia whimpered in terror. Cheerfully, she would sacrifice her own life to protect her child. Yet, she could not let herself be killed; who would care for him if aught happened to her? Desperately, she pelted through the emptiness, hoping to find safety somewhere in terrain she could not see.

Suddenly, she realized that her cradling arms were empty and she stopped and looked around wildly. She wanted to call out to the baby but she could not -- she realized that she had not yet given him a name. How very stupid! Everything was so dark; how was she to find him?

She saw her son and the monstrous Septha in the same instant. The awful beast reared over the horizon, moving with unbelievable speed, and her baby was running toward it as fast as his little legs could carry him. She started to run after him; he was only a baby, she should overtake him in a few seconds. But she found she could not catch him, no matter how fast she ran.

Wait! *she called out to him in anguish.* **Please, wait!**

I cannot wait, *came the piping voice of a very small child.* **I am sorry, Mother.**

Still running, she watched in horror as the valiant infant cast himself right into the face of the beast. Dia stretched out an arm in a sort of protective reflex but there was nothing she could do.

And then he was gone.

Dia's face was wet with tears when she struggled out of a fitful sleep with shudders wracking her body. The very first thing her eyes fell upon was the cradle beside her bed and she stared at it for several heartbeats before she realized that it was empty. With the awful dream vivid in her memory, and with panic in her soul, she looked around the room frantically.

Nothing had changed since she fell asleep except that ominously empty cradle and Dia leaped from her bed, only vaguely noticing that her body seemed to have almost completely healed from the delivery as she had slept, so that it was as if the pregnancy had never been. She ran through the bedroom, pausing to look here and there, and on into the sitting room, and there she found Phoenedra holding the little bundle in her arms.

Just as she uttered a profound sigh of relief, she heard an outraged roar of unspeakable loss and fury. Startled, she looked around but saw nothing. She turned back to the priestess and met her eyes. "What?" she demanded, quivering inside at the sorrowful glance bent upon her. "What has happened?"

Again, she heard that awful roar, just as Phoenedra, in a voice choked with tears, said, "The child has died."

CHAPTER FIFTEEN

Dia was numb. She leaned heavily upon Phoebus' arm as they entered the inner sanctum of the Temple, for she had never been so exhausted in her life. Her brother's corruption, followed by the deaths of Caelon and of their newborn son had left her heart an echoing barrenness of grief. She retained her grip on sanity only by holding the dreadful, burning pain at bay and, since it seemed to her that her heart and mind held nothing but her terrible sorrow, she was left with nothing at all -- or so she thought.

The inner sanctum was actually quite small, with rows of benches to seat perhaps fifty in comfort. Before those benches rose the dome of the temple, which could be seen shouldering its way into the sky from the outside of the building, and under which were the altars and the plain, carved wooden chair from which the Phoenix presided over the Temple. A pair of huge, elaborately cast golden pedestals held twelve equally huge candles, and their golden light touched the faces of the living and the dead with an impartially gentle hand. With dull eyes, Dia noted that Caelon's body had been placed upon the central altar and that her infant son reposed on a marble bier off to the left.

The lone hope still lighting her heart was that perhaps Caelon was intended to be reborn as the next Phoenix, and it was for this purpose that she was attending this ceremony. They would have attended to this as soon after she had arrived as was possible, once she had had a chance to rest, but had been interrupted by the birth of her baby. Involuntarily, Dia found herself wondering if her son would have lived, had he been born after Caelon had risen to be Phoenix. Sharply, like wincing away from pressure on a deep bruise, Dia pulled her mind away from that thought.

Phoebus seated her in the center of the front row with tender care and then joined his fellow TimeKeepers under the dome. There was stately Phoenedra ... rotund, merry-faced Phoeday ... youthful, serious Phoetar ... and Phoebus, steadfast and familiar. The four archpriests took up positions around Caelon's body and, surrounding them, the underpriests formed an outer circle with very precise care. When they were all in position, there was a moment of silence and Dia felt a wave of profound serenity wash over the Temple, emanating from the TimeKeepers, like the warmth of a hearthfire. She waited.

Finally, the four archpriests lifted their hands to their chests, fingertips touching, and bowed their heads. The underpriests raised their arms slightly, extending their hands toward their neighbors on each side, one hand facing front and the other turned back, so that each priest stood palm to palm with his neighbor, although their palms did not touch. They stood so for a moment, whether to sink further into that central peace or to commune silently, Dia could not tell. And then, they began to sing.

Dia had never heard this song before. The archpriests began with a simple melody in a mournful minor key that seemed eminently appropriate to Dia, for it sounded like every broken heart in the world. Then the underpriests joined in, singing their harmony and turning the dirge into a yearning, questing plea.

As she listened, Dia felt tears sting her eyes as she recalled all that she had done since arriving at the Emperor's palace at Ormaerand, all in obedience to a prophesy she did not understand, in the service of a Phoenix who still did not come. No one had been able to explain to her what any of this -- the rift with her brother, her affair with Caelon and his subsequent murder, the child she had carried and his subsequent death -- had to do with the Gaerud. So many times during those recent events, the scant instructions she had received, the instincts she had obeyed, the expanded senses she had trusted had led her into situations and behaviors with consequences that seemed senseless to her and her blood still burned with the pain of their aftermath.

And yet, she had plodded on blindly; not even in the nadir of her despair over her son's death or her bitterness over Caelon's had she seriously considered simply refusing whatever had been required of her in this peculiar series of events. And, as the second chorus of the TimeKeepers' song came to its lingering, longing close, her spirit rose with it, renewed, shiningly renewed. She knew now that she would continue on this path, whether Caelon rose or not. She had paid too dearly for the birth of this New Age to abandon the process now. Phoebus had taught her no more than truth when he had told her that the ways of the Phoenix were not the ways of men. He would come. In her heart, she knew that He would come and, when He did, she would be prepared to serve Him. In that sense, she had been surrendering to the light all along.

Dia remembered her caustic complaints to Phoebus when they were journeying to this place. She winced, a little ashamed as she recalled her raw bitterness in the wake of Caelon's death, and how pointless everything had seemed to her then. How very odd it was, that one could still serve the Sacred Way of Time in spite of oneself -- even if one was in rebellion against it, as she had been, even if one did not believe, as Caelon had not.

Perhaps, she thought, she was not so very unworthy. Perhaps her faith was stronger than she had suspected.

And still Caelon's body remained still and unresponsive as the TimeKeepers swung into the third repetition of their longing hymn. Her eyes still full, Dia drew a deep, shuddering breath. Really, she ought to have known that Caelon's resurrection had been only a remote possibility, largely born of her desire. Caelon was dead and their infant son was dead, as well. Her shoulders slumped in defeat. Daerus had won.

One of the underpriests, less disciplined than the archpriests, gasped. Startled, Dia blinked the tears from her eyes. Caelon still lay cold and dark but, following the direction of the young priest's glance, she looked at the marble bier on the left side of the dome, where the body of her dead child lay.

Dia blinked. No, her eyes were not deceiving her. The tiny body had begun to glow with a soft golden light, a light that had nothing to do with the candles burning in the Sanctum, a light that grew steadily brighter as the TimeKeepers' singing continued. At the end of this final verse of their song, the glow abruptly intensified for several heartbeats before there was a brilliant flash as the child's body flared to ashes in an instant. Into that momentary silence, Dia's heart began to pound.

Suddenly, the TimeKeepers began the final chorus, lifting their faces and their voices to the rafters in a joyous hymn of praise and thanksgiving. Those faces, in the soft glow of the candlelight, looked exalted, uplifted. The ashes of what had been her dead baby began to stir, sifting gently at first, as if touched by the lightest of breezes. The movement grew more pronounced, wafting about in the air in rhythm with the hymn that filled the Sanctum. Finally the ashes seemed to flow together into a moving, flowing, changing mass of energy that congealed into the naked figure of a boy.

Dia stared up at him, trembling so violently that it seemed her bones would be shaken to pieces. He looked to be some sixteen years of age, slender and well-made, just budding into manhood. His features were a blurred combination of hers and Caelon's; this was their son! It was!

She could not see his eyes, for they glowed with the same light that had consumed the dead infant he had been. But she could see that those glowing eyes were turned upon her, and she was suddenly overwhelmed with joy and humility, the abject hope of the faithful and the boundless love of the mother for her son. He stood before her in glory, reborn from the ashes of bleak death to embody radiant life, and all the confusion and anguish and loss no longer mattered to her in the least. The Phoenix had risen!

The four archpriests had retrieved the ceremonial robes of the Phoenix and brought it to the foot of that marble bier, where they stood, waiting. Gracefully, He allowed them to help him to the floor, and to garb Him as He held himself proudly, chin high and back straight. Then he turned to them and they knelt before Him to receive His blessing.

Having concluded these small but important ceremonies, the Phoenix walked over to where Dia sat and gently took her hand, drawing her to her feet. The brilliant light in his eyes had faded and she saw now that they were as blue as Caelon's.

As if he had discerned her thought, he smiled a gentle smile that washed over her like a benediction. "Thank you, Mother," he said to her in a pleasant tenor voice. "I know this has not been an easy thing for you, and I am grateful."

Dia was speechless, her eyes devouring his face hungrily. *It does not matter in the least, dearest,* she said silently.

His smile widened slightly before He looked around expectantly. "But, where is my father?" He then asked in brisk accents.

Sorrow once more swept over her as she indicated the altar where Caelon's body lay.

"Dead?" The Phoenix seemed surprised, and displeased. "Now, how can this be?" Purposefully, he turned and strode to his father's corpse, retaining his clasp of his mother's hand so that Dia, perforce, came with him.

Together, they stood over the violated body of Caelon of Aerandos. The Phoenix placed a hand over the dreadful wound in the silent chest, shaking his head severely. "No, no, no -- this will never do," he muttered to himself. A thoughtful frown spread over his face.

An impossible hope sprang up in her heart and she turned her gaze on her son in anticipation. A momentary surge of disbelief again possessed her; it seemed quite impossible that *she*, of all the women of this world, should have given birth to the Phoenix! She shook her head, disconcerted, and turned her eyes back to the body of her lover. And then, she gasped in astonishment.

The wound in his chest was almost gone and, even as she took note of that impossible feat, the last vestiges of it disappeared from his chest. A quick glance at the Phoenix showed Him to be wearing His gentle smile once more, as He performed this miracle without visible effort.

A cough drew her glance back to the gentleman lying on the altar. Dia saw his chest rise and fall and rise again. Once more, she was trembling violently, her eyes filled with tears, and, when she felt the return of his presence to her mind, a sob of relief escaped her. And once again, she recalled her bitter doubts with a feeling of deep shame. Without a second thought, she fell to her knees, lifted the hem of the Phoenix's robe and kissed it.

"Mother!" He reached down and gripped her hands, pulling her back to her feet. "Please, do not!" He looked terribly embarrassed.

She looked into His eyes searchingly, her own still swimming with tears. This was going to cause some major revisions in her religious thought, she realized. The Phoenix of the Last Age was to be worshipped; the Phoenix of this Age was her son, and He was to be loved. She lifted a hand to his cheek. "I have no wish to confound you, dear heart," she told him shakily, "but you will at least allow me to thank you."

"Really, there is not the least need," He said, adorably flustered.

This tableau was abruptly interrupted. A string of curses, uttered feebly but with great feeling, came from the recumbent figure on the altar. A startled gasp was collectively uttered by the TimeKeepers, who looked quite shocked -- except Phoebus, whose shaking shoulders indicated that he was laughing silently into his cowl. Dia looked into the eyes of the Phoenix and was surprised to see amusement and mischief there. In that instant, He seemed less like the focus of a religion and more like the child she bore. Their eyes held for a long moment and then, together, they giggled.

Dia moved to stand by Caelon's head and, seeing that his eyes were still closed, she called to him softly, "Caelon."

His eyes fluttered open. After staring at her for an uncomprehending moment, he said, "Where am I?"

"You are in the Sanctum of the Temple of the Fires," she said gently.

He continued to stare at her, his eyes roving over her face, and she remembered that the last time she had seen him, he had been in her bed. Then, still apparently struggling to understand what had happened, he said, "I remember. I was dying -- murdered."

Dia nodded.

Caelon frowned. "And now I live?"

Dia nodded again before tenderly helping him to achieve a sitting position.

He put a hand to his head, still frowning at her. Then his eyes widened. "Really, my lady, you are an unending treasure of unsuspected ability," he said with a tentative smile. "Clearly nothing is impossible for you."

Dia grinned. Death did not appear to have changed his lordship noticeably. A smothered giggle behind her informed her that her thoughts had been clear to their son. "This was not my doing, my lord," she told him demurely. She then turned and drew the Phoenix forward, somewhat amused to see a touch of shyness in the boy's gaze. "You owe your restoration to this young gentleman."

"Indeed?" Caelon said in some surprise. His voice was thickened from disuse, as if he had just roused from a long sleep, but the eyes he turned on the young boy-god were as alert as ever. "Well, you are certainly Talented for one so young. How may I call you, sir?"

"I am the Phoenix," the boy said hesitantly, a touch of shyness lingering in his smile.

Caelon blinked.

"He is your son," Dia added.

CHAPTER SIXTEEN

Colonel Lord Caelon, heir to the Grand Duchy of Aerandos and future commander of the finest army in the Empire of Ormaeranda, was a gentleman of quick wit and decision; the education provided by the Grand Duke Saeros had seen to that. His lordship had been in more than one situation in which rapid thought and decisive action had saved his life, and he could always be counted upon not to lose his head in an emergency. There had been a time when he had thought that there was little his life could throw at him that he could not assimilate and act upon immediately.

But, of course, that was before he had become acquainted with Lady Dia of Shae.

The last thing he remembered was his encounter with Lord Daerus in the dusky halls of the Imperial Palace, and the searing pain of a sword piercing heart and lung. He distinctly remembered feeling the seriousness of the wound and becoming aware that he had been killed. Yet, here he was, confronted with my lady, who looked just as he remembered her and who was introducing as his son a young gentleman who claimed to be the fabled Phoenix. His son! Why, the lad had to be quite sixteen or seventeen years of age! Try as he might, he could make no sense of these revelations.

He fixed his eyes on Dia and ventured upon a question. "Who," said his lordship, "is his mother?"

"I am," she replied promptly, blushing rosily.

"You are remarkably well preserved, my lady," he said, beginning to smile. Clearly, he had gone insane when he had entered the House of the Dead. "Either that or I have been absent for a great many years. How old is he?"

The lad -- that Ancient Phoenix, who was the focus of an important element of the world's religious devotion -- giggled.

"To own the truth," my lady said, somewhat diffidently, "he was born yesterday."

"*Yesterday?*" Shock reduced Caelon's rusty voice to something of a wheeze.

She looked at him with a curious expression that combined amusement with concern and something else which Caelon could not at that moment identify. "Are you all right?" she asked him.

Given all that she had just told him, the question seemed so preposterous that he recovered from his shock instantly, falling into laughter. "Yes, certainly, I am fine. Here I have been reclaimed from death by my son, the Phoenix, and nothing could be more common, after all! Indeed, I do not know why I was not expecting something like this!"

A sympathetic grin spread over Dia's face as she said, "Oh, dear! I suppose this is rather a lot to throw at you so suddenly. A great deal has happened since you died."

That statement made him laugh all the more. He still did not in the least understand the impossible thing that seemed to have happened but, all things considered, he really had little to complain of. "I find myself in complete agreement with you, my lady," he said finally. Then, he looked at the young man and said, "I have never believed in you, you know."

Dia winced but the boy continued to smile. "Do you believe in me now?" he asked ingenucusly.

"I suppose I shall have to," Caelon conceded.

"Well, no, you do not *have* to," he said judiciously.

"No?"

"Not if you continue in the belief that you are simply mad," the boy said, grinning again. "Or if you come to the conclusion, as I see you mean to, that you have conjured up a splendid fantasy with which to entertain yourself, having found Death to be a bit boring."

"Oh!" Dia broke into scandalized laughter. "Caelon, you did not!"

"Not yet, but I was about to," he admitted, warming to the sound of her laughter.

"Never mind," the lad said magnanimously. "I do not mind. It is a very great deal to take in all at once, particularly when one was predisposed not to believe in any of this. I think it would be a very good thing, Mother, if you were to tell my father all that has befallen you since you saw him last."

"And what of you, young sir?" she asked him with a gentle authority that was so very maternal that Caelon grinned.

"There are preparations I must make, Mother, and instructions that I must give to my children," and he indicated the hovering priests with a careless flick of one long-fingered hand. Then, he gave his parents a shrewd glance and added, "Besides, I fancy the two of you have many things to say to each other. You will require a few moments of privacy." With that, this child who called himself the Phoenix turned to the knot of priests clustered nearby, saying, "Come." With his retinue trailing behind him, the boy exited through one of the doors behind the altar.

Caelon then turned his gaze to Dia, who was still looking after the boy with so much tenderness in her face that he felt an irrational surge of -- what was it? Not jealousy, he realized as she turned back to him. There was naught of the lover in her manner towards the boy. He took a breath and then had to laugh a little. "I never thought I'd hear myself ask this of anyone," he said with a rueful shake of his head, "but how long was I dead?"

She chuckled. "How very odd that sounds, doesn't it?"

"Very."

"Do you want to know how much real time has elapsed or how long it has seemed to me?"

He frowned slightly, wishing she would stop talking in riddles. "Is there a difference?"

"We are outside time at this moment," she said in the most matter-of-fact way imaginable.

"Indeed?"

"Yes, have you not noticed how dull and grey everything looks? That is because of the peculiar time we are in. So, when we return to real time, almost none of it will have passed since you fell in the Emperor's palace."

Very well, he thought. *I suppose I followed that.* "And how long have you been in this peculiar sort of time?"

"It has seemed like a matter of several months," she said, her gray eyes watchful, "although I was surprised at how quickly the baby came."

She stopped and for a moment they simply sat surveying each other in silence. He could not imagine at first why she was looking at him so oddly, until finally she said, "Are you vexed with me?"

"Vexed with you?" he repeated, surprised at the question. "No, how should I be?"

"Because I ... because of ... of the baby," she said with considerable difficulty.

He shook his head vaguely, a bit surprised that she would worry about that. "Now, how could you have helped that, my lady?" he asked, quite reasonably. "Indeed, it is I who should beg your pardon for using you so shamefully."

She blushed rosily and her smile was full of tender mischief. "I did not mind."

"Perhaps not," he said sternly, summoning the self discipline to push away the memories her smile evoked, "but one should have more respect for a daughter of Shae." He saw that she was still looking doubtfully at him and realized that she would misinterpret his austerity. "I do not blame you for that, you know," he explained gently. "It was I who ... "

"Oh, stop that!" she said with sudden impatience. "You had no more choice in the matter than I did and if you mean to sit there and spout such noble, meaningless stuff at me, I shall be very much inclined to murder you all over again!"

This unexpected harangue not unnaturally rendered him speechless. Under any other circumstances, such a bizarre threat would have made him laugh heartily, but he could see the angry tears in her eyes and he prudently swallowed his mirth. What under the sun was she so upset about?

"What, indeed?" she snarled at him, making him aware that she was listening to his thoughts. "Of course, I have not the least cause to be upset with anyone about anything at all! How can you ... oh, never mind! Permit me to *show* you what has been happening, my lord!"

She spoke violently, uttering these last words in much the same tones Caelon would have expected to hear from a fellow offering to knock his teeth down his throat. He felt her mind at work and braced himself.

He was used to the experience of her mind slowly melding into his, like a shy and inexperienced maiden who was eager not to give offense. On this occasion, she was not gentle. She plunged into his mind with the abruptness of a knife thrust. Then she was expanding into his awareness, consuming him, and her thoughts became his. As did her memories.

He saw and felt it all in an instant, everything she had experienced from the moment she had felt his death until the moment of his resurrection. As if it had been his own, he endured the bereavement and betrayal, the anger and bitterness, and a pain that burned like acid; the surprised tenderness when she learned of her pregnancy, the fear of a young girl deprived of support during her first childbearing experience, the lingering sorrow over a boy who would never know his father. Then the consuming pain and exaltation of the birth itself, followed by the devastating blow of the baby's death. And finally, battered numb by so many terrible losses, the rebirth and renewal of her own faith and willingness to serve the Phoenix, whatever else He required of her, the amazed humility of watching her dead child rise to become the new Phoenix, and the unexpected bounty -- her inexpressible joy and relief, the release from regret and guilt, when their son had given her the gift of restoring his father's life.

Into the vaults of his mind came her voice. *Do not speak to me of anything so petty as the honor of Shae after all I have endured!* she told him, with all the contempt of one who had learned, through bitter experience, of things that were far more important than the honor of the Great Houses of Ormaeranda.

Shaken, Caelon stared at her as her mental presence dwindled to a faint touch, and he found himself wishing she would not leave him. Her face was as calm and unmoving as a quiet pond on a summer day, but her eyes were dark with emotion. Any of the obvious platitudes that he might offer her in comfort would be meaningless to her, he knew; she did not blame him for any of what had befallen her, however much he might blame himself.

He shook his head in bemusement. "What can I possibly say to you?" he said softly, his throat still tight from the avalanche of emotion she had shared with him. Her eyes fell away from his and she shrugged but, when she would have turned away, he caught her wrist, preventing her. "Do you turn away from me now, after all I have just seen? Come, my lady," and he smiled ever so faintly, "this is less than honest of you."

To his delighted surprise, vivid color rushed into her face at this gently teasing reproach. "That is not at all fair of you, my lord!" she protested.

At that, Caelon laughed outright. "What is not fair? You have been making it all seem so very easy, this heeding of prophesy and such, that I fear I had been taking you thoroughly for granted. And now, I have come by my just deserts, for I am rendered quite speechless"

"Not noticeably," was Lady Dia's wry interjection.

"And how is it that I have sunk to 'my lord' again? I am quite certain I heard you call me by name but a few moments since," he continued, his quivering lip the only indication that he had heard her quip.

Grey eyes sparkling, she gravely replied, "Very well, Caelon."

"Thank you," he said as seriously. "I was very much in earnest, you know. I have no notion of what to say to you after all that has passed. I would not want you to think I make light of what you have done." Then he smiled again and lifted the hand he still held to his lips.

Her only reply to this speech was a return of the pressure of his fingers on her hand. She then guided him to the temple door and placed him in the hands of one of the priests, informing him that very likely the Phoenix would be sending for them both soon enough and no doubt she would see him then.

He did not truly have any wish to leave her just then but, taking this dismissal in good part, Caelon followed the priest to an unadorned apartment nearby, in which he was installed with very little fuss. The young priest, a fellow of about his own age named Phoelan, suggested that he might like to rest for awhile before midmeal was served and enquired whether he wished to be served in his chambers or conducted to the dining hall. On another occasion, he might have been curious to see more of this Temple that he had come to believe did not exist. However, it occurred to him that he would like a bit of privacy to sort out his scrambled wits. He elected to take his meal privately.

Caelon was not much given to introspection but he could not deny that the notion of having a son almost grown was going to take some getting used to. That that son turned out to be fabled Phoenix, whom he had thought someone had invented to justify the existence of a theology, unsettled him further. How could he have any sort of paternal relationship with a religious icon?

For that matter, how could he be father to a boy that most of the continent prayed to, that he would have prayed to himself, if he had been that sort of man. Clearly, his religious thought was going to need major adjustment. Much more difficult for him was the unwelcome notion that his son was unlikely to need much in the way of a father. He found himself resenting that. He had been looking forward to fathering sons -- granted, not for some time yet -- and all that entailed. Now, he was to be done out of that role and it did not matter in the least that he would have been pleased to play it.

Brooding over that was unlikely to produce much more than a headache, and the other matter begging his attention was much more pleasant to contemplate. What was he to do about Dia?

He had spoken nothing but the truth when he had told her that he did not know what to say to her. When he considered all that she had done, all that she had suffered, for the sake of her faith in her

God, he felt strangely humbled -- a sensation that was new to him. On the other hand, when he recalled the boundless love of which she had proved herself capable, and the terrible pain she had endured, for himself and for their son, his heart filled. He had no words for these overwhelming feelings. And, of course, when he remembered that magic time when he had shared her bed, had loved her and then held her as she had slept, he knew his fumbling with language did not matter in the slightest. She was his lady, his mate, and all that remained were the formalities.

Caelon smiled ruefully. He still did not like being led about by some inscrutable Fate, very much preferring to believe that he controlled his own destiny. And, for the most part, he knew that he did. In the matter of Dia of Shae, Fate had proved too much for him -- but never mind. Caelon was willing. Dia was worth it.

After he had washed and dressed himself in a robe that was the only clean garment to hand -- his newly bathed skin cringed away from the clothing he had been wearing, which was crusted with his own blood -- Caelon was seized by a sudden, compulsive restlessness. Accordingly, after he had eaten the midmeal that had been brought to him by the obliging Phoelan, he emerged from the room and began striding along the corridors in his usual decisive fashion, even though he had no destination in mind. He roamed about, ignoring the closed doors in the halls of the Temple, for he had no wish to offend anyone by inadvertently invading their privacy, and no real wish to encounter anyone, either. Those he did encounter did not speak to him, although one and all gave him a low, reverent bow as he passed. The gesture irritated him. Why in the name of ashes were they bowing to *him*? he wondered. Then he remembered that he had sired their Phoenix and so unwittingly earned a place of honor among them. He sighed. The obeisance disturbed him, for he felt he did not deserve it.

Such was the thought in his head when he absently turned into the only open door he had thus far encountered. Once inside, he stopped short, for he had come face to face with his son. "I beg your pardon," he murmured awkwardly, preparing to leave.

"No, please, do not go," the boy said.

Caelon saw again that shy smile that had greeted him when

first he had regained consciousness. He looked more closely at the lad, noting that he had Caelon's own blue eyes and Dia's slight frame. He looked to be delicately built, although Caelon saw some evidence that he would fill out nicely as he grew older -- or whatever it was that a Phoenix did. What struck him most forcefully, however, was the timid innocence in those blue eyes. Perhaps, he thought, growing more cheerful, the boy *did* need a father ... at least, for a little while.

"I would not intrude upon your privacy," Caelon said formally, not quite sure how to proceed.

Somewhat to his surprise, the boy blushed rosily. "Well, sir," he said with a deference that Caelon found even more surprising, "as to that, your arrival was not quite accidental, you know."

"Indeed?"

"Well, you see ... I called you."

Caelon surveyed his offspring in considerable amusement. Really, the boy was as nervous as if he expect his father to deliver a clout to the head for insolence. Caelon could not imagine himself so severe a parent. Even less could he imagine being able to bring himself to offer violence to the Phoenix. "How may I serve you -- you know, this is most awkward," Caelon interrupted himself to complain. "How shall I call you? I really cannot address my young son by his title -- even if I could so address an unknown demi-god with whom I had little acquaintance."

The boy grinned. "Well, if I had lived longer than a few hours, my mother would have called me Caerad," he supplied. "You may call me so, if you wish."

Caelon returned the grin a bit ruefully. "Splendid, Caerad," he said, already feeling a bit more normal. "Now, then, how may I serve you?"

"Serve me?" Caerad repeated, looking nonplussed. "Oh, no, no, no, sir. It is just that I was hoping to become better acquainted with you before we go our separate ways." He paused, thinking. "I shall be forced to go about my duties with no real experience of having lived with my family, and that is not what was intended, you know."

"Oh!" That startled Caelon. "Do you know, I did not know that. I had thought all this was foreordained."

"It was destined that you and my mother should produce me," the lad agreed, "but not in the manner in which it has come to pass. In fact, you two should have met some three years ago ... and would have, if she had accompanied her brother to court when first he did journey to Ormaerand, as her parents suggested to her at that time."

Caelon's amusement deepened. "Well, yes, but I was not at court three years ago," he pointed out.

"You would have been. I expect some matter concerning the defense of the Empire would have come up, so that Lord Saeros would have found it necessary to see the Emperor personally. You would have accompanied him. However, since my mother refused to go, there was no need for you to be there," Caerad explained earnestly. He hesitated, looking at Caelon in some uncertainty. "I love her dearly but I must confess that she can be *very* stubborn," he added.

"Indeed?"

"Not that I mean her any disrespect," the boy went on hurriedly.

"No, of course not."

"She really is an extraordinary woman."

"I quite agree."

"It is just that she can sometimes be a bit uncooperative ... "

"Not to say, obstinate." Caelon chuckled. "No, lad, there is no need to stare at me so warily. You seem to know her much better than I do and I am perfectly willing to take your word for it. No doubt I shall encounter this stubborn streak soon enough. It is as well to be forewarned."

"Oh, dear!" he said, sounding so dismayed that Caelon laughed outright. "This has all become so excessively awkward that I really do not know what is to be done."

"Why? To be sure, you should have been here some time ago but, surely, that is of no moment. You are here now ... "

"Oh, so much is different. That is why the Gaerud will be much more difficult for us. You should have been wed to my Lady Dia some two years since, and have been well enough acquainted with her brother to be willing to lend her your aid now that he has been ensnared by Septha. You would have liked him very well, you know."

Caelon recalled that brief encounter with the trapped mind of Lord Daerus of Shae. "I expect you are probably right, but I am willing to lend Dia my aid in any event, as indeed I have," he said, gently reproachful. "Besides, no one should be left to have their thoughts embalmed in such a stinking darkness as we found in the mind of Daerus of Shae. Is he so very crucial to this Gaerud of yours?"

Caerad nodded. "Indeed, he is quite crucial, Father," he said and Caelon felt an odd, wistful pang at being addressed so. "And Septha has been in Ormaerand unhindered for so long that He will be difficult to overcome. His instrument is the Princess Kera and He has strengthened her hand so that she has become almost impossible to withstand."

"And yet, your mother managed to withstand her rather handily," Caelon pointed out.

"Oh, that was your doing, sir," his son told him ingenuously.

"My doing?"

"Why, yes." The boy smiled. "Did you never wonder why , on the two occasions on which you actually felt that terrible darkness invading your mind, you were able to obliterate it with but a thought?"

"I was?" Caelon asked, stunned. "I had thought that must have been your mother's work."

The boy shook his head. "You are invulnerable to them, Father. Septha did not recognize you were when you arrived at court -- which, I will confess, has me in something of a puzzle. That is why they did not kill you until they learned that they could not control my mother so long as you were about to protect her. If they had known who you really were, they would have been making attempts on your life before you had even unpacked from your journey south."

"I see."

"In any event, I should have spent a bit of time in the lap of a loving family, for that would better have sustained me -- and the two of you, as well. I only hope I can overcome the Dark One, for I am ill prepared for this battle," Caerad said worriedly.

Caelon digested this in silence for a few moments, for he found himself visited by a series of conflicting emotions. Most vivid among these was the image, generated by Caerad's words, of the loving family that would have been forged by his union with Dia. Without realizing it, he sighed wistfully and, unnoticed by him, his son's lips twitched. "And what would become of you if you were to fail?" Caelon asked finally.

"I would be no more," the boy replied simply.

Well, that was assuredly not an option. A surge of protectiveness welled up in Caelon that was just as primitive and primal as his feelings for Dia. Caelon eyed his offspring speculatively. The boy looked much too innocent and unworldly to warrant the suspicion, but Caelon nonetheless had a notion that he was being very cleverly manipulated. Not that it really mattered. His son would *not* be sacrificed to monstrous Septha.

Then he realized that Caerad was watching him. "I should be quite angry with the two of you, you know," he remarked.

"Sir?"

"As difficult as it may be to believe -- I can hardly believe it myself, for I had not considered the matter -- I was looking forward to being a *father* to my son. Between you, you and my lady have cheated me of that," Caelon explained.

"There will be other sons, sir," the boy said soothingly. "I, too, regret the necessity, but it had to be this way."

"Very well, my boy," Caelon said cheerfully, and managing to sound much like his own father. Other sons? Fathered upon Dia? "What now?"

"Now," Caerad replied, smiling his mother's impish smile, "we make my mother welcome."

An instant later, Dia entered the room. Like him, she wore one of the robes which adorned the underpriests of the Temple and the severe, utilitarian garment served as an excellent foil for her luminous beauty. She was looking at Caerad as she entered the room and Caelon noticed that motherhood had added a tenderness and depth to her eyes that had not been there before. He wondered dazedly if his son was tampering with his mind but rejected the notion. Perhaps he had never allowed himself to look at her before. Slowly, he drew a deep, much-needed breath.

Dia turned her gaze to him and searched his eyes. Caelon could not know what she found there but whatever it was seemed to please her. She fetched up before him and dropped a curtsey. "My lord," she murmured formally in greeting.

Caelon took her hand and kissed it. "My lady," he replied.

She smiled in some mischief. "You pursue your acquaintance with your son?"

"Indeed," he said, returning the smile, "the hour has proved most instructive."

That made her laugh. "Really, my dear," she said over his shoulder to Caerad, "it is unkind of you to tease your father so."

The boy blushed. "Mother!" he protested.

That made them both laugh. "Come, we have plans to make, do we not?" Dia said when she recovered her composure.

"All in good time," Caelon replied, placing a chair for her.

Flicking a glance toward the Phoenix, he made due note of the expression of satisfaction on that young gentleman's face. Caelon mentally shrugged. Before any of this began, he would resent being so shamelessly manipulated, but he found he could not summon up the righteous anger he might have expected of himself. That did not really matter to him anymore. This was his mate and here was their son, and Caelon had no desire to resist the bond of the small family that was speaking to him so loudly. There was no rush. This instant would last for as long as the Phoenix allowed it to last. And, if this would help them all to face Dark Septha and prevail, then it would be time well spent.

They spent the equivalent of a month or so in that timeless place in which the Temple had dwelt since the death of the last Phoenix. As matters evolved, all three of them found the experience of being together as a family to be very instructive indeed. More than anything else, they managed in that short time to forge a bond of love and mutual togetherness that made the approaching separation difficult for them all to contemplate. They all knew that, once this time was over, they could be family no more, and that awareness lent a certain poignancy to their gatherings.

It was the Phoenix who finally said, "It is time, I think."

"Time?" Caelon said, looking blank.

"Oh, surely not so soon," Dia protested at the same time.

The boy smiled his gentle smile and said, "This will only get more difficult the longer we postpone it, Mother."

"What of the plans we were needing to make?" Caelon asked, quizzically eyeing his son.

"There are really no plans to make, Father," the boy replied. "Septha will instigate this battle and without much delay; the longer I remain, the more strength I will gain. He will want to challenge me when he thinks I am still weak enough to be easily vanquished."

Dia saw Caelon scowl and his eyes took on a look of such implacable determination that she regarded him with satisfied pride. "What do you want us to do?" she asked her son.

"You will do what comes very naturally, Mother," the boy replied. "It may very well be that you will engage in this Gaerud and triumph over the Dark One without even knowing it."

"Do you know," Dia said with a laugh, "somehow I envision the scene being a little too spectacular for that."

The Phoenix smiled and then sighed. "Know that I love you both and I do believe the darkness stands no chance against the two of you."

Caelon and Dia exchanged a smiling glance, both thinking the same thing. There spoke the adoring child to adored parents, and it did not seem to either of them that there was much point in disabusing Him of the trust He had in them.

Caelon then asked, "We return to the palace?"

The Phoenix nodded.

"Do we ride out?" Dia wanted to know.

"Now, really, Mother," the boy reproached her gently, "would I ask you to needlessly exhaust yourselves so? I shall open a time window and you shall step back into real time. You will arrive at the time shortly after you left the city. Once back in the palace, you will know what to do."

"And may we tell anyone of the rise of the new Phoenix?" Caelon asked meekly.

Dia and her son both grinned, for Caelon had come in for a great deal of teasing from them for his earlier skepticism. "Of course, you must tell them," He said, "although I do not know that you will wish to tell them ... er ... how I ... I mean, where I came from ... if you know what I mean ... "

Now Caelon grinned. "Yes, my boy, I do know what you mean, so you need explain no further."

"Phoebus and Phoeday accompany you back to the palace," the Phoenix went on, having speedily recovered from his embarrassment. "They have received certain instructions and have their own tasks to perform. I have sent for them ... and here they are," he added as the two archpriests entered the room. "Now, I will bring the Temple back into time and then open the window for you ... oh, no, wait. I think perhaps Phoenedra had best go out to the front courtyard, do not you? There is that poor fellow watering his donkey at the stream, you know. No doubt the sight of the Temple appearing from nowhere will give him quite a fright ... "

CHAPTER SEVENTEEN

Dia stepped out of the time window and into her own sitting room in the imperial palace with Caelon, Phoebus and Phoeday close behind her. She swallowed against the tightness in her throat. It had been difficult to bid her son good-bye, particularly when he was afraid and could not say so. Dia was afraid, as well, not for herself but for Caerad. *I really must stop thinking of him so*, she chided herself, trying to insert a practical note into her thoughts. Squaring her shoulders, she looked around, trying to get her bearings, for she was separated from this place now by so much time and distance that she needed to assimilate the current *now* into her thinking before she could do anything else.

"One wonders how anyone can see in this palace through this curst darkness," Phoeday grumbled, looking around uncomfortably.

Dia smiled faintly. "The whole city is like this, good Phoeday," she told him. "No doubt they do not even know this darkness is there. Lord Septha has done his work well in this part of the Empire." She looked around at them, her eyes seeking and finding Caelon's. "Come. We each have things to do and have no occasion to dawdle here."

Dia had received no further instruction from her son and she suspected that Caelon also had been told nothing. Yet, somehow, they each knew that they had business in separate parts of the palace and, with no further words, Caelon, followed at a discreet distance by Phoeday, left her, striding purposefully down the corridor. She watched him for a moment, smiling wistfully and thinking nothing in particular but feeling a very great deal.

Your pardon, my lady, but I believe you have your own business to attend to as well, Phoebus gently brought her back to reality.

Nodding once, she started toward Lady Tamia's sitting room.

As well that Phoebus reminded her, she thought. She could not allow maudlin sentiment to cloud her mind or prevent her from the performance of her tasks. She still did not know what those deeds would consist of, but she very much doubted that any of them would prove as pleasant as the first of them was like to be.

In real time, only about an hour or two had elapsed since she had left the palace, but it seemed to Dia that she had not talked to her Grace of Aerandos for some months, and she found that she had missed the lady. When she reached her Grace's sitting room door, she tapped gently and, upon being bidden to enter, did so without ceremony, quickly crossing the room to her hostess. "Your Grace," she said, stopping just before she had flung her arms around Lady Tamia. In some confusion, she dropped a low curtsey.

"Gracious, child," Lady Tamia said, observing her disorientation in a considering fashion, "I had thought you and Caelon must be leagues away from here by now! Certainly, I am glad to know that you have not yet departed, for I made sure Caelon would have come to my sitting room to bid us good-bye, and when he did not I was prepared to give him a very severe scold. But, surely, I cannot have been mistaken. Did you not mean to start for Shae just after firstmeal had been served? How do you come to still be here?"

By this time, Dia had risen from her curtsey. Her eyes met Lady Tamia's and her Grace suddenly gasped. Dia smiled; almost, she had no need of even saying it. She nodded. "There is no need for me to leave this place, now, your Grace, and every reason for me to stay. The Phoenix has risen!"

"Oh!" Lady Tamia lifted a trembling hand to her mouth and her eyes filled with tears. Then she quickly rose from her seat and came to Dia, giving the girl the embrace that Dia had been too shy to initiate herself. "Oh, this is the most wonderful thing anyone could have told me just now, my dear! How had you the news? Is it all over the court yet?"

Dia grinned. "I very much doubt it, your Grace. I know of it only because I was there when it happened."

That announcement caused Lady Tamia to freeze, staring at Dia in astonishment for a moment. Then her eyes narrowed and the shrewd gaze her Grace usually kept hidden emerged from behind the facade of the fluttery chatterbox once more. Lady Tamia took a deep breath and those keen eyes alighted upon Dia's companion.

Blushing, Dia made haste to repair an omission. "I am very sorry, your Grace. Do allow me to introduce Phoebus, of the purple, who serves us at Shae."

But that introduction seemed unnecessary, as Lady Tamia slowly walked over to Phoebus and raised her hand in the traditional greeting gesture that Dia had seem him exchange with Phoenedra at the Temple of the Fires. Then she turned back to Dia, and suddenly Lady Tamia of Aerandos was gone. In her place was ...

"Phoetara," her Grace supplied, informing Dia that her thoughts were clear to one trained in the Secrets. "It has been a very long time since any have either called me by that name or even thought of it in connection with me. But that is neither here nor there." Again, Lady Tamia swept Dia with her glance. "Yes, you were there when it happened. I can see that in your face -- as I can also see that there was a great deal more involved than just having been there, is that not so?"

"Well, yes ... ," Dia hesitated. Surely, she could not be contemplating divulging the entire, shocking story to the Grand Duchess Tamia of Aerandos? Then she smiled. Possibly not, but there was no reason why she could not tell the entire tale to Phoetara, priestess of the Phoenix. TimeKeepers, Dia knew, were not easily shocked.

And so, Dia poured forth the whole story of all that had befallen her since she had seen the Duchess last. She told her Grace of Prince Maermat's attempt to rape her and how she was able to hold him off until Caelon had arrived; she spoke very frankly of the moment when she had realized just *how* she was to surrender to the light, and how she had joyfully welcomed Caelon of Aerandos into her bed. Dia recounted how she had awakened alone, to the overwhelming sense of danger that had sent her scurrying to the palace stables, where she had met Phoebus; of how he ultimately told her of her pregnancy, and of the shock, pain, guilt and bitterness she knew when she had felt Caelon die at her brother's hand. Her Grace learned of Dia's journey to the Temple of Fires, of her fears, of her loneliness, of her ongoing feelings of guilt over Caelon's death, of her sudden compulsion to return to the palace to retrieve Caelon's body, through a time window that she should not have been able to open. Dia, losing herself in her narration, spoke of her arrival at the Temple, of her confinement and of the almost immediate death of her infant son. And, finally, eyes glowing, Dia told of the glorious aftermath of all that pain -- the rebirth of her son as the Phoenix and His restoration of Caelon's life.

"And the Gaerud?" Lady Tamia asked. Dia had noticed that her Grace had not had an easy time listening to this tale. When she had heard of her son's death, she had paled alarmingly and, upon learning that he had been brought back, a small sob had escaped her. Now, she was composed and serene, and her expression showed nothing except the shadow of the same implacable determination Dia had seen before in Caelon's eyes.

"That is in the hands of Lord Septha, your Grace," Dia replied to the question with a little shrug. "I am not entirely sure, even, that He and His minions are yet aware that we are back in the palace. Although ... " and here, Dia exchanged a glance with Phoebus, who nodded. The archpriest also felt the approach of a familiar, though altered, aura. "It would seem that my brother, at least, has felt the return of my presence, for he comes."

"Here?" Lady Tamia asked, brows lifted.

Dia nodded, smiling absently with her eyes on the door.

"Well, I very much hope that I can keep my nails from the

boy's eyes," was the Duchess' surprising comment. "Perhaps, if I keep reminding myself that Caelon is hale and hearty, and that I shall be seeing him shortly ... ?"

Dia, still smiling, turned her attention back to her hostess. "Indeed, you shall. For the moment, I believe he has sought out Lord Saeros. No doubt, he will join you both for midmeal."

"And do you join us as well?" asked Lady Tamia.

Dia was about to decline, thinking it would be best for her to rest herself well before she was required to appear for endmeal, but Phoebus forestalled her. "Indeed, my lady, you should be here."

At that moment, a polite knock was heard at the sitting room door. They all knew that it was Daerus seeking admittance and, further, that he had come alone. Phoebus looked questioningly at Dia and she nodded. While she did not have anything to say to her twin, she thought she might do herself, Caelon and their son some good if she were to give ear to whatever Daerus had come to say to her.

He entered the room trailing clouds of darkness, and fixed her with a brooding stare, nodding off-handedly at Lady Tamia and wholly ignoring Phoebus. That alone would have told her that this was not truly her brother, if any doubts had remained with her. "How did you do it?" he asked without preamble.

"Do what?" she asked, raising a brow.

"I killed that man with my own hands, sister," Daerus said, eyes and voice flat with hostility. Lady Tamia stiffened.

"Yes," she agreed pensively, retreating into a calm that brought a faint smile of approval to her tutor's face, "and someday you will have to explain to me why you should have done such a thing."

"At the time, it seemed preferable to killing you," he said, sneering.

Dia lifted her eyebrows. "Now, why would you wish to kill me?"

"I have already explained the matter to you, Dia," he said impatiently. "You must be wed to Maermat, or at least allow him into your bed."

"My choice is to submit my body to Maermat or to die?" she asked. "How would murdering Caelon of Aerandos have accomplished my cooperation?"

"It was obvious to us that he would interfere for as long as he was about. My Master decided that he must be removed."

"He would interfere?" Dia repeated. "Lord Caelon was not present when I held his Highness at bay with my daggers, twin."

"Your daggers?" It was Daerus' turn to repeat her words.

"Well, yes, dearest," she confirmed in some amusement. "Can it be that you are surprised to discover that I was unprepared to cooperate with my rapist?"

Oddly -- or at least, Dia found it odd -- that gentle question wiped the sneer from his face. "Your rapist?" he asked her, frowning.

Dia said nothing for quite a long moment. She was not mastering her temper or any other emotion, so much as she was wondering if he would say further what was on his mind if she remained silent. Also, she felt she had some small advantage in adding to his discomfort by her silence. When he began to fidget, she said, "Was there some part of that description that you did not understand?"

"You cannot have been such an idiot as to have attempted to resist him?" Daerus asked her incredulously.

He seemed so astonished that, try as she might, she could not help laughing. "Really, Daerus, I am already *quite* convinced that you have taken leave of your senses. You need no longer work at it this hard." Sobering, she added, "Surely, you cannot have expected anything else of me?"

"But, he is the crown prince!" Daerus said, apparently very much shocked. "You cannot refuse an imperial command!"

"As I recall the scene, Prince Maermat did not trouble himself to issue an imperial command," she informed him with sedate good cheer. "And, in any event, he has no authority to issue such a command to me."

If you had had the slightest doubt that this man is not, in truth, your brother, Phoebus said quietly, *this conversation must surely provide it, my lady.*

Indeed, she replied, *I would not have had to explain this to Daerus.*

"Come, sister," Daerus was saying, "the Emperor has absolute authority and, as his heir, Prince Maermat should have been obeyed. I am ashamed of you."

"Somehow, your shame fails to distress me, my dear," she said, calmly. Then, her eyes narrowing, she spoke directly to the Dark God. "It would have been much better, my Lord Septha, had You taken the trouble to understand our ways in Ormaeranda before You embarked on this elaborate scheme."

There was a moment of pregnant silence, during which Dia felt a swirling darkness slowly gathering momentum and whipping around her with increasing fury. Lady Tamia and Phoebus watched her with almost identical expressions of startlement in their eyes. A gasp came from her brother's lips and echoed through the vaults of her mind like the slow death of a rumble of thunder. *"Thou art impertinent, Muphoen,"* said a deep, heavily powerful voice that reverberated around the room, bouncing off the stone walls and sinking into silence.

"I am bored, Dark Septha," she replied, suddenly more irritated than prudence suggested she should be in the presence of a God. "We neither of us accomplish anything by forcing me to explain things to Daerus that he really ought to know. I am sure he came to her Grace's sitting room in search of me for some reason. Do please instruct your instrument to get to the point."

Phoebus blinked.

"Enjoy this, thy last waking, then, Muphoen!" the voice came roaring at her from Daerus' still and uncomprehending face. *"Before next thou seekest thy bed shall the battle be joined. Even now do my instruments prepare to celebrate next endmeal by giving over the souls of all Ormaeranda to me. With such power, thy Phoenix shall find me invincible."* There was an ominous pause. *"Be assured that thou shalt feel the weight of my displeasure for thy presumption when the Gaerud is done and I am its victor! Foolish woman, canst thou not feel how great is my strength and how feeble is thy new-hatched godling? Fear me and tremble, Muphoen, for I* **shall** *prevail!"*

Having delivered himself of this ominous promise, the enraged God caused her brother to turn from her and, with a gait that was curiously wooden, stalk from the room.

"Well!" said Dia, after a moment of stunned silence.

Fire and ashes, Dia, have you taken leave of your senses? Caelon snapped in her head, clearly incensed.

No, she replied calmly, *why?*

That was very dangerous, my lady, Phoeday informed her. *Septha* **is** *a God, after all. He could obliterate you with but a thought.*

And very likely will, if He gets the chance, but not until after next endmeal, Dia told them, smiling roguishly at Phoebus. *So you heard all that, then?*

I feel certain they must have heard it as far off as Nedalia, Caelon said sardonically. *And you could not have known that you would not be struck down when you spoke to Him so.*

Enough of these reproaches, she said impatiently. *Let us address the heart of the matter. We know now that our battle will be joined in a matter of a few hours. I expect there are some preparations that we will need to make and,* and here she looked pointedly at Phoebus, *some instructions that will need to be given.*

She was rewarded with Phoeday's robust chuckle. *Very well, my lady,* he said wryly, *we will leave off these remonstrances. What is done is done, and my good brother Phoebus and I have our work to do.*

With that, his presence and Caelon's faded from her mind. She turned bright, expectant eyes upon her companions. She saw Phoebus exchange a glance of rueful amusement with Lady Tamia before turning back to her. "I suppose there is not the least use in advising you to try to restrain your temper?" he asked her.

"Well, really, Phoebus, I do not plan these things, you know," she pointed out reasonably. "I had the firmest of intentions of maintaining such an unearthly calm as must have made you proud of me. It is just that everything about this business has been so tediously indirect, and nothing moreso than my alleged brother's dealings with me. I am used to speaking my mind to him and old habits, after all, are very difficult to break."

Reluctantly, he began to laugh. "It well may be that our most excellent Phoenix knows you even better than I had thought," he said cryptically.

At that, Lady Tamia laughed as well. "One can only hope so," she said. "I will confess, I had thought for a moment that we would all be incinerated by lightening bolts or some such thing." She rose and stepped over to Dia, reaching out to clasp her hands. "My dear, if courage alone is all that is needed in order to prevail, we have nothing at all to fear. It is not every lady who would so address Septha the Destroyer. Accept my compliments, *Muphoen.*"

Dia grinned. "Gladly, your Grace," she said.

In another part of the palace, Caelon tried to unobtrusively compose himself. He had been attending his father as Lord Saeros conferred with Giseth of the Chosen, Ambassador from Lemantia, when he had heard Septha's mighty voice roaring in his mind. He had not been alone in his perception, he knew, if the priestess' pained wince were any indication. Indeed, once he had finished his brief, rapid conversation with Dia, she had looked at him gravely and said, "Thy lady is perhaps unwise to goad One who is feeling His strength more fully than has been possible for Him for longer than thou couldst imagine."

"So I have given her to understand," he replied grimly.

Lord Saeros observed this exchange with no more change of expression than he had evinced when Caelon had walked into the sitting room in which Giseth received visitors. "Ah, Caelon, good of you to join us," his Grace had said, just as if he had not been expecting his heir to have been leagues away from the palace by then.

Caelon had nodded his greeting to them both, a faint smile appearing on his face. "I fear I am sadly tardy," he said with an apologetic air that was slightly overdone.

"Lord Caelon," had said Giseth reproachfully.

Lord Saeros had raised a brow at that. "It would appear that you need no introduction," he said.

"Indeed," Caelon agreed, eyeing the priestess speculatively.

"I am Giseth," the lady had then said, anticipating his Grace, "of the Chosen."

"And how am I to call you, ma'am?" Caelon asked politely.

"We of the Sisterhood do not indulge in such formality, my lord," she said. Then, she surprised him further. "I am happy that thy journey has been fruitful."

"Thank you," he had replied, falling back upon ritual civility in order to resist the temptation to cast a wildly appealing glance at his father. "Have I missed very much of your discussion?" He affected not to notice Phoeday's silent laughter.

"Giseth has been briefing me on the Lemantia situation," Lord Saeros had replied.

Caelon accepted the seat that his father offered, listening with only half an ear to the discussion of the massing of the Throk on Lemantia's eastern border. He did not quite know what he was doing there, but he did know that strategic positioning had little to do with it. He had wanted to give forth his news, except that it seemed unnecessary; this Giseth seemed to know already, and Caelon knew better than to interrupt his father when that gentleman was immersed in military matters. Caelon was tense, knowing that the Gaerud was but hours away and knowing, as well, that he had no notion of what part he himself was to play in the battle. Like Dia, he had no fear for himself. All his anxiety was focused upon the frail newly-born boy called The Phoenix. The waiting was making it difficult for Caelon to focus his attention on the discussion.

All this worrying does neither you nor your son any good, you know, Phoeday told him, *and it is curst tedious besides.*

The simplest solution to that complaint, good Phoeday, would be for you to get yourself out of my head, said Caelon with a sad want of respect for the priesthood.

Giseth, in the midst of describing what steps were available to the Chosen of Lemantia to protect themselves, choked and erupted into a fit of coughing.

Be sure that I do not abide in your mind of any desire of my own, halfling, Phoeday returned. *I obey the injunctions of my Master. If you object, you may take up the matter with Him. Considering your relationship with our Phoenix, he may even listen to you -- but I doubt it.*

Caelon ducked his head and covered his grin with his hand. It would never do for Lord Saeros to see it.

The discussion continued, and Caelon did his best to attend to it, until his attention had been captured by the anger of The Destroyer. Now, Lord Saeros continued to watch him in mildly bewildered annoyance, causing Caelon to suppress another grin. Finally, his Grace said, "I cannot imagine what has come over you, Caelon, but it is very plain that you will not be able to contain yourself until you have spoken whatever is on your mind."

Now that the moment was upon him, Caelon surprised himself with the discovery that he felt very happy in spite of his tension. He straightened, and threw his shoulders back and his head up. Gathering himself to deliver his message, joy and pride flooded him. "Indeed, I do have news, sir, although I am ashamed of having been so impolite as to interrupt you here."

Lord Saeros, who listened to this speech with an expression of growing irony, merely said, "Yes?"

"The New Age is upon us, sir," Caelon told his audience solemnly. "The Phoenix has risen."

Caelon had spoken diffidently, half expecting his father to demand in irate tones why he had been interrupted for *that.* He realized, even as he was making this brief statement, that he had never discussed matters of faith with Lord Saeros and had no notion of what his Grace's beliefs might be.

Lord Saeros stared at Caelon for a moment, blinking rapidly. Then, taking a deep breath, he sank back into the comfortable chair in which he was sitting. "Great Gods, boy!" uttered his Grace, obviously shaken. "Why did you not tell us this at once?" Then, completing Caelon's astonishment, his gaze returned to his hostess and he said, "This explains the Throk."

"Indeed, your Grace." Giseth, smiling radiantly, suddenly reentered the conversation. "I do beg thy pardon. I could see, of course, what had occurred immediately Lord Caelon entered the room. I had hoped that he would be so delighted with bearing such glad tidings that he would share it without delay." Then her expression turned slightly impish as she added, "Thou wilt forgive me if I suggest that his lordship is *very* well trained."

Caelon felt that he had somehow wandered into another universe as he watched his father laugh sheepishly at that oblique criticism. *I wonder if I know him at all,* he found himself thinking.

Actually, you know him rather well, considering that he is your father, Phoeday opined.

Oh, be quiet!

Lord Saeros then turned to his heir. "Does your mother know of this?"

Caelon nodded. "I expect my lady will have informed her by now," he said, having no idea of how he knew that was what Dia had done when she left him.

Lord Saeros was eyeing him consideringly again, a smile growing on his face. "In that case, I expect we shall be entertaining your lady to midmeal," said that perspicacious gentleman blandly. "Have you any notion of when the Gaerud shall begin?"

"I have a few suspicions," Caelon replied with a quizzing smile that caused his Grace to chuckle.

"In that case," said Giseth, "it is of the first importance that these few hours before battle is joined be spent reinforcing the loving bonds that join House Aerandos and House Shae. Lord Saeros, thou and thy excellent son must away at once."

"Indeed," Lord Saeros agreed, his eyes full of laughter, "and excellently well-put, Giseth."

Once again, Caelon pretended not to notice the merry laughter that echoed in the vaults of his mind.

Dia was seated in Lady Tamia's sitting room engaged in quiet converse with her hostess and her mentor when Caelon returned with Lord Saeros. For the briefest of instants, her eyes sought his of their own volition. There was no private message to be read in the glance they exchanged; rather, she just felt the need to refresh herself with his gaze, even after so fleeting an absence. Absently, she wondered if it would always be so between them.

Lord Saeros crossed the floor toward her in his leisurely way, saying, "Well, my dear, it seems that you have no need to rush off to Shae after all. I am glad to know that I have not yet seen the last of you."

Dia grinned with mischief. "Oh, well, I expect that you would not have seen the last of me in any event, your Grace," she said. "Allow me to present the archpriest Phoebus, who serves us at Shae."

Lord Saeros nodded in acknowledgement and Phoebus politely returned the gesture. Then he looked around at them all. "And have you concluded, then, how you mean to pursue this Gaerud? Shall you have need of my services?"

"I rather expect that we shall," Caelon replied, his expression suspiciously bland but his blue eyes twinkling wickedly. He had crossed the room to his mother and now took her hand and kissed her cheek. "How do you do, Mama? I vow, it seems I last saw you months ago, rather than just a few hours since."

Lady Tamia's eyes laughed up at him. "You are a very wicked boy, my dear," she murmurred reproachfully.

"Me?"

Meanwhile, Lord Saeros was staring at his son as if he had never seen him before. "I see," said his Grace. "And might one enquire as to *how* one might best be of service?"

"Yes, of course, you may enquire, sir," Caelon said, feigning astonishment at the question. Then he turned back to his mother. "And here is my lady to bear you company once more. Tell me, do we increase our covers for midmeal, ma'am?"

Lord Saeros audibly sighed, although his eyes were losing impatience in amusement.

"Indeed, your lady has been so good as to promise herself to us for midmeal, " Lady Tamia told him, adding in an undervoice, "as I expect you know very well, you naughty boy!"

"Do you not think, good Caelon, that it might be of some use to know what to expect?" Lord Saeros was asking with uncharacteristic meekness.

With exquisitely slow movements, Caelon turned his head toward his father to show that gentleman an expression of such comical astonishment that Dia was hard put to it to keep from laughing. "I expect it very well might, sir, but surely there is no need to discuss such a dreary subject when we are entertaining a guest."

By this time, Lady Tamia was clearly in dire straits and Dia, pained to see such a want of chivalry on the part of her lord, thought it prudent to intervene. *Caelon, do stop baiting your father like this!* she said to him in tones of the greatest reproach.

Why? he asked her, in very good spirits. *I expect it is doing him a great deal of good to be on the receiving end for once.*

That is all very well and good, but only consider your poor mama, Dia pointed out to him, glancing meaningfully at the sorely afflicted Duchess.

An excellent observation, my love.

Oh, stop it!

Phoeday and Phoebus both erupted into coughing spasms.

Meanwhile, Lord Saeros glanced at his heir sardonically. "I

suppose all this is designed to give me my own back again," he observed in wry accents. "No doubt, when you have finished playing these games, we might be able to discuss the matter at hand."

At that, Caelon burst into pent up laughter. "And I suppose I should know better than to imagine that I shall ever get the best of you, sir," he admitted handsomely between guffaws. "Truly, there is little to tell, Father. I gather that my lady and I both have tasks to perform in the furtherance of this Gaerud, but all the instruction either of us have received," and here, he glanced severely at the two archpriests seated demurely in a corner of the room, "is an assurance that those tasks will flow very naturally from who we are and will therefor require no preparation."

Armed with this information, a considering look descended upon Lord Saeros' face. "Aye, I can understand that."

"Indeed, sir?" Dia asked in some surprise, for the continued withholding of instruction had rankled.

"Yes, of course, child," replied his Grace promptly. Then he cast a beetling gaze at his heir. "There is such a thing as over preparation, you know."

Once again, Caelon began to laugh. "Touche, sir."

CHAPTER EIGHTEEN

Caelon opened his eyes and took a deep breath. He felt curiously lightened, as if he had somehow become a floating aura of consciousness surrounding his earthbound body. At the same time, he felt preternaturally alert and extraordinarily well-rested. Inhaling deeply once more, he finally focused his eyes upon his companion.

Phoeday returned his gaze calmly but with an approving twinkle in his eyes. Everything about Phoeday was round: eyes, face, belly and form. He did not exude the sort of unquenchable calm that Dia's Phoebus did; Caelon got the impression that the serenity of the TimeKeepers was hard work for Phoeday. *Trying times*, Caelon thought irreverently, *to be forced to maintain that iron calm in the face of such momentous events as the rise of a new Phoenix, the birth of a New Age and the incipient Gaerud*.

"Trying times indeed, my lord," Phoeday replied aloud. "I have found the meditation technique you have just practiced to be invaluable recently."

"I wonder how long it will take for me to grow used to having my companions reply to statements which I do not utter," Caelon rather pointedly mused.

Phoeday's eyes glinted. "Perhaps, when we have more leisure, I will show you how to shield your thoughts to guard your privacy," he said. "For now, I expect it must be time to join your parents for endmeal."

Caelon laughed. "And, of course, Phoeday never misses a meal."

"Not when I can help it, Impertinence," he replied with the assumed severity of a tutor, which fooled neither of them. "I cannot think what Lady Tamia can have been doing to have so neglected your education that you are freely disrespectful to the priesthood, my lord."

"I fear I am a sad disappointment to her," said my lord meekly as he sauntered to the door.

Phoeday chuckled. "I do not doubt that she did her best with you," he said, "and cannot be faulted at the way you have turned out."

Caelon grinned. He would have been astonished if anyone had suggested to him that he could become so entirely comfortable with the constant attendance of a TimeKeeper that they could wile away idle moments exchanging affectionate insults, but so it had been. "There is something I had been meaning to ask you, good Phoeday," he said as they walked together toward his mother's sitting room.

"Well, and what might that be, my lord?"

"Septha referred to Dia as *Muphoen*," Caelon recalled. "Is that a title or an insult or some other obscure name?"

Phoeday smiled absently. "It is a title, my lord. Loosely translated and summarized for brevity, it refers to her position as the mother of the Phoenix."

Caelon grunted in response. He was still unsettled by that vicarious encounter with the God of Chaos. It had given him quite a start to suddenly hear that roaring, rasping voice in his mind as he had been soberly attending his father in Giseth's sitting room. There had been so much unbridled fury in His voice that Caelon had experienced an instant of raw terror for her -- followed (very naturally) by an overwhelming desire to throttle the girl for giving him such a fright.

"There is not much point in brooding over the incident, my lord," Phoeday told him gruffly. "No doubt you will have ample opportunity to make her very sorry for her foolishness when, once this business is over with, you have settled into wedded bliss and can torture her in private." After Caelon laughed delightedly at this sally, Phoeday continued, "Indeed, my lord, I should prefer not to intrude upon your mental meandering, but you do not have the leisure to walk about with your head in the clouds just at this present."

"As if I should be so rude to my parents," Caelon murmured reproachfully.

"No," Phoeday muttered, "you save such rudeness for me. I believe we have arrived, sir."

Shoulders shaking with suppressed mirth, Caelon knocked politely and then entered the room.

His Grace, the Grand Duke of Aerandos, along with the Grand Duchess, were in the room, preparing to go down to endmeal, as expected. What Caelon had not expected was that they would be entertaining a very welcome visitor in the person of Colonel Braeden, one of the top officers in his father's army. As Phoeday effaced himself with deceptive meekness, Caelon entered the room and said, "Braeden, you are a sight for sore eyes!"

Colonel Braeden, ramrod stiff and very proper as always, smiled faintly and bowed. "It is my pleasure to be of service to Aerandos, as always," he said politely.

Caelon shook his head as he lounged over to his mother's chair to bow over her hand. "One of these days, I really must get the good colonel inebriated," he said to no one in particular. "Either that, or I will have to do something really desperate, like slip a toad into his trousers."

"Caelon," Lady Tamia said, mildly chiding him as she batted at his hand playfully, "do leave the colonel's trousers alone, I pray you."

Since he knew that Lady Tamia found the colonel daunting for the very reason that he was always so extremely correct, he did not take her admonitions too seriously. "Well, but surely there must be some way to relax that barge pole he calls a back," Caelon said, lowering his voice.

Her Grace stifled a giggle behind one elegant hand. "You are very naughty, sir!" she said, raising twinkling eyes to his.

"Indeed, I cannot think where I came by such an irreverent sense of humor," he said with loving amusement.

"Braeden is a very good soldier, which is all your father requires of him," Lady Tamia said firmly and with dignity. "You shall not tease him in this ridiculous way when Saeros has summoned him in his official capacity."

"You are very right!" Caelon said, apparently much struck. "I shall have to wait until he is off duty to make him a present of that toad."

"Caelon!"

"Caelon, your attention, if you please," Lord Saeros interrupted them.

Automatically, Caelon straightened to attention and all softness faded from his face. "Sir?"

"It would appear that we have rather more than two regiments at our disposal," Lord Saeros told his son, "thanks to the kind offices of the newly risen Phoenix."

For once thoroughly and completely amazed, Caelon's jaw dropped.

Close your mouth, boy, Phoeday instructed him tersely.

Caelon's jaw snapped shut.

Lord Saeros did not comment upon his son's facial contortions, only the faint twitching of his lips betraying that he had remarked them. "Colonel Braeden tells me that, shortly before he arrived at the palace with the seventh and ninth infantry, a TimeKeeper visited him with another message -- that we would have need of a show of force -- and an additional three regiments, traveling through time windows."

"Indeed?" Caelon said faintly.

"Judging from your reaction, I would surmise that you had no hand in this change of plans," his Grace continued smoothly. "I had thought that you might have requested a favor of this new Phoenix who, I am led to infer, might view with favor one who was instrumental in bringing His rise about. And I cannot think," Lord Saeros added with a hint of asperity, "why you arc staring at me as if I had suddenly grown another head. If you perceive that some discretion should be exercised in this matter, I would not think of asking you to betray such a trust but that does not mean that a normally intelligent man might not surmise what has been left unsaid."

Still dazed, and with Phoeday's unsympathetic laughter echoing in the vaults of his mind, Caelon said, "Allow me a moment to pull myself together, sir. I am less surprised at your perspicacity than I am at a military initiative by the Phoenix. I wonder what He can mean by it?"

"I rather expect," Lord Saeros said placidly, "that He knew we shall have need of them, my boy."

Caelon frowned thoughtfully. So far as he knew, the entirety of the battle between Septha and the Phoenix would be decided by the simple choices of the Shae twins. One did not need armies for that sort of thing. "And what need do you expect we shall have of them?" he asked his needle-witted sire.

"As to that," his Grace replied, unruffled, "I could not even venture a guess."

Caelon gave a short laugh. "In that event, I have no need to feel quite such a simpleton as I did a moment ago," he said ruefully. "Er ... what *do* you mean to do with them -- now, that is?" Caelon asked, beginning to smile.

"Do?" asked his Grace, eyeing his heir as if Caelon had lost his senses entirely. "I shall inspect them, of course ... after next firstmeal."

Caelon settled himself in a chair to await Dia feeling distinctly humbled. He had told her -- by the Fires, it seemed an age ago! -- that he was a soldier and so felt uncomfortable without a plan of battle. His father, who Caelon knew to be ten times the soldier that he was, apparently did not need such a plan. The Phoenix provided. It would be up to Lord Saeros to take advantage of that provision, should the need arise. That was all his Grace seemed to require. Caelon, having had no notion of the simple and profound faith which his father had always had, found it disquieting to meet with this wholly new facet of Lord Saeros' complex personality. Of course, his Grace had no way of knowing it, but in that moment he showed more faith in the

Phoenix than he who had sired Him. The thought made Caelon feel unutterably sad and shamefully unworthy.

Think you that faith can be demonstrated only by breast-beating and loud protestations? Phoeday asked him.

Do not mock me now, good Phoeday, he replied, subdued.

There was a brief pause before Phoeday spoke to him again, more gently than was his wont. *Now, why do you think I would mock you?* he said. *We each serve in our different ways, after all. Do you not see that you have unthinkingly and unhesitatingly acted with much more faith than this simple and fairly easy gesture of Lord Saeros'?*

Caelon did not reply but he could not help wondering what the TimeKeeper could possibly be thinking. He had not even believed in a Phoenix until he had met Him, and his religious thought was still unformed and not very profound.

Phoeday seemed to feel the instant and instinctive protests that remained unvoiced in Caelon's mind. *Recall, if you will, my lord,* said the priest in a droll tone of "voice", *that you have done everything from mildly inconveniencing yourself to acting against the dictates of your own conscience -- and suffering the consequences in unneeded guilt -- to getting yourself killed. And, in the end, all was done to provide what aid you could in the rise of the new Phoenix and the birth of the New Age.*

Nonsense, Phoeday, said Caelon brusquely. He had no wish to be credited with deeds of faith and martyrdom for which he had not earned such accolades. *I did nothing to aid in the rise of the new Phoenix.*

Indeed? Phoeday returned, clearly amused. *And why are you involved in this business, then?*

If we are to believe your prophesies, then my involvement was fated to be, Caelon reminded him. *Or, if you prefer, you may take my word for it that I lent my aid to Dia of Shae and, while my motives for doing so are not precisely clear to me, they had nothing to do with the rise of the Phoenix. Even now, as we approach your Gaerud, I am less willing to enter into battle on behalf of the Phoenix than I am to fight for the life of my son.*

You act, you tell me, of kindness for Dia of Shae and of a father's love for his son. Given what you have already suffered on their behalf, did you never think perhaps that something more might have been at stake?

Mentally, Caelon sighed. *Say what you mean, sir, if you please.*

All you have done, Phoeday told him, *you have done because it was* **right**. *Nothing Dia of Shae could have said to you would have moved you to assist her if you had not felt it was the right thing to do. And, whatever your motives may have been, my lord, it is results that matter.*

Unconvinced, Caelon said nothing.

You are the most easy-going fellow in the world, are you not? Phoeday remarked with a resigned sigh. *You are perfectly willing to tolerate or endure everyone else's weaknesses except your own. You are a harsh taskmaster, my lord -- and, if you mean to hold yourself to standards of such height that you spend your spare time wallowing in feelings of unworthiness, then you are a fool besides!*

This speech, ending as it did on a note of considerable asperity, unaccountably raised Caelon's spirits and he began to wonder if Dia meant to keep them waiting much longer. After all, Septha had as much as told them that this Gaerud was take place sometime within the next hour or so; Caelon would need to keep up his strength. So engrossed was he in contemplating his upcoming victuals that he did not see Phoeday, standing in his inconspicuous corner of the room, with a great deal of affection in his glance and his entire pudgy form shaking with suppressed laughter.

Dia arrived in Lady Tamia's sitting room in due course, accompanied by the faithful Phoebus, looking more stern and, at the same time, more queenly than he had ever seen her. She wore the silken leggings and overdress that was usual for young ladies of fashion and breeding, in a rich purple -- the color of the archpriests of the Phoenix -- and the deeply cowled overdress it boasted gave it the look of an ecclesiastical robe.

There was little conversation when she arrived. His parents gravely bid her welcome, and Caelon walked over to her and took her hand, bowing over it as he had so many times since the two had met. His eyes sought hers, their glances held, and he said, "Are you ready, my lady?"

She said nothing, replying with a solemn nod.

"Then, let us go and greet the Emperor," he said to the room at large, nodding in his turn. "No doubt he is anxious for this game to begin."

With Phoebus and Phoeday trailing a respectful distance behind, the two noble couples left the apartments.

CHAPTER NINETEEN

"Their Grace, Lord Saeros and Lady Tamia of Aerandos," the herald announced, sounding very formal for some reason. "Colonel Lord Caelon of Aerandos and Lady Dia of Shae."

Aware that he was making more of an entrance than was his wont, Caelon took a deep breath and followed his parents into the throne room. And, as soon as he had crossed the threshold, he *knew*, for a wave of cold darkness swept over him and chilled him to the marrow of his bones. *It is now,* he thought.

Prepare yourself, advised Phoeday.

Lord Saeros was bowing before the throne, as Lady Tamia and Dia sank into deep curtseys. Caelon performed his duty to the Emperor, his eyes taking careful inventory of the three people standing behind the throne.

Daerus of Shae was suffering from some sort of intense perturbation, and Caelon would have given a great deal to know what was going through his mind. The young man's skin had assumed a greenish cast, he was breathing as hard as if he had just run a few miles during the height of HighSun, and his upper lip was faintly dewed with sweat. His nervous eyes -- so like Dia's, Caelon realized unwillingly -- darted around the room and over its occupants, restlessly searching for something he clearly could not find.

Prince Maermat stood erect, wearing an expression so prideful that he appeared smug. But when Caelon looked at the Princess Kera, he was forced to suppress a gasp of revulsion.

Like her brother, she stood tall and proud, the tilt of her chin proclaiming absolute arrogance. Her arms and face -- all the skin on her body that was exposed to his sight, in fact -- was almost black, for the darkness of Septha had consumed her utterly, so that there was nothing left of the young girl she had been not so long ago. Black and, yes, shiny, as if her skin had been transformed to scales or some such thing. The expression in her eyes almost defied description; there was smug superiority, inhuman cruelty and a touch of insanity there. She turned those eyes on him and smiled and Caelon's spine rattled. Once more, he was forced to sternly control his reactions.

There was a peculiar stillness about the courtiers scattered about the cavernous room that suggested to Caelon that he and his parents had arrived on the heels of a startling pronouncement and he wondered what had happened. Had Septha somehow decided to begin this battle without awaiting the arrival of his adversaries? Had they somehow made a crucial first move that he and Dia would have to counter, placing them in the sort of defensive posture from which few wars were ever won?

All these questions of yours will be answered soon enough, my lord, Phoeday told him in trenchant accents. *You must be very calm now; let nothing disturb your inner sanctum of tranquility.*

"In a good hour, Saeros," the Emperor declared with a terrifying geniality. "I am told that your troops have arrived, in good order and more than you had given Us to understand you would be able to spare. Indeed, you are commended for your willingness to serve your Emperor."

Lord Saeros bowed again in acknowledge of that imperial approbation. "I am happy to know that you are pleased, your Majesty," he said smoothly. Then he looked around appraisingly. "Can it be that we have interrupted your Majesty by our arrival? If that is so, then I can only ask your pardon and express the hope that we are not too late to receive whatever tidings have startled your entire court into immobility."

"Not tidings for you, Saeros, for you were briefed on this day's work along with the rest of the General Staff." Emperor Kaerkas then lifted his eyes to the remainder of the occupants of the room. Grimly, he smiled. "It is gratifying, however, to note how eagerly my subjects welcome the embrace of their new God."

An uncomfortable shuffling filled the room, stating louder than any words that the courtiers, who gave little thought to any form of religion in any event, were not yet ready to change their allegiance to the God of Chaos -- even if their allegiance to the Phoenix was more the product of habit than of faith.

"Remains but one small formality in order to deliver us into the hands of our God," his Majesty continued, seeming to derive some obscure pleasure in the discomfort all around him. He turned then and, very solemn and oddly respectful, nodded to his daughter.

The hideously altered Imperial Princess bowed in a curiously ceremonial way and began to chant, weaving her hands in a series of curious gestures. After a few moments, the room darkened further as the candles in the wall sconces and candlabras flickered and dimmed, and a deadly chill that seemed to consist of fear and confusion and uncertainty filled the room.

An inky blackness appeared near the vaulted ceiling of the throne room, circling the dome, slowly at first and then with increasing speed. And then, as the princess' chant seemed to reach its climax, the swirling shadow hurled itself to the ground, coalescing into a creature such as Caelon had never even imagined before. It had the body of a powerfully muscled man, but its head was that of a beast of nightmare: horned, fanged, with slitted eyes that glowed red and chilled the blood of anyone unfortunate enough to catch its eye.

Septha the Destroyer had arrived. The battle was upon them.

"Bow down to Dark Septha," the Emperor ordered. "Fall to your knees in awe and gratitude, and worship the new God of Ormaeranda!"

There was neither awe nor gratitude apparent in the terrified faces of the courtiers standing before the "New God", Caelon thought with a flicker of amusement. No one moved.

"Kneel!" said Kaerkas the Beast ominously.

Slowly, hesitantly, the men and women of the court sank to the floor, bowing their heads as they did so -- perhaps in respect, perhaps in an effort to avoid looking upon the hideous being that, they had been told, was to be their God -- except the party from Aerandos and Dia of Shae.

Affronted, the Emperor stared at them as if he could not believe his eyes. **"Kneel!"** he screamed at the four of them, as if they could be subjugated by the power of his voice alone. Phoebus and Phoeday, standing quietly behind them, seemed to have escaped his Majesty's notice.

Lord Saeros stepped forward with all his usual aplomb. "I am afraid I cannot, in good conscience, bow to your new God, Sire," he said blandly.

"You -- *what?!*" demanded the Emperor in apparent astonishment.

I wonder if Lord Septha really thought that we should all instantly drop to our knees in adoration, should Kaerkas the Beast only snarl at us? Caelon heard Dia mutter in his head in disgust.

I cannot make any guesses about Septha, Caelon answered her, *but snarling has been working for Kaerkas for years.*

"We of Aerandos will not worship the God of Chaos, my liege," his father was saying firmly.

"Indeed?" the Emperor said in threatening tones. "You stand before me in mine own throne room and throw your treason in my teeth?"

"Treason? No, sire," Lord Saeros disagreed. "I have no wish to usurp your throne and wish you not the least harm in the world. But Aerandos does not pray to any God upon the orders of the throne, although we willingly grant you all *worldly* allegiance and respect."

"So you say," Kaerkas uttered, eyeing them through narrowed eyes. "But, if you will not bow to my God, you will not defend Him in this realm, cither, in open despite of my orders, is that not so."

"That is so," Lord Saeros agreed with calm audacity, "but since you have the Imperial Army to serve you in this way, my army is free to serve you in other ways -- such as dispatching the Throk, who may be poised on your northeast border even as we speak. Each to his own craft, your Majesty."

But the Emperor did not seem to be appeased, and a tense silence filled the room. "Very pretty words, Saeros," his Majesty grated out, "but what you tell me, in effect, is that I have given an imperial command that you choose to ignore." Again, there was a brief silence. Softly, into that silence, the Emperor said, "Tell me, your Grace, do you know the penalty for treason?"

For an instant, this gentle question hung amidst an appalled silence. The courtiers glanced from one to the other, still frightened but watchful. Caelon remained as outwardly impassive as his sire, while silently giving vent to a wide-ranging sample of the less genteel expressions in his vocabulary. He might have continued in that pastime indefinitely, and derived considerable relief from it, but that he recalled that those colorful descriptions of the Emperor and his likely genealogy were being overheard.

Picturesque, my lord, commented Phoebus after a particularly scurrilous metaphor.

A bit inaccurate, though, wouldn't you say? added Phoeday to his brother TimeKeeper.

Yes, certainly it is inaccurate, acknowledged Phoebus, *but you must admit that it* **was** *evocative of some rather extraordinary imagery.*

Oh, stop it, the pair of you! snapped Dia, apparently every bit as incensed as was Caelon.

"Indeed, I know it well, your Majesty," Lord Saeros replied, his voice as gentle but his eyes glinting. "I have even carried out that penalty on behalf of your Majesty upon occasion." Boldly, but still in tones as gentle as the Emperor had used, he added, "One wonders whether your Majesty has considered the penalty for forcing an issue in flagrant despite of the established rights and privileges of the Great Houses of the Empire?"

It is as well that someone remind the madman of the realities of his situation, Caelon thought savagely.

Softly, my lord, Phoeday warned. *Remember, you* **must** *remain calm.*

There was another lengthy silence and the tension in the room swirled about the company like a thick, milky fog that is disturbed by a fast moving steed. "Aye," the Emperor finally growled, menace in every line of his face, "in that you are no doubt quite right. I can see that I must look to defend myself, for like the treacherous cur that you are, you have been busily creating alliances with the other Great Houses these many years. Gedbaen is in your pocket since you married your sister into that House, and now, it seems, you seek to breach the friendship between Ormaer and Shae by marrying your son to a daughter of that House -- also in defiance of my wishes."

Given the fact that his alleged betrothal to Dia had originally come about because of his Majesty's insistence on wedding her ladyship to the crown prince against her wishes, it was difficult for Caelon to hear his father dishonored by it. Heated protests formed on his lips but he was not given a chance to speak.

Calmly, my lord, Phoeday reminded him. Caelon wondered irritably if this was the archpriest's task, of the Phoenix had spoken. *One of them,* replied Phoeday, amused. *If you are weary of hearing the admonition, my lord, then you would do well to make it unnecessary for me to make it.*

"Unjust, sire!" To Caelon's surprise, Dia was moved to come to his father's defense. "His Grace had no hand in bringing about my pledge to Caelon of Aerandos! No doubt," and here, she cast a bitter glance at her brother, "we should not have felt it necessary to make an announcement until after we had leisure to consult my parents, were it not for the fact that my hand was forced and my rights ignored."

"Your rights ignored?" purred his Majesty, pinning her with his glance. "Indeed? As I recall, you made your announcement a refusal to wed my heir. Your own foolish choice and now, child, you speak of rights." Dia scowled and he continued sympathetically, "I know how difficult it must be for you to admit, my lady, but it would seem that you have contracted a most ineligible alliance into a dishonorable House. There can be no doubt that it would have been much better had you accepted

Maermat, rather than refusing him in order to promise herself to the heir of the serpent Aerandos."

These words, uttered in paternal accents, had much the effect of a flame applied to dry kindling. "Oh, indeed, how much better for me it would have been!" the lady exploded, seeming to completely forget the respect due the Emperor. She hurled herself forward to plant herself at the foot of the dais with angry defiance. "I wonder I did not immediately see the advantages of such a match? Had I accepted him at the outset, no doubt Maermat would have found it unnecessary to then inveigle his way into my chambers for the purpose of assault and rape. I expect I am incorrigible, for I fear I have failed to learn my lesson and still would not wed Maermat were he the last man on earth!" Sarcasm dripped from her voice, vying with the bitterness she made no attempt to disguise.

"How dare you!" roared Prince Maermat with as much wounded, innocent outrage as if Caelon had not himself ousted the fellow from her ladyship's chambers. "You come to this palace, behave like the most unrepentant whore with this guttersnipe from Aerandos, and refer to my attempts at persuasion as rape and assault? As well for me that you refused me, *caethera*, for I was quite in error. You are most unworthy to wed into Ormaer!"

"You are still in error, Highness," said Dia sweetly, rage narrowing her eyes and pride lifting her chin. "It is Ormaer who has proved unworthy to marry a daughter of Shae."

No one spoke or moved. The entire court knew what must follow such deadly blood insults. Caelon, locked in a stasis over which he had no control, fought against it, struggling to speak.

Finally, Prince Maermat, who had appeared on the verge of an apoplectic fit, uttered an inarticulate snarl of pure fury and said, "Choose your champion, Dia of Shae!"

She stood tall and proud and unafraid -- and every bit as angry as the prince. "I fight my own battles, *pathaed*!" she snapped, profound contempt in her voice.

As guards were dispatched for short swords -- Dia's choice -- Caelon fought even harder against the unknown power that held him immobile in its grip. *Let me go!* grated Caelon, coldly furious.

No! All trace of amusement had left Phoeday's "voice". *Don't interfere. This is not your fight. If you go blundering into this now, you will only succeed in getting her, and yourself, and your son, killed.*

And, to Caelon's considerable astonishment, gruffly kind Phoeday suddenly gripped his mind with a strength and ruthlessness that bespoke of unshakable resolve. The archpriest dragged him down, down, deep into himself, down to that incorruptibly calm kernel of himself, where he existed in pure and untouchable integrity, where nothing could harm him or even reach him.

When Phoeday had introduced Caelon to that part of himself after midmeal, Caelon had wondered what the purpose of the exercise had been. While he was fully prepared to admit that contact with that profound and innocent part of himself was reassuring and refreshing, it had seemed to serve no useful purpose. Now, he saw that Phoeday had wanted him to know, practically, what steps to take when he needed to calm himself. And it seemed terribly important -- at least, to Phoeday -- that he remain calm.

Dia had divested herself of her overdress while she waited for the delivery of the dueling swords, and now paced the stone floors wearing only leggings and her undertunic. The garb was starkly utilitarian but also left no doubt in anyone's mind that its wearer was splendidly female.

Not even that, my lord, said Phoeday, laughter marring the sternness he tried to inject into his tones.

Spoilsport. He felt a certain sort of wistfulness as he watch the girl furiously stalking about the throne room, awaiting the arrival of sharp-bladed steel. *May I not even touch her mind?* he asked, realizing suddenly that her presence had faded from his thoughts.

Certainly, you may, Phoeday promptly assured him, *if you wish to utterly destroy her concentration and give Maermat an easy opening. You would do well rather to focus upon yourself, my lord, for when the time for your task comes, you must be ready.*

That was plain enough and the thought that Dia might prevail in this duel and win through for the Phoenix, only to have him fail in his task for lack of preparation, was not to be thought of.

The swords arrived then and neither Dia nor the Prince wasted any time in choosing their weapons. In that moment, they were really very much alike, mused Caelon; both exuding an aura of crisp purposefulness that was powered by the energy of fiercely controlled fury. Once they were armed, they faced each other in the center of the room and, after the briefest of salutes, engaged in dueling combat.

Prince Maermat was a better-than-competent fencer, displaying the precision and control that bespoke the well-trained swordsman. Certainly he was not a master but, Caelon saw with some misgiving, he was an opponent to be reckoned with. He had the advantage of strength and reach, it was true, but as the fight progressed, it began to be apparent that those advantages were only of marginal use to him.

For my lady of Shae did not favor the gentlemanly style of the crown prince; Dia was a trench fighter, Caelon saw immediately, perfectly willing to throw a leaping kick or a glancing blow when she saw an opportunity to do so. After the first few times she had surprised him with her astonishing agility, Maermat apparently decided that he needed to stay out of range of her blows, which effectively extended the length of her reach to almost equal his.

Dia fought like a wildcat, taking enough recklessness chances that Caelon's breath caught more than once in fear for her. She felt the lash of Maermat's blade more than once glancing across arm or shoulder -- cuts not serious enough to incapacitate her but he drew her blood nevertheless. And, while Maermat seemed to derive considerable satisfaction every time her skin felt the bite of his blade, she did not seem to care. Watching her, Caelon thought he understood why.

For all that she seemed crazed, darting here and there, moving constantly in a way that might serve to convince one that she was needlessly tiring herself, her eyes were not the eyes of a berserker. She was watching her opponent very carefully, he realized, measuring his every move, testing his reactions, gauging his reflexes. Her experiments cost her a few drops of blood but she seemed perfectly willing to pay that price. *Let Maermat have his petty interim victories,* he could almost hear her thinking, *since he is so easily amused.* She did not want his blood; she wanted his life.

And the sheer unpredictability of her swordsmanship was, indeed, taking its toll. Maermat, coldly correct, found her style wholly baffling. He began to grow frustrated and, as she continued to almost easily thwart his efforts to inflict more telling injuries, his detachment began to suffer. He was tiring, Caelon could see, getting sloppy with his parries, taking longer to recover from his thrusts.

And then Dia, still with that tireless, darting agility, combined a spinning kick to his kneecap with a backhanded slash across that beautiful, imperial face. For the first time since the fight had begun, the Prince's skin tasted the kiss of her blade. He had seemed to believe that he would pass the entire duel without a single nick, and his misplaced contempt for her warlike skills betrayed him into carelessness.

For now, he gave a bellow of pure rage and began to swing wildly, so infuriated by her unexpected proficiency that he stopped fencing altogether. Dia, her eyes narrowed measuringly, danced clear of his flailing sword and, as soon as she had given herself the room, loosed the light dueling sword she wielded with a smooth, underhand cast. It spun, whistling through the air, penetrating the rhythm of thrashing arms, until it met its target, punching through Maermat's breastbone with a sickening thud. The crown prince never knew what hit him.

Maermat stared stupidly at the woman whose sword hilt protruded from his chest. Blood suddenly belched from his mouth. And then he swayed, and then he fell.

Dread Kaerkas the Beast, Emperor of Ormaeranda, started to his feet with an incredulous gasp. Caelon looked at him sharply. For just a few moments, Kaerkas was no longer the barely sane ruler who struck terror into the hearts of all who lived between here and the Sea of Akkad. For now, he was just a man who had watched his son fall to the sword of another.

"Maermat!" he cried, and his voice resounded with anguish and loss.

The herald uttered the cruelly necessary epilogue to the duel. "The honor of Shae is won," he intoned.

Silence fell.

CHAPTER TWENTY

Tear-blinded, Emperor Kaerkas stumbled from the dais to the center of the floor and fell to his knees beside the still body of his son. No one spoke; there was nothing to say.

It was during that silence that Caelon felt the first touch upon his mind. He thought at first that it was Dia and his instinctive reaction was to respond to it, to rise from where he dwelt in that core of himself to meet it, but Phoeday retained his mental grip and would not let him go.

You cannot do what you need to do until you have prepared yourself, my lord, Phoeday instructed him with unusual gravity. *Seek the weapons you will need inside yourself.*

Caelon might have been tempted to argue with Phoeday about such interference, but he had felt the beginnings of a touch he knew. The languid, cloying, sickening blackness was descending into his mind and, as instructed, he retreated father into his essence.

That was where he found a seed of glowing light that he had not noticed before, beckoning to him with its promise of warmth and safety. He responded to its silent invitation, diving into it, bathing his mind in it, clothing himself in it. It both surrounded him and penetrated him. It throbbed in rhythm with his heart beat. He breathed it into the depths of his lungs.

By the time that cold blackness found him, he was ready.

This need not be, Caelon of Aerandos, a voice said to him. *Will you die with your father here and now?*

Caelon recognized the touch of Daerus of Shae. *Am I in danger of dying just at this present?* he asked, injecting a note of tolerant amusement into his "voice".

You know that once Kaerkas recovers his composure, you will all stand accused of treason in the death of his son, Daerus told him.

Well, and even if that is so, why do you concern yourself with my fate? he asked, venturing into the sticky darkness, slowly, slowly, piercing the enveloping blackness ever so gently in search of the imprisoned mind buried in the mire.

Daerus of Shae did not seem to notice. *Do you care nothing at all for my sister, sir?* he asked. *She will not stand against you.*

And what do you imagine I can do appease the Emperor and, I must suppose, make up to him for the loss of his son? Even as they carried on this conversation, Caelon felt the enervating darkness settling over his body and only the fiercest concentration kept it from creeping into his mind.

The mental voice of Daerus suddenly increased in depth and volume, and the pressure against his mind abruptly grew so heavy that Caelon felt a little dizzy. *All that is needed is for you to renounce your father and swear your loyalty to the Emperor,* Daerus told him. *I am very sure that, in that event, both you and Dia will be spared.*

While my father, meanwhile, goes to the headsman's block, Caelon said ironically. He became simultaneously aware of a spurt of anger at such a suggestion and of the sudden surge of triumph in the mind touching his. That was when he fully understood Phoeday's repeated assertions that he must maintain his calm. He took a deep breath and, with quiet stealth, continued his exhausting journey.

Moving like a very old man, the Emperor slowly rose to his feet. He looked wildly at House Aerandos and Dia of Shae as they stood before him. "Traitors! Traitors!" he shrieked at them. "Dare to raise steel against the heir to the throne? Think you that the Great Houses are entitled to such perfidy as their birthright? Then it is time for the Great Houses to be no more!"

Carefully, wondering if he could accomplish so delicate a maneuver, Caelon left that anger in his outer mind and burrowed further still into the tranquility of his inner soul. *Tell me, does my loyalty to Kaerkas include loyalty to the God he has chosen?*

Of course, Daerus said with calculated indifference.

Really, Caelon complained, feigning considerable annoyance, *you must think me the most complete clot! Should I make such a pledge, it will not save Dia's life, for no power in this world will make her stand with me if I choose to stand with Septha.*

And still he plunged down and down through the muddy darkness of Daerus' mind. This stodge seemed to go on forever and he was getting so tired, so very tired ...

"Gather the men," the Emperor was ordering his generals, who stood among the crowd of courtiers. "Take them out the west gate and fall upon Aerandos stealthily. Give them no hint of your approach and see you kill them all, to the last man! I want no prisoners."

"Yes, my liege," ashen-faced General Kraetus said mechanically, "but ... "

"Make no excuses to me, sir!" Kaerkas stalked back to his throne. "When you have exterminated that force, prepare the men to march north to Aerandos. Kill every living thing you find within its borders! I will wade to the hips in the blood of Aerandos before I will feel I have been avenged for the death of my heir!"

Leave Dia to me, Daerus was saying urgently, watching carefully as Caelon began to sway slightly. The darkness had by this time so enveloped him that Caelon could no longer see the throne room around him. Inky coldness surrounded him, exhaustion threatened him, and he felt his will to resist insidiously crumbling. *I can persuade her and all the more easily if you will only choose your Emperor and the might of great Septha over the sickly boy-god Phoenix.*

And that may have been the last, fatal mistake which the Princess Kera -- for Caelon was certain she was the force behind this effort at temptation -- would make. He might have been persuaded to turn his back on his father in order to save Dia -- although, even now, he could not be quite sure of that. However that may have been, nothing would have persuaded him to hand his soul over to dark Septha, thereby condemning his young son to annihilation. With a final, heaving surge, he pushed through the heavily encrusted blackness into the inner mind wherein Dia's twin remained trapped. *Daerus,* he called urgently.

"And why should Aerandos pay for the death of Maermat?" Dia was demanding, moving toward the throne with such a combination of menace and pride that she could only have been said to swagger. "They had no hand in it. I am yet a daughter of Shae." Then her lips curved into an uncharacteristic sneer as she added, "For that matter, none from Aerandos thought to try to compel me into a marriage with the crown prince -- either by imperial order or by conspiring to ravage me into it. Let Ormaer bear its share of the blame for the death of one of its own!"

"You would have consented fast enough if not for Caelon of Aerandos," the Emperor asserted, scowling at her.

"I would not," she returned, her voice flatly contradictory, "even if I had never heard of Caelon of Aerandos."

Come, Daerus, Caelon said to the mind he had found huddled miserably in the ever-shrinking center of its being, where the darkness could not encroach.

Caelon? said a hopeful, hopeless voice. *Caelon of Aerandos?*

None other, Caelon said lightly. *We must hurry for the time is nearly upon us.* Unnoticed by himself, Caelon had sunk weakly to his knees. Lady Tamia rushed to him in some alarm, taking his arm and speaking to him words he could not hear.

"Perhaps, my liege, if you feel a need to place blame," Dia was saying with quiet force, "then blame your New God for the death of your son. In the end, it was He would have me wed to Maermat, being too arrogant to accept that there are some things that cannot be forced. The Destroyer is aptly named."

"How dare you!" the Emperor said in a voice that shook with passion. "If indeed it was Great Septha that desired such a union, then you were doubly at fault for refusing the choice of your God."

"Septha is not my God," she told him without hesitation, "and never will be. My heart belongs to the Phoenix."

Emperor Kaerkas loosed a bellow of pure fury. "*How dare you!*" he said again, screaming this time. "There is no Phoenix! The Phoenix abandoned us, we were forsaken and godless until Mighty Septha found merit in us! The Phoenix is no more!"

"Not so, Sire," Dia replied, still in that flatly emphatic tone of voice. "The Phoenix has risen."

A collective gasp rattled around the throne room and a few of the more brave courtiers got to their feet. The more timid exchanged tentative glances and a great deal of rustling of silks and satins was heard. The Emperor shrieked a denial of that news that was remarkable for the desperation laced into his threatening manner. "How dare you bring these lies before our God!" he screamed.

"I was there, your Majesty," she maintained. "I saw it with my own eyes. The Phoenix lives and Shae lives with Him."

Come, Daerus, Caelon was saying, only vaguely aware of what was going forward around him, *join with me.*

No! a woman's voice intruded upon them suddenly. *No, my beloved, do not. It is a trick, they will destroy you.*

Kera! he said despairingly, trying to push Caelon away.

Daerus, who do you think is the author of the predicament in which you find yourself? Caelon said impatiently.

But I love her! the boy cried.

It was as well that this encounter was purely spiritual; if Daerus of Shae had spouted such sentimental twaddle during a similar physical encounter, Caelon would have been very sorely tempted to knock such nonsense out of him. *You would have me believe that you are willing to sacrifice the world for that?*

Yes! Daerus cried hysterically. *I love her! I cannot bear to leave her behind!*

Do you? Do you really love her?

Yes! Yes!

How do you know?

That home question was greeted with complete, profound and stunned silence.

You have never seen her, Caelon told him, boring in inexorably, *for you have spent this whole time with your mind obscured by this murky black slime. Before you declare yourself ready to throw the world away for her sake, you owe it to the rest of us to at least look upon her with an unobscured vision. If, when you have seen her as she really is, you find yourself still enamored of her, you will still have the option to choose allegiance with dread Septha.*

Daerus, no! wailed the Princess. *Do not leave me!*

Come, Daerus, Caelon said again, not knowing how he knew what to say. *Surrender to the light.*

"It is not for you to say whether Shae stands with the Phoenix, girl," the Emperor told her contemptuously. "In the absence of your father, that is for your brother to decide." And, with that, Emperor Kaerkas turned to Lord Daerus. "Well, my lord?" he barked at him. "Does Shae stand with this new-risen, weakly Phoenix or do you accept glorious Septha as your God?"

Caelon felt Daerus touch him hesitantly, and he waited no longer. The moment of choice had arrived and Caelon would not risk Daerus having second thoughts about this. He poured himself and the light he carried into the mind of young Daerus of Shae and, as their contact strengthened and grew in power, the tiny seed of light grew more brilliant. Together, finding trust and affection in common purpose, they fed that light until they could contain it no longer.

It began suddenly to expand, roaring out of the inner reaches of Daerus' mind, burning away the darkness in seconds, clearing the fog from both their minds and giving them back to themselves. Slowly, back in the throne room, Caelon rose to his feet. Up on the dais, Daerus look at him and their eyes met, both glowing with that holy fire.

The Princess Kera's dismayed gasp was heard throughout the throne room, breaking the little tableau. Her father turned to her to say irritably, "What ails you, girl?"

She did not reply, staring instead at Daerus. *Very well, then,* Caelon said. *Turn and look at her as she really is. Is this the face of your beloved?*

"Choose!" the Emperor bellowed at Daerus.

That young gentleman ignored him, turning to look at the woman he had said, not so very long since, that he would wed. But when he beheld her, Daerus could not stop himself from jerking back with a violent start, staring at her in dismayed revulsion.

Caelon did not blame him, for the spirit of the Dark God possessed her utterly and, to those possessed of the special perceptions of the Talented, she appeared to wear the horned, scaled, fanged face of her Master. Daerus shook his head and, swallowing nausea, stepped away from her.

Come, Daerus, Caelon heard Princess Kera say insistently and cajolingly, *the moment of choice has arrived.*

Yes, Caelon agreed, *it would not do to keep Septha waiting.*

Daerus of Shae took a deep, shuddering breath and, for a moment, his eyes sought out those of his twin sister. It had not escaped Caelon's notice that the younger man had avoided looking at her until now. Dia did not speak, but her lips twitched faintly and Caelon wondered what they had said to each other. She gave a slight nod and her brother smiled, a relieved, happy smile.

"Choose!" raged the Emperor once more.

"Very well, Sire," said Daerus, squaring his shoulders and turning to face the Emperor, suddenly looking like the twin brother of Dia of Shae, proud master of himself once more. "I am sorry if you believe it to be disloyal or disrespectful, but I will stand with my sister and Shae will stand with the Phoenix."

For a few more moments, no one either moved or spoke. Then, as the Emperor continued to stare at Daerus of Shae, the hideous spectacle standing behind the throne, which had been immobile until now, began a faint wailing that quickly grew almost unbearable in volume. It was a soulless wail of unmitigated fury, seeming to come from nowhere and everywhere at once. The Emperor began jump up and down, literally dancing in his fury, and to scream, "No! No! No!" He appeared, Caelon thought clinically, to have finally and completely lost his mind.

A time window opened just left of the throne.

"The Choice has been made, Septha," said a disembodied female voice, gentle and sensuous, that seemed to come from nowhere and everywhere.

"No!" The terrible wailing broke off long enough to utter that fierce denial. *"I do not yield! I* **will** *not yield!"*

"Those were the terms of the agreement, Septha," said another disembodied voice, this one male, stern, disciplined and powerful

as the roiling waves of an angry sea. *"The Choice is made, the contest is done. You must yield."*

From the time window stepped the youthful Phoenix.

"No!" roared enraged Septha. *"I do not yield my place in this world to this half-human godling! It is not fitting that I should be displaced so."*

"You were displaced many Ages ago," the female voice reminded the Dark God, *"by just such a half-human godling. He is the keeper of time and of order, and he thus works his powers in furtherance of* **our** *goals. The contest is done, Septha, and you have not prevailed. Accept the choice with what grace you can muster."*

"I **will** *not!"* snapped Septha, who did not appear to be very popular with His peers. *"Thus do I claim my rightful place among the Gods of this world!"*

The boy-Phoenix of this age was struck in mid-step. Dark Septha, permitted uncontested sway in this world for two whole years, had grown great with power and that power seemed to swirl almost visibly around the Phoenix. He gasped and paled, wilting.

"I do not yield to this weakling!" gloated Septha gleefully.

"No!" cried Dia, running forward with terror in her eyes. The boy held up a restraining hand and she stopped, straining against his unspoken admonition and wringing her hands in agitation.

Caelon, his stomach quivering and his heart in his throat, looked around the room wildly in the same instant. "Help him!" he shouted at the unseen deities who seemed to have been observing the Gaerud all along.

"We cannot," the unknown Goddess said regretfully. *"We, too, are bound by rules during these encounters."*

"What odds does that make?" Caelon said furiously. "Septha breaks these rules at will, unopposed, and You stand by doing nothing?"

"There is much justice in his words," the Goddess mused thoughtfully.

"Indeed," agreed her companion God, *"but how may We keep the universe from flying apart in the wake of our many contentions, if We decide that We all can break the rules whenever any one of Us does?"*

"Sophistry!" snapped Caelon, never pausing in his fear for his son to consider his temerity in so addressing a God.

Caelon! Dia's desperate voice came into his mind in the same moment. He knew what she wanted, and he joined his thought with hers without hesitation. Her thought was focused on Caerad, gallantly struggling to regain his feet but gasping with pain in the grip of whatever torment Septha visited upon him. While he had been fruitlessly arguing with Gods, she had been pouring her own energy into their son, trying to hold him up with the sheer strength of her own will. As she had grown tired, she had called to him for help.

Unconsciously, he stepped up behind her and laid a hand on her shoulder. Touching her had always seemed to help.

Septha gave a baffled growl of incredulous anger. *"And still these puny humans do not submit to the might and insurmountable will of an omnipotent God?"* he said. *"Foolish ones! See how easily you are overcome!"*

Joined together as they were, they both felt the power of the Dark God increase, pushing against them as they continued to pour all their hope and love into the heart of their son. Dia groaned as if she were trying to move a mountain and, as best he could unschooled, Caelon increased his support.

And then, he felt the touch of Daerus of Shae. And then, of Phoebus and of Phoeday. Giseth of the Chosen, apparently with the permission of her Goddess, added her strength to theirs. And, to his complete amazement, his mother, the Grand Duchess Tamia, joined her mind with theirs, all of them focusing their strength and will upon Dia, giving her unstintingly of all the power they could gather.

Dia's concentration never faltered or wavered, and she continued to give to her son all that she had. So iron hard was the determination he read in her mind that she fully intended, Caelon realized, to give the boy the whole of her life force, if that was what he needed in his deadly struggle.

No! he thought, his own resolve matching Dia's, *I will not lose you both!*

He joined his mind more firmly with hers, holding her up, shouldering her burden as best he could. As a result, his contact with both his son and the Dark God increased. He saw, as Septha was required to bend more and more of His will to His fell purpose, that the Dark God was baffled by the difficulty He was having in dispatching the Phoenix, whom He held in utter contempt. Clearly, Septha had underestimated one of the most awesome, unwavering and inextinguishable forces in the whole of the universe: the love of a mother for her child.

This is not working, he heard Dia mutter to herself. *I must ... I must ... oh, Gods!*

Must what?

Caerad! she cried suddenly, her heart weeping.

It is well, Mother, the boy replied, sounding strained and tired. *I know, have always known, what it is that you must do.*

A whimper greeted that statement and Caelon felt the wave of anguish that washed over her. *I shall try not to hurt you, beloved,* she told Him, her heart overflowing with love and her mind afire with pain.

The Phoenix did not reply. And then, something changed, some quality in the energy Dia was pouring out altered in a way that Caelon could not assess. And now, as the seven of them continued to pour their strength into Dia, and as Dia funneled it into the Phoenix, the boy began to glow.

Septha gave a howl of astonished fury, redoubling His efforts so that, as one, they reeled at the immensity of His will and at the task of doing battle with it. And still the Phoenix glowed brighter and brighter. Dia was panting now, and Caelon himself was beginning to feel the first treacherous tendrils of exhaustion. With a shrill bellow of triumph, Septha, sensing their weariness, could be felt gathering His will for one final barrage that would, no doubt, dispatch them all. Caelon tensed himself, not knowing what to expect, except that it was likely to be quite final.

But before Septha could unleash whatever He had in mind for them all, the Phoenix flashed one brilliant, stunning flash, as bright as an exploding star. *"No! NO!"* roared Septha. *"It cannot be!"*

When the brightness faded, the robe of the Phoenix sat forlornly crumpled amidst a pile of ashes. Caelon gasped, slowly shaking his head in instinctive denial. Unconsciously, his grip on Dia's shoulder tightened until she cried out in pain. He did not really see her. He did not feel the tears that streamed down his cheeks. He had eyes only for the remains of his son. His only thought was that he had failed and his son was dead.

Dimly, he realized that Dia was talking to him and he turned to look at her. "You killed him?" he asked, still in shock.

She was crying but her eyes glowed with happy triumph. "I had to," she told him simply.

"You *killed* him?!" Caelon said again, suddenly grasping her shoulders so forcefully that she winced.

"Will you ever learn to trust, my lord?" she asked him tenderly. Then, laughing lightly, she said, "It's alright, Caelon."

How could she say that? He shook his head again, releasing her so abruptly that she almost fell, and managing only to stammer, "But ... but ... "

"She is quite right, my lord." Pale and shaking, Phoeday came to stand beside him, looking tired but no less exalted that her ladyship. "Please do not grieve so," he added with that surprising gentleness, "for, truly, there is no need."

"But, how ... ?"

"Watch," Phoebus said, exultant, pointing.

Following the direction of his hand, Caelon looked again at the ashes on the floor. Then he frowned, blinking the tears from his eyes so that he could see clearly. Surely, he had not ... no, he *had* seen it! The ashes were moving, stirring faintly as if a gentle breeze had blown over them. As Caelon continued to stare incredulously, an impossible hope stirring in his heart, the agitation of the feather-like particles grew more violent. They seemed, he realized, to be gathering back together, rising within the robe, drifting first this way and then that, apparently looking for just the right way to adhere together.

Finally, they seemed to reach a certain point that was enough, and they came together in a rush, coalescing into the form of a man. Caelon saw that the young man looked to be about his own age and he sighed harshly in disappointment. But, a moment later, when the fellow turned to gaze at them, he still wore Dia's impish smile. Dazed, Caelon stared. Yes, this was his son, he thought with a gasp. Older, certainly, but it was. *It was!* The father's heart sang for the rebirth of his son.

And he was still the same Caerad. He looked at the two who had been most instrumental in helping to defeat dread Septha, not once but twice that day, with an indecipherable expression in his eyes. And then, incredibly, unbelievably, Ancient Phoenix -- chosen partner and instrument of the Gods -- winked at them.

CHAPTER TWENTY-ONE

Dia stood slightly to one side of the Imperial Throne of Ormaeranda, her eyes upon the man who had been her child -- the Phoenix. The various exertions of the past half hour had bedewed her with sweat, causing the various cuts and abrasions which Maermat had inflicted to burn and sting, and she was so tired that she could hardly stand upright. But none of that mattered. They had won through, despite the great strength Septha had gathered upon himself during the Interval. Daerus had been retrieved from the abyss of darkness into which he had fallen, and the Phoenix was restored.

She could not but be glad, but she ruefully admitted to herself that a tiny seed of regret still lived in her heart. Gone was the infant whose tiny fist had curled around her finger while he nursed; gone was the innocent man-child she had petted and teased and grown to love. This man -- the Phoenix -- was fully grown and his powers were now in full flower. He had no further need of her, and that was as it should be. But their ways lay apart and the fact that the world called to her child meant that he would have little time to humor Dia's maternal longings. There would be other children, of that Dia was certain, but the Phoenix had been her first and it seemed that, no sooner had she come to know him than she was forced by circumstance to say farewell.

The Phoenix, having delivered himself of that extremely familiar gesture, stepped around the throne, upon which the Emperor of Ormaeranda was screaming insanely, and said to t the hideous apparition behind it, *"The contest is done, Septha -- twice done."*

"You tricked me!" Septha howled, infuriated.

"Nonsense," the Phoenix said, mildly chiding. *"There was no trick involved; you were so determined to destroy me before I acquired enough strength to defend myself that you neglected to consider what happens every time I die."* He smiled, then. *"You would have been better served had you left matters as they stood, you know. As weak as I was, I could not have kept you out of this world, and you would have been* **very** *well placed indeed to challenge the next Phoenix for mastery over the Next Age."*

"I will be avenged, petty godling," snarled Septha. *"I will punish you and your chosen for my downfall this day."*

"Yes," the Phoenix replied, managing to sound both faintly amused and slightly bored, *"that is what you always say. Perhaps, during some Age or another, you will be able to carry out those threats. At least, it will give you something to consider during this Time."* He straightened and drew back his shoulders. *"And now, begone,"* He commanded, almost negligently. *"Return to your throne in the House of Chaos and take with you the ones who served you here."*

And, as simply as that (for One who has the power), Septha fled, howling, into some unimaginable void. The Princess Kera shrank back, but she had only the time to shriek one long, despairing "NOOOO!" before she, too, vanished, along with the body of Prince Maermat.

Dia, curious, glanced over at Daerus and surprised a wistful expression on his face. *Do you mind very much, dearest?* she asked him tenderly.

A melancholy sigh echoed in the vaults of her mind. Almost shy, he replied, *I really did love her, you know.*

Was that before she was subverted by Septha?

Yes. Again, the sigh. *She was a lovely, spritely girl, full of delightful whimsy -- much like your charming self, in fact.* He paused. *It was only later that ...*

Never mind, love, she said, not quite knowing what to say. She perceived that her relationship with her brother had changed subtlely; it would take some time for them to regain their former level of mutual comfort. *There will be others.*

The Phoenix was now looking over his shoulder at the throne. Then, he said sympathetically, "Someone really ought to do something about that poor fellow."

"What shall we do, dread Phoenix?" asked one of the courtiers, going down on one knee before him.

"The first thing you must do," said that demi-god, "is to remember *never* to call me 'dread' anything. Indeed, I very much hope that I shall be no such thing!"

"Sorry, sir," the gentleman muttered hastily.

"Very well," the Phoenix nodded, satisfied. "Now, then. I expect you shall have to confine Kaerkas and perhaps request that Lord Thraetor of Ormaer find someone to care for him. He is hopelessly insane now." He shook his head sadly. "That is a part of what Septha and His minions did to him."

"Can you not reverse it?" asked Lord Saeros.

"There is no need."

"No need?" repeated his Grace in mild protest. "Now we shall be ruled by a madman?"

"Trust me, good Saeros," said the Phoenix soothingly. "All shall be well." Then he strolled forward into the center of the room.

"Very well done, young Phoenix," said the watching God, proud approbation vivid in His rolling tones.

The young man bowed in the general direction of that resplendent voice. *"Thank you."*

A feminine chuckle sounded. *"Yes, this was very well played out, indeed,"* she said, evidently much amused. *"Your predecessor would seem to have chosen your instruments without much thought; they served you surprisingly well."*

"Not so very surprising," the Phoenix disagreed blandly, shrugging.

*"***I** *am surprised,"* the Goddess said, the laugh still in her voice. *"It certainly took a great deal of contrivance to persuade them to fulfill their destiny."*

At that, the Phoenix grinned over at Dia and Caelon. *"They are stubborn. That is one of the reasons why they were chosen."*

Dismayed, Dia blushed furiously and knew not where to look -- but she did catch the grinning glance exchanged by her brother and her lord. She gave them both to understand that she was not amused, with imagery that was as vivid as it was macabre, but that only seemed to add to their amusement.

"Is it all over then?" asked Lord Oshaed, sounding almost respectful for once, and looking more wizened than ever after the compound shocks of that day.

"Not quite yet," replied the Phoenix, looking meaningfully into that empty space in the middle of the throne room which evidently held Beings that He alone could see.

"Ah, well ... yes," said the unseen God with a great deal of throat-clearing.

"Come, Father," chided the gentle Goddess, *"You gave Your word."*

"I know that!" He snapped testily. *"I simply do not see ... "* He began in a blustering sort of way.

"Trust me," the Phoenix intervened, *"it will be much easier this way."*

There as a brief, exasperated silence. *"Oh, very well, then,"* said the God, giving in. *"Stand forth, Saeros of Aerandos."*

They all turned to look at Lord Saeros, who surprised Dia by flushing with self-consciousness as he stepped forward to take his place beside the Phoenix.

"Know that I am Rei, Father to the Gods of this world, and I speak for Them in concert," He went on. *"It is Our will that Ormaeranda shall be no more. Henceforth, this land shall be known as the Empire of Tamaeranda, and thou shalt be its ruler. Thus shall the House of Aerandos sit upon the throne during this the Sixth Age, as was intended."*

Dia smiled gleefully at this pronouncement. *How* Papa would be pleased! She exchanged a single, long glance with her twin. As one, they moved to stand forth and, shoulder to shoulder, went down on one knee before the new Emperor. "Hail Saeros, Emperor of Tamaeranda," they said in unison.

"Hail Emperor Saeros!" the former members of Kaerkas' court intoned dutifully.

"Know further," Daerus continued, standing and turning to face the assembled company, "that, on behalf of the Grand Duke Loraed, the House of Shae pledges its unswerving fealty to the Imperial House of Tamaeranda, as its loyal servant and defender. Let all of Tamaeranda know that he who plots treason against Aerandos shall face, as well, the wrath of Shae."

A wave of deep bows and curtseys swept around the room. And then, Rei spoke further.

"Caelon of Aerandos, stand forth and take thy place at thy father's side, as heir to the imperial throne of Tamaeranda," Rei commanded.

Caelon did as he was told, pausing to drop to one knee and, grasping his father's right hand, to kiss the ring bearing the Great Seal of the House of Aerandos.

"Caelon," said Emperor Saeros, deeply moved.

"Sir?" replied Caelon, smiling affectionately at his sire.

The newly-appointed Emperor returned that smile. "I am more proud than I can say," he said softly, "for the privilege of calling you son."

"And We share thy pride in thine heir," said the gentle voice of the Goddess. *"I am Istha, Goddess of earth and fertility, patron to thy neighbors in Lemantia. Giseth, my daughter, stand forth."*

At that command, a fair young woman in a deeply cowled white robe stepped forward, her face radiant at this divine visitation. "I hear Thee, Divine Istha," she said in a throbbing voice.

"Thy sisters in far-off Lemantia have sorely missed the quiet strength of thy presence, my daughter," Istha went on, *"but they have held the Throk and, now that my Brother is once again banished, I can lend them mine aid. Thy work here is almost done, gentle Giseth. Know that I am pleased with thee."*

Tears streamed down Giseth's face at these words of approval. Dia clearly heard the woman's thought: *I am not worthy.*

"One last task awaits thee here, Giseth. By thy hand shall Prince Caelon of Tamaeranda be joined with Lady Dia of Shae, and with thy hand shall I bless them and their increase. Dia of Shae," She continued as Giseth drew Dia forward, *"I have watched thee at thy task since first the Princess Kera's deceptions set thy feet upon the path that brought thee to this place. Truly, thou and thy companion-in-arms, Caelon of Aerandos, have earned the honor of the titles of Muphoen and Tiphaen for this Age. Know that We stand in thy debt."*

Dia sank into a deep curtsey of acknowledgement. "It is an honor to have been among the chosen of the Phoenix," she said demurely, disconcerted but too well-bred to show it. Then she turned her head to meet Caelon's smiling eyes and forgot about embarrassment and Goddesses and imperial politics. Here was her lord, as she had considered him since she had first welcomed him into her bed, and there was nothing coy or ambiguous in the completely honest glance they shared. Her heart was full.

"There is nothing quite like being declared man and wife by a Goddess to make the whole thing feel quite definite and final," murmured the Phoenix with considerable satisfaction.

That statement unmercifully broke the solemn mood. Caelon choked. Dia looked around the room wildly, trying desperately to still her twitching lips.

Emperor Saeros and his Empress exchanged a startled glance before they both fell to laughing. "Indeed, I expect that must be very true," chuckled the Emperor.

"Aye," agreed her Majesty, "and I expect our new Phoenix will require some growing accustomed to." She gazed at Him in considerable amusement. "I had been wondering how to persuade these two to stop huffling about and finish the business. My compliments on so easily accomplishing the feat for, as you said, good Phoenix, they are both stubborn."

Dia's eyes widened and she blushed rosily. "Your Majesty!" she cried indignantly. The echo of Daerus' laughter in her mind did not help to ease matters, either.

"I believe the proper form of address for your marriage-mother would be 'Mother Tamia', dear," smiled that lady, not in the least apologetic.

"Now, then, good Phoenix," said mighty Rei, *"if all these matters are arranged to your satisfaction, We will be on Our way."*

"Indeed, this will all do splendidly," said the Phoenix warmly, *"and I thank You both."*

"No thanks are needful, young sir," Istha told him blandly. *"I expect my Father found the experience quite educational."*

"That will be enough of that, young lady," said the Father of the Gods.

"Well, but, Father ... "

"In private, miss!"

A vast silence followed that testy order.

"Well, that conversation certainly had a familiar ring to it," commented Daerus to his twin.

"Indeed," she agreed.

That made them all laugh. Then Caelon turned to the Phoenix and, looking a bit melancholy, said, "What now, sir?"

The man who had been their child looked at them both, and His eyes were also a little sad and regretful. *Know that you and my mother will always be in my heart,* he told them privately. *I wish there were some words I could offer to adequately express my thanks ... and my love. I shall miss you.*

Dia felt her eyes stinging again, and she blinked rapidly as Caelon placed a comforting arm about her shoulders. *I love you, my darling,* she whispered in her heart to her baby.

Be well, Caerad, added Caelon softly.

The name made Him smile. Then He turned to the rest of the company. "I shall leave you now, for I know that you must have found all this quite exhausting -- and none moreso than my ... er, than the Prince and Princess here. Phoeday will inform me of whatever arrangements you have made, and I shall return to perform the coronation myself." With these words, He opened another time window. "Rest now, my children, and live well always," He added.

And then, he was gone.

CHAPTER TWENTY-TWO

Eight hours later, Dia and Caelon stood silent together on the parapet of the Imperial Palace of Tamaeranda. The first day of the New Age was drawing to a close, and they watched in silence as, in a glory of gold and crimson, the sun finally set.

THE END

About The Author

Dawn Rivers Baker grew up in Philadelphia, where she had many outlets for her artistic impulses. She studied dance at the Philadelphia School of Dance Arts, studied voice while on scholarship at Foxcroft School in Virginia, and got thoroughly involved in theater with various student productions at the schools she attended. It was not until after she married and started a family that she turned her considerable creative energy to writing. The Rise of the Phoenix is her first novel. She is also the editor and publisher of Wahmpreneur News Magazine (www.wahmpreneur.com), an online business news weekly for small and home-based businesses.

Ms. Baker lives with her husband and four children in the Catskill Mountain region of New York State.

Printed in the United States
3809